The three [friends emerged] from the piney woods [and paused at a rock outcropping] near a bend in the trail. Jane's chest expanded as she took in a deep breath of the crisp mountain air. "Someone lives over there." She shielded her eyes with one hand and pointed with the other across the narrow box canyon to a log cabin nestled in a fluttering aspen grove.

Smoke puffed in white clouds out of the short chimney stack and sailed to the east. A lone man with a German Shepherd lumbered out the door. She waved both arms above her head in greeting, but the man was staring the other way, down into the short ravine.

"What's he looking at?" Jane's gaze fell to the bottom of the gully just a few more steps down the path. Next to the shallow, winding creek, an amphitheater with rows of gray, splintered wooden benches encircled a smoldering fire pit.

Near the pit, a man lay still, his legs crumpled underneath his body.

Her heart flew into her throat. She raced down the steep trail, her friends on her heels. "Are you okay?" she shouted as she came close.

Libby drew in an audible breath, and Wes mumbled, "What the heck?"

Jane recognized the campground host. Dark red blood stained his light jacket and pooled beneath his back. Tracked in the blood were several large animal prints.

No Grater Evil

by

Karen C. Whalen

Dinner Club Murder Mysteries,
Volume 3

No Grater Evil

Cover Art by *Kim Mendoza*

The Wild Rose Press, Inc.
PO Box 708
Adams Basin, NY 14410-0708
Visit us at www.thewildrosepress.com

Publishing History
First Mainstream Mystery Edition, 2017
Print ISBN 978-1-5092-1738-0
Digital ISBN 978-1-5092-1739-7

Dinner Club Murder Mysteries, Volume 3
Published in the United States of America

Dedication

To all veterans,
especially our Viet Nam vet friends,
Pete and Russ,
and our son in Special Forces

Chapter 1

A whisper of movement stirred the woods on the other side of the canvas. Were the mother bear and her two cubs in the campsite? The movement flitted away in the direction of the pond. Tightening the sleeping bag around her neck, Jane tensed and wiggled deeper into the down-filled flannel. When the wind rattled the dry evergreen boughs releasing the sharp pine resin, her eyes darted around in the dark, but they must have dropped closed as her mind fell into nothingness.

A fearful scream jerked her back from sleep. She scrambled out of her bag and tore the tent flap open, but hesitated, crouching low. "Olivia? Are you awake?"

"Yes." Olivia and Doug stood with flashlights outside the tarpaulin. "What was that?"

"Did a bear get somebody?" Jane's voice came out as a squeak.

They flicked the light at Jane's face for a moment, then pointed their flashlights into the woods, the light beams throwing shadows around. Jane stretched behind for her flashlight and bear repellant, then emerged from her minuscule tent, shivering in the cold night air. They leaned together without speaking, listening to the blowing wind for several heartbeats, then Doug spoke, making her jump. "I'm going to look around." He strode off in the direction of the latrines.

She squinted at Olivia, who was holding a brave

face while flinching at every gust of wind. Both women were middle-aged, but Olivia managed to look youthful with smooth, olive skin and her thick, black hair in perfect place. Even while camping. And in the middle of the night. Olivia started to turn away. "I'm going back to the tent."

"Wait for Doug." Jane aimed the flashlight in her friend's direction.

"All right, scaredy-cat." Olivia trembled.

"Like, you're not scared." Jane's knuckles showed white as she gripped the flashlight tighter at the sound of crunching footsteps on gravel. "Who's that?" she shrieked. The hair on the back of her arms stood at attention, and her heart thumped.

Doug popped out of the dark. "The campsites look quiet, and I didn't see a thing. Someone was probably having a nightmare."

Jane let out a long breath, as Olivia asked, "Do you want to bring your sleeping bag over? We have plenty of room."

"Thanks, but I'll be fine." Jane fluttered her hands around. "See you in the morning."

Twice widowed, she had not camped since her first husband passed away a few years earlier and had never slept alone in a tent, but wasn't going to be afraid of the dark. With the bear repellant clutched in her right hand, she fell sound asleep.

It seemed like only moments later her eyes opened. She peered out the mesh fabric that served as a window. The sun had not yet topped the mountain range on the horizon, but in the twilight-before-the-dawn she was able to make out her friends' palatial tent on the other side of the old, weathered picnic table. A welcome mat for wiping dirty camp shoes lay on the ground in front of the zipped-shut awning, and a bright red hummingbird feeder swayed from one of the stately tent poles.

The temperature was chilly outside her warm bag. After climbing into her worn blue jeans and a T-shirt, she grabbed her fleece jacket and stepped out into the brisk, fresh air. A beautiful day in the Colorado Rocky Mountains was about to begin.

Coffee first. She pumped up the gas on her Coleman stove. Something grabbed her, and the pot slipped from her grip and slammed down on the burner.

"Jane, it's me. I need some coffee." Olivia was outfitted in L. L. Bean camping apparel.

"Good morning, Miss Fashonista. The coffee will be ready in a minute." Jane lugged her giant cooler from the secure, bear-proof, metal container. She lifted out a jumbo-sized plastic bowl of chopped jalapeño peppers, bell peppers, onions, and tomatoes.

"Hmm. I'm hungry." Olivia eyed the plastic dish. "What's all that for?"

"Huevos rancheros." Jane held out a block of cheese. "Darn! I meant to pack *shredded* cheese. How am I going to grate this?"

"I've got a grater."

"You do?" Jane peeled bacon out of its wrapping, as her friend went to get it. "Of course, she does," she said under her breath.

Olivia returned with a compact grater that had sharp, stainless steel ridges. "Give me the cheese. I can do this while you fry the bacon." Jane handed her the cheese block, then banged an over-sized, cast iron skillet down on the stove. "Ouch!" Olivia yelled, "I just

3

shredded my knuckles instead of the cheese."

"Oh, sorry." Jane grabbed antibiotic ointment and Band-Aids from the first-aid kit and treated her friend's cuts.

Olivia surveyed her bandages. "That grater's evil."

"Or the cook's not fully awake." Jane adjusted the camp stove knob, and the blue flames leapt higher. She dumped the slab of bacon into the pan, and soon the aroma of bacon, mingling with the fresh-air scent of the pine trees, filled her nose.

Doug poked his head out of their tent. "That smells wonderful."

"Good morning." Wes strolled into the campsite, rubbing his bald head. He was wearing brown camping pants with endless pockets and a camouflage jacket. His wife, Libby, cruised up behind him in blue jeans and a flannel shirt, her chin in the air, nose quivering. A sun visor topped her short, spiky blonde hair.

Doug said, "Morning," as his full body broke away from the tent. He brandished a pistol in his right hand. Everyone gaped at him. The jalapeño pepper mixture dropped from the bowl in Jane's hand into the pan with a plonk.

"Jane, I want you to go to the firing range with us after breakfast." He handed her the gun, and she numbly took hold of it, as Wes and Libby lowered themselves onto the picnic bench, their eyes wide.

With the revolver in her left hand, Jane stirred the huevos rancheros with a spatula in her right. "Take this back, Doug. I'm not going." She stuck her left arm out straight, dangling the gun from the trigger guard pinched between her fingers.

"Did you get up at the crack of cranky? After all

4

the danger you've put yourself in over the past couple of years, you of all people should learn how to shoot. Especially since you live alone."

The revolver still dangled from her fingers. "I'm never going to own one of these things, so why should I learn to shoot?"

"That's not how to hold a gun!" Doug's hand whipped around, snatching the pistol from her. "It's not loaded, but still, you have to be more careful." He rechecked the safety before shoving the revolver into its leather holster and snapping the buckle shut over the barrel. He returned the gun to his tent, while Libby poured coffee for herself and her husband.

Jane removed the heavy, steamy skillet from the stove to the table. Olivia sprinkled the grated cheese on top and jabbed a large spoon into the pan. "Everyone help themselves." The hungry campers dug in without much to say this early in the day. The chill burned off as the morning sun ascended higher into the sky.

Soon, Doug threw down his napkin and stood. "I'm heading over to the firing range. You coming, Olivia?" To Jane's surprise, his wife nodded. "Anyone else want to come?" Smiling, Doug glanced around the group.

"I don't think so." Wes shook his head. "But if you'd like to shoot a 9-millimeter, you can take mine. It's kind of unusual, a Ruger."

"Sure." Doug clapped him on the back.

"I'll stay and help you clear, Jane." Libby wiped the table with a damp, checkered dish cloth, as Wes trotted off. He returned in a matter of moments with a gun case the size of a trade paperback.

"Thanks." Doug extracted the pistol, checked the safety, and tucked the gun into his pocket.

Jane scraped the plates into a garbage bag while reminding him, "We're taking the short hike to the fishing pond and amphitheater this morning. Don't be long."

"You three go ahead and we'll catch up to you." Doug tugged on his wife's arm.

"All right. The trail marker's over there." Jane motioned toward the signpost, as Doug and Olivia gave a farewell wave.

A few minutes later the campsite was tidy and clean, with the garbage bag deposited into the rusty iron dumpster and the food locked inside the metal bear-proof container. Before long, the crack of gunshots sounded in the distance. Wes's body twitched, and a vacant, distant look came over his face. Libby's hand flew to her husband's shoulder. "You okay, honey?"

"I'm fine. Leave me alone." His voice was fierce.

Jane sucked in a breath. "Is everything all right?" Wes rarely lost his temper for no reason. He was like a big teddy bear.

Libby shook her head and mouthed, "I'll explain later." She rose from her seat and trailed after him toward their site.

Jane filled a squeeze bottle with water and a miniature backpack with rain gear, listening to the shots resounding from the range. Yes, she had taken risks in the past, walking into danger because she was too trusting. But maybe there was something else she could do—self-defense classes, perhaps.

She banished those thoughts as she breathed in the fragrance still in the air, a pine and bacon blend. This was a day to enjoy and savor, no worries in the world. After only being gone a short while, Wes and Libby reappeared, backpacks on their shoulders. Jane unfolded herself from her seat. "Let's go. The Ladners can catch up later, like they said."

"Sounds good." Wes looked back to his normal self. Their feet carried them over the stone-peppered path. They trudged along in single file until they reached the pond. "Let's take a break. Maybe Doug and Olivia are on their way and will meet up with us here." Wes gestured to a spot in the shallow water. "See all the fish just below the surface?" He stepped onto a fallen log to get closer, but the log rolled, and his feet went out from under him. With a splash, he went down on one knee in the cold, glacier-fed water.

"Wes! Look what you've done." Libby grabbed hold of his hand, but he was wet all over by the time he sloshed out of the pond.

"You're going to freeze. Should we turn around?" Jane tried to hold her lips still, so she wouldn't burst into laughter.

He shook himself like a dog. "Nah. It'd be quicker to keep going."

Libby brushed some of the moisture off his sodden pant legs, but he pushed her hands away, then took the lead as they continued past the pond. The sun traveled behind a low cloud and the wind kicked up, as they climbed upward. Soon, large, icy drops of rain sprinkled onto their heads and shoulders and made circles in the dirt on the trail.

"Did you bring rain gear?" Jane opened her small pack.

Libby slung her pack off and unzipped the pocket. "No, but I did bring a hoodie." She dragged the gray sweatshirt over her head and fitted the hood around her face, while Jane slipped into her thin plastic poncho.

A flat cap with a brim covered Wes's bald head. "The storm will pass quickly, you'll see."

He was right. They only hiked about a quarter of a mile more before the rain stopped. The quick-drying raindrops spotted the otherwise dusty ground, giving off an after-rain, wet-earth smell. Jane shook her rain gear to shed the few beads of water clinging to the plastic before stuffing the poncho into her pack. The three friends soon emerged from the piney woods and paused at a rock outcropping near a bend in the trail. Jane's chest expanded as she took in a deep breath of the crisp mountain air. "Someone lives over there." She shielded her eyes with one hand and pointed with the other across the narrow box canyon to a log cabin nestled in a fluttering aspen grove.

Smoke puffed in white clouds out of the short chimney stack and sailed to the east. A lone man with a German shepherd lumbered out the door. She waved both arms above her head in greeting, but the man was staring the other way, down into the short ravine.

"What's he looking at?" Jane's gaze fell to the bottom of the gully just a few more steps down the path. Next to the shallow, winding creek, an amphitheater with rows of gray, splintered wooden benches encircled a smoldering fire pit.

Near the pit, a man lay still, his legs crumpled underneath his body.

Her heart flew into her throat. She raced down the steep trail, her friends on her heels. "Are you okay?" she shouted as she came close.

Libby drew in an audible breath, and Wes mumbled, "What the heck?"

Jane recognized the campground host. Dark red blood stained his light jacket and pooled beneath his back. Tracked in the blood were several large animal prints.

Chapter 2

Libby started to sob, taking deep gulps, and covered her face with her hands.

Wes's eyes raked over the dead man. "We need to get out of here because the blood will attract bears. Actually, I'll wait here and you two go find Doug." He tugged his cellphone out of his pocket.

Jane couldn't pull her eyes away from the blood-red animal prints. "Are those a big dog's or a bear's?"

Wes peered closer to the ground. "Whatever it was had claws, but I've never seen bear tracks up close, so I don't know." As Libby stood there trembling, he punched in numbers on his phone, then repeated, "Jane, take Libby to the campsite. It's just through those trees over there, and go get Doug." Phone to his ear, he nodded in the direction of the tall pines.

"Can't we stay here with you?" Jane's vision swam, and her ears rang.

"I don't...want to...leave you...either." Libby gulped, then drew in a long quivering breath.

"I know this is upsetting." Jane patted Libby's shoulder as Wes's voice boomed into the phone. He reported a man down on the trail and gave the dispatcher directions to the amphitheater at Yellow Mountain Campground. Disconnecting the phone, he said, "The dispatcher told me it won't take long for them to get here because some forest rangers are just down the road."

"Good." Willing her eyes away from the blood, she asked, "Do you think it could've been a bear that killed him?"

"No. He was shot, there." Wes's hands hovered over the man's bloody chest. "He'd be mauled if a bear got him."

Libby was blubbering now, and Jane had to take a deep breath to pull her own self together. Wes steered Libby by her elbows to a rickety bench and wrapped his arm around her shoulder.

Jane gave Wes a sideways glance over his wife's bowed head. "My God, shot? Can you tell when it happened? Do you think the shooter is close by?"

"I imagine he's long gone."

"What's this?" Doug burst out of the woods with Olivia right behind him.

"The campground host has been shot!" Jane's voice sounded shrill to her own ears.

At first, the Ladners appeared stunned into silence, then when Libby let out a wail, Olivia rushed over to her. The three women sat close together, side-by-side, on the worn bench. Jane held one of Libby's hands and Olivia held the other. Doug bent low to study the scene with Wes leaning over his shoulder.

Where was the man from the cabin? Should she backtrack up the trail and ask him for help?

After what seemed too long a time, crashing in the trees from the direction of the campsites made everyone suck in their breath and stare into the pines. Was a killer bear heading their way? But only the national park rangers in green uniforms advanced through the underbrush with two state troopers on their heels. And following the troopers were search-and-rescue paramedics in white carrying a stretcher.

"What happened here?" One of the rangers pointed to the dead man.

Wes's chest swelled. "We have no idea what happened. We were hiking and found him like this."

"Sit on the bench and don't leave."

Doug and Wes backed away from the body as the rangers took their places.

Olivia hissed to Jane, "We tried to catch up with you guys, but we got lost." She drew a strand of her jet black hair behind her ear as her worried eyes darted over to the campground host on the ground.

"How in the world could you get lost?"

Doug piped up. "Olivia couldn't find her reading glasses, so we looked all over the path thinking she might've dropped them." He turned to his wife. "I don't know why you would've brought your reading glasses when you didn't bother to bring the trail map. We wouldn't have gotten lost if we had a map."

Olivia gave an exaggerated sigh. "I told you, Douglas, I'm not sure where I lost my glasses."

"You two quit sniping at each other. A man's dead here." Libby's eyes were swollen and red, her breath ragged.

Olivia exchanged a puzzled look with Jane, who resumed patting Libby on the back. Doug handed Wes his gun. "Thanks for letting us shoot this."

Wes shoved the gun into one of his pockets, fast. A holstered revolver peeped out from an inside pocket in Doug's open jacket and he yanked it shut. A state trooper marched up to Doug. "Please hand over your gun. Anyone else have a firearm?" His steely eyes moved from one of them to the other.

Jane's mouth dropped open when Olivia said, "I do." From her pocket she slid out a leather holster housing a small-barreled handgun.

Doug handed his gun over, too. "You'll find the guns have been fired. We went to the firing range just outside the camp this morning before we hiked here." The trooper's head swiveled around, and his eyes bored into Doug's.

"Mine has been fired, too." Wes gave his pistol to the officer. "I didn't go to the firing range, but I lent my gun to Doug to use."

"That's right. My wife and I both shot his revolver at the range." Doug crossed his arms and tucked his chin low as the paramedics lifted the heavy, blanket-enveloped body onto the portable gurney. A couple of the rangers stalked around in the woods, and others poked the ground near the fire pit.

The officer placed the three revolvers into evidence bags. "A special agent from the National Park Service is on his way here, and he'll take your statements."

The dinner club members appeared to own a number of firearms. How many others at the campground had also brought guns, since the firing range was so close?

A ranger walked over with a pair of purple glasses in his gloved hands.

"Those are mine!" squawked Olivia. "Where'd you find them?"

"Under the body."

Olivia's frightened eyes bulged. "No way! I haven't been to the amphitheater before this." The friends shot alarmed looks at each other. Olivia shrugged with her palms raised upward, as if saying, "What the…."

The trooper stationed himself with feet spread apart and hands on hips. "Two of the park rangers will escort you to the campsites. You will wait there until we can question you. Everyone is to leave their backpacks on the benches, and we'll return them later. Before you leave, the rangers will search your pockets." They stood up and submitted to being searched, then trekked to Jane's campsite, with one ranger in front and one in back.

Jane tapped her friend on the shoulder. "Olivia, are you hurt? You're limping."

"As if enough hasn't happened. I tripped over a tree root on the trail and stepped down funny on my ankle."

"Maybe you shouldn't be walking on it."

"When we get back, I'll prop it up."

"Wrap it in ice, too."

Once they'd reached the campsite, Jane hastened to the cooler, but a ranger stopped her when she lifted the lid. "We're going to test for gun residue, so don't put your hands in any water."

Jane frowned. "I want to make an ice pack for my friend over there."

"I'll do it." He scooped some ice and wrapped the cubes in the dishtowel lying on the picnic table. The ranger passed the ice pack to Olivia, who rested her foot on top of the picnic bench and balanced the homemade pack on her ankle. "Someone planted my glasses at the crime scene," Olivia said in an undertone to the group, sitting in their camp chairs near the fire pit.

"Shhh, be quiet." Doug shook his head slightly, his eyes darting to the ranger.

Libby touched Olivia's fingers. "What happened to your knuckles?" The back of Olivia's right hand was no longer covered in bandages and was red, scratched, and scabbed.

"I scraped my knuckles when I was grating cheese this morning. I can't keep the Band-Aids on."

"Ouch." Libby made a face. "That looks nasty."

"I've done that before," said Wes. Everyone stared at his big, meaty hands. Olivia held out her long, slender fingers, with beautifully manicured nails, and a large diamond ring on her left hand, scabs on her right.

"Do you want some more Band-Aids?" Jane started to get up.

The ranger standing by the fire pit said, "Sit down and refrain from speaking. The federal agent will be here in a moment to take your statements." The other ranger checked his cellphone, while the first one looked fixedly into the remains of the campfire from the night before. He poked a stick in the pit and stirred the ashes around. "What's this?" He lifted the stick into the air. The charred remains of a disposable latex glove hung from the end.

"It's mine." Olivia reached for the hand sanitizer on the picnic table. "I wore disposable gloves to handle raw fish last night. That's what we had for dinner—"

"Olivia, quit talking," snapped Doug. The three women's heads swiveled toward him.

"Give me that hand gel." One ranger snatched the bottle from her, while the other jerked an evidence bag from his capacious jacket pocket and thrust the charred glove inside. Olivia's face turned white, and they all sat with their mouths shut.

In just a few more minutes, a group of state troopers and a man new to the scene marched into the campsite. A trooper announced, "This is Special Agent Marshall who will be taking over the investigation."

The agent, in a crisp, khaki green uniform and Smokey the Bear hat, handed the troopers a duffle bag. "Swab everyone's hands for gun residue. Here are the kits."

Once that was done, the agent asked the group to change their clothes and place what they were wearing in evidence bags. After that, he passed around clipboards and pens. "You need to fill out these forms with your statements and be sure to include your contact information."

Jane sat next to Libby at the picnic table as they scribbled on the pages. Jane said in a low voice out of the side of her mouth, "It's a good thing he's not a federal marshal or his name would be Marshal Marshall."

That got a smile out of Libby. "Like Dr. Doctor in the movie, *Spies Like Us*."

"Or attorneys whose last names are 'Law,' or worse yet, 'Lawless.' "

"Please stop talking and fill out the forms." Agent Marshall spoke in a clipped voice.

"Are we in kindergarten?" asked Olivia. "Jeez."

Doug cast them a warning glance, then continued to write.

Once they finished, Agent Marshall collected the clipboards. "We'd like permission to search your tents and vehicles."

The group gave questioning looks to Doug, who

asked, "What you are looking for?"

"Firearms and bullets. Clothes and gloves with gun residue."

"I think you've taken all the guns already. But you have permission to search my tent and car." Doug took his wallet out of his pocket, extracted his gun permit, and handed the piece of paper to the agent.

Wes led Agent Marshall over to his pickup truck and opened the locked glove box where he kept his gun permit. The investigators gathered the bullets for all the firearms.

As several troopers went in and out of the tents, the dinner club members took turns giving separate evidence at Wes and Libby's campsite across the graveled road from Jane's and the Ladners' shared site. When it was Jane's turn, Agent Marshall read the statement she'd just completed out loud to her, then asked, "Describe all your conversations with the campground host."

She carefully recounted everything she could remember, including the sounds in the night. "First I heard a rustling outside my tent. The noise seemed to move in the direction of the trail to the fishing pond. I was afraid it was a black bear, but it could've been a person. I didn't look out to see what it was. By the way, can you tell me the host's name? It seems so callous not to know."

"Michael Quadtrini. What time did you hear the noise?"

"I don't know. I didn't look at the time. After I fell back asleep, Olivia, Doug, and I heard a scream. We came out of our tents, and Doug walked around with a flashlight, but didn't see anything. Olivia and I waited here. After that, I didn't hear anything more until I woke up. Did anyone else tell you about the scream? Do you think it was Mr. Quadtrini?"

Agent Marshall ignored her question. "You didn't hear a gunshot during the night?"

"That's the one thing I didn't hear. But you see, I could hear shots all day yesterday from that firing range, even after dark. Maybe it just didn't register as an unexpected sound."

"How long was Doug gone?"

"Not long, just minutes."

"Did you know Quadtrini before you came to the campground?"

"No."

"Did you see anyone else on the trail this morning?"

"No. Wait, yes I did. There's a cabin not too far from the amphitheater, just up the hill, and I saw a man come out, right before we spotted the body. I didn't see anyone else."

"Did you go to the firing range?"

"No. I don't own a gun, and I'm not interested in learning to shoot."

"That's all I have for now. Please let us know if you think of anything more that might be helpful." He spoke in a slow, no-nonsense manner, and didn't crack a smile.

"We're all innocent bystanders here."

"There will be a meeting at the amphitheater within the next thirty minutes, as soon as the state troopers are done questioning the other campers. We'll be back to gather everyone."

"Oh. All right." Jane stomped over to the group

waiting at her campsite. The investigators had gone, and the friends were finally alone.

Doug whirled his hands around. "How on earth did your glasses end up with the body, Olivia?"

"How should I know, Douglas?" she howled, plucking at the towel wrapped around her ankle.

"Where did you last see them?"

"I can't remember. I must've set them down somewhere and forgot about them. I only use them for reading." Olivia stretched her foot out and winced. "I hope no one at the firing range tells the police I'm a good marksman. A sharpshooter."

"What? You?" With her jaw open, Jane pulled her head back and fixed her eyes on her friend.

Olivia's chin shot up. "I took classes for my conceal-carry permit. I'm really good at hitting the target, and I have strong wrists."

Libby scratched her head. "What do your wrists have to do with it? I would think all that matters is your trigger finger."

Doug tugged on his mustache. "Most women don't have wrists strong enough to handle the kick-back of a large caliber. Even Olivia, strong as she is, shoots a standard caliber."

Jane nodded along with the others, but didn't understand what he meant.

As if on cue, gunshots cracked from the firing range.

Olivia leaned closer. "I'm surprised the police haven't closed the range down."

"Me too." Jane widened her eyes.

Doug crossed his arms. "I'm sure they will soon. Did anyone hear a shot in the middle of the night?"

Wes's expression looked grim. "I did around four-thirty this morning. Did anyone else hear it?"

"I sure didn't, but that might've been when we heard the scream." Jane drew her fleece tighter around her middle. "Does anyone know what time that was?"

The sound of gunshots ricocheted off the mountains. Wes vaulted out of his camp chair. He grabbed the coffee pot off the camp stove, but the pot slipped from his fingers and crashed down onto the burner. He muttered a few swear words under his breath. "Sorry. I'm so clumsy, but it's empty anyway."

"I'll make some coffee." Jane stood.

Libby stared at her husband. "I sure wish they'd close off that firing range." Her foot bobbed up and down after she crossed one leg over the other.

Jane patted Wes's shoulder, his trembling running up through her fingers, then busied herself measuring the coffee grounds and filling the pot from the water jug. What could be bothering him? He must be upset about finding the body, but maybe there was more to it. After the coffee brewed, she poured the steaming hot liquid into blue enamelware mugs.

Libby added sugar to Wes's. She clutched her husband's arm for a moment, then said, as if by way of explanation, "That marshal made a big deal about Wes falling into the lake. He said the gun residue could've been washed right off his hands."

"He's an agent not a marshal," Doug reminded them.

Olivia blew out a big breath, puffing out her cheeks. "Wes isn't the only one in the sticky wicket. That marshal went on and on about my glasses. He asked over and over how they got under the body. And the fact that I twisted my ankle and have cuts on my hand. Like, maybe I was in a fight with the campground host. He actually asked me if the host roughed me up."

"Why in the world would you have a fight with him?" Jane was about to sit down, but paused in mid-air.

"Why anyone would. He was an obnoxious bastard." Wes stuffed his hands in his pockets and scowled.

Doug crossed his ankles. "I didn't think he was friendly either, but why do you say he was obnoxious?"

"He wouldn't let me use my military discount to pay for our campsite, for one thing."

Jane sank into her chair. "Well, he charged us extra because we had two vehicles at our site. I explained we're sharing this spot, and I checked to make sure it was okay to put up two tents, but he said there was still an extra fee."

"You were too nice to him, Jane. I would've argued and refused to pay more. But I thought Wes was going to punch him out. The whole campground could hear you yelling, Wes." Olivia chuckled, then her laugh faded when no one else joined in. Libby looked pallid, and Wes was absorbed in his own thoughts.

There was a long silence. Jane could no longer hear shots from the firing range. "If Quadtrini was rude to everyone, and he probably was, that agent will soon hear about it from the other campers."

"Quadtrini?" asked Doug.

"Yes. His name was Michael Quadtrini." Jane narrowed her eyes. "Agent Marshall told me, but he wouldn't give away any more information. He was so serious, never even smiled once."

"He scares me to death." Olivia scowled. "I'm sure he suspects me. Between my glasses and the burned gloves. Plus, he asked several times if I washed my hands with the sanitary hand gel. He thinks I put on my glasses to shoot while wearing the gloves, accidently dropped my glasses in the woods by the body, burned the gloves to destroy the gun powder residue, and washed my hands with the sanitizer. All this while limping around with a cut hand because Quadtrini beat me up first."

"And when were you supposed to have done all this?" Wes puckered his eyebrows.

"Marshall said the murder most likely happened in the early morning hours. I got the impression it could've happened even during the time we were on the hike this morning."

Doug ran the back of his fist across his upper lip. "The body was not cold all over when we found him, but the heat from the fire pit may have kept him partly warm. His legs and feet were stiff, though. It'll make time of death harder to determine."

A shiver went down Jane's spine. "You touched the body, Doug?"

"Yes, but I didn't move him."

Wes added, "And I touched him, too. I pressed his neck for a pulse."

Libby wrung her hands. "None of us have an alibi during the night, except for our spouses."

"Libby, you and Wes have me for an alibi during the hike, anyway." Jane blew on her coffee before taking a sip. "And Olivia, think harder. When did you last see your glasses?"

"I noticed they were missing while we were on the

hike, and I thought they could've dropped out of my pocket. But the last time I remember using them was at dinner when we were sitting right here at the picnic table. It's possible I didn't even bring them into the tent with me when we went to bed."

"If you left them out on the picnic table, someone could've come through the campsite during the night and taken them." Doug sank down on the bench and ran his fingers the length of the rough wood surface.

"And continued down the trail to the fishing pond and the amphitheater to kill Quadtrini, leaving your glasses with his body," added Jane.

It was not looking good for Olivia.

Chapter 3

"Come with me!" The agent was back with his regiment.

The club members followed his lead to the amphitheater, joining a group of six other adults and two young children, evidently the other campers. One of them, a man possibly in his thirties, with horned-rimmed glasses and wearing a red pullover, was standing next to a mousy woman holding the children's hands. An elderly woman was assisting her husband as he sat down on a park bench.

Agent Marshall stood at center stage as the campers watched him with interest. Yellow crime scene tape fluttered behind him. "You can collect your backpacks." The club members plucked their packs from the tail end of a Forest Service pickup truck someone had driven in on the service road.

"As some of you know, the road closure of last night has been reopened, and you can leave the park now. You are free to go, but we may call you for further questioning."

A murmur went through the small gathering.

"What's this about the road being closed?" Doug stood facing the agent.

"Last night around six o'clock a large sinkhole developed clear across the access road connecting the park to the highway. A gravel detour was put in place this morning. The hole is stable, and the state's road department has now determined the temporary road is safe."

"So, no one could've entered or exited the park and the campground from six last night until this morning?" asked one of the other campers.

"That's right." Marshall gave them a curt nod. "At least not by vehicle."

"So, how did you get in?" asked the oldest child, a boy wearing a pint-sized fishing vest and plastic Crocs on his feet.

"We cut the trail in our jeeps. We were already at the sinkhole this morning when we got the emergency call."

"Can you tell us what happened? When was he shot?" asked the boy's father, a man with a deep voice, the one in the red pullover. He nudged his glasses up his nose.

Jane glanced at the young children. Their mother drew the smallest child, a girl with brown curls, into her arms.

"You can go onto the U.S. Forest Service website for more information. A press release will be posted later today. Also, for those of you whose revolvers have been confiscated, we have your receipts. Once we are done with ballistic testing, you can pick up your firearms, unless we have a reason to hold them. We will let you know when, or you can call us to check."

The campers examined each other with curiosity.

"That's all. Unless you have more questions."

No one said a word. The federal agent, state troopers, and park rangers took off in different directions, and the elderly couple ambled along the trail toward the campsites.

Doug strode over to the remaining campers. Jane turned to Olivia and asked with a rise in her voice, "Does Doug know these people?"

"We met that man in the red jacket at the firing range." Olivia's eyes darted from face to face. "I recognize others from the range, too."

The man's deep, bass voice carried over. "So, one of the campers had to have shot the campground host, since no one else could've gotten in after six last night."

"I suppose someone could've walked in and out." A woman in a gray sweatshirt held up both palms of her hands.

Wes stood up to join them. "But it's a good twenty miles to the highway."

The campers' eyes pinged from one to another.

"Well, we're packing up and going home," said the mother of the children.

Libby shot a look at her husband. "Can we leave too?"

Jane tugged on her friend's arm. "Please don't go. Let's stick together. I'd like to stay until tomorrow like we planned." She'd put hard work into this camping trip—making park reservations, planning meals, packing—plus all the fun would be cut short.

"There's a killer out there, and your guns have all been taken by the rangers." Libby ran her fingers through her spiky hair.

"Most likely the murderer will be the first person to high-tail it out of here." Doug stood with his hands on his hips, staring into the woods as if watching the killer escaping.

Olivia looked to Doug. "I'd like to stay."

Wes stood in silence for a moment, then acquiesced with a shrug. "I guess I don't want to leave, either. After all, Libby and I are done with our turn to cook, since I caught and fried the fish last night." He winked at his wife, but she didn't look happy.

Jane heard a ping from her pocket and checked her cellphone. She walked a few paces away and sat on the hard bench to scroll through her text messages. There was one from Dale Capricorn, her on-again, off-again boyfriend. *How is the camping trip? Having any excitement?* She tapped a return message. *Lots of excitement! Tell u about it when I get home.* Her cellphone battery was low—she would have to charge her phone in the car, but decided to turn the phone off for now.

She rejoined the dinner club to head back to the campground. "Let's take the longer hike up to the high mountain lake like we planned. It's five miles round trip, so it will take a couple of hours, and we should get going soon."

"Good idea. We should enjoy the rest of the weekend and put this out of our minds," Doug said, with Olivia limping behind him, and Jane taking the rear. "Olivia's made sack lunches. I'll get the box of lunches out so everyone can grab one."

Olivia added, "Each sack has something different, so be sure to look inside the bags and choose the lunch you want."

"Is there a Cracker Jack prize in one?" Jane laughed.

"You'll have to look inside to find out."

The friends each went into their own tents for their gear and to get ready for the long hike. Jane needed to visit the latrine before setting out, so she stashed a tiny packet of hand wipes into her pocket and wended her way over to the primitive outhouse. She went in, closed the door and slid the bolt, then heard two people talking at the back side of the wooden structure.

"What did you tell that federal agent?"

Jane had heard that deep bass voice before—from the man in the red pullover and glasses.

"What? I didn't say a thing," a woman answered in a high, tense voice Jane didn't recognize. "What are you worried about?"

"They'll be looking at me, as you know."

"I'm sure there are plenty of others with motives. I don't doubt he ruined other people's lives, not just ours."

"But who else had the opportunity because of that sinkhole? Bad luck there."

"Remember the killer could've walked in."

Jane tried to find a knot hole to see out. There was a small one, but not placed so she could see anyone. She positioned her ear near the wall without actually touching the wood, because it was covered with flies. Her ear hovering over the knot hole, she heard, "Maybe, but how likely is that? The police will focus on the campers." It was the man's voice. A moment of silence stretched out.

The woman sounded suddenly nearer. "Quadtrini caused plenty of grief to both our families. I'm glad he's dead. No regrets there." Jane jerked her head back, then tried to peek out the hole once again. What looked like a gray fleece or sweatshirt blocked the aperture.

The voices went quiet, and she heard nothing more for several minutes. Jane was stuck inside the stinky outhouse until she could be sure the man and woman had left. Was she free to leave her concealment? Someone rattled the door handle and she jumped.

"Just a moment." She rubbed her hands with the wipe from her pocket and tossed the tissue into the overflowing trash basket. Using another hand wipe to cover the door handle, she turned the knob and slunk out. Only the mother of the young children was waiting outside. She wasn't wearing a gray sweatshirt, and she seemed safe.

Jane took a deep breath of clean, fresh air and gave out a sigh of relief, but glanced behind the outhouse on her way to the campsite. No one was there, only a bare gravel road and scrawny bushes.

"We were waiting for you." Olivia grasped both of her elbows, her arms folded across her chest. "What were you doing at the outhouse so long?"

After throwing Olivia a look, Jane retold the conversation she'd overheard. "And the man was the one you talked to, Doug, the one with the horned-rimmed glasses and the red jacket, because I recognized his voice. Was he also at the firing range?"

"Yes." Doug rubbed his jaw.

"Did he introduce himself? Do you know his name?"

"Ben Malkon. We even traded guns, and he let me fire his revolver, a .357 Magnum." Doug exchanged a look with Wes.

Olivia let go of one elbow and propped her chin in her hand. "You were in the outhouse long enough to hear their conversation?"

Jane rolled her eyes. "I was stuck in there."

Doug stood up. "You need to tell the ranger what

you overheard. I'm walking over to the ranger station right now. Come with me."

Leaving the others behind, their feet ate up the gravel road as they bustled over to the park's entrance. Inside the booth, built out of logs with windows on all four sides, was a ranger, a young woman wearing a crisp uniform with her hair in a ponytail. Jane explained the conversation she'd overheard between Ben Malkon and the unknown woman, and the ranger called Agent Marshall on the phone, leaving him a message.

Doug took Jane's place at the window. "Our group is hiking to the homestead near the high mountain lake, but my wife twisted her ankle and can't go. Could you keep an eye on her, please, while we're gone? We'll only be a couple of hours." He peered clear through the windows of the wooden booth out the other side and nodded toward the day-use area. "If she set up her camp chair in the shade over there, you'd be able to see her from here."

"Yes, that's fine. Someone'll be here all day, and we can check on her."

"Okay. I appreciate it." A smile creased his face. With that, they headed to the campsite at a trot.

"Grab your sack lunches, we're ready to go." Doug quirked his chin in the direction of a square cardboard box crowded with brown lunch bags. They peeked into the sacks and made their choices. Jane's contained a roast beef sandwich, an apple, a bag of homemade granola, and a chocolate chip cookie. The other bags held cheese and crackers, pop-top cans of tuna, fruit, and other healthy or sweet snacks. Libby choose a bag containing a Suzy-Q cake.

"I'm not going. I need to rest my ankle. I can't take

a long hike." Olivia gave them a wan smile as she rubbed her foot.

Jane knew this, but Wes and Libby stopped in their tracks, and Libby said, "I can stay with you."

Doug explained, "Olivia will be fine by herself. I talked to the ranger and asked them to keep an eye on her. She's going to hang out at the picnic area in view of the ranger station the whole time."

"Are you sure?" Libby wrinkled her nose.

"Sure, nothing's going to happen." Olivia flipped her day pack upside down and spread out the contents on the table top. "I have a book to read, but darn it, no reading glasses. I guess I only brought one pair."

"I've got extra. I'll get them for you." Jane retrieved her readers from her purse in the car. After she returned, the campers stuffed their backpacks with their lunches and went on their way—sans Olivia—to a wooden post pointing in the direction of the homestead and mountain lake.

"This trail is sign-posted and marked well according to the map." Jane hitched her backpack higher onto her shoulders. The rest followed her, trudging behind. Overhead, birds chirped in the trees, and underfoot, dry pine needles softened their steps. Before long, they stopped at a fork in the trail to take long drinks from their water bottles. Doug turned the pages of a pocket-sized book on birds, Wes took selfie photos of himself and Libby, and Jane sank onto a low, flat rock to rest. The area appeared so peaceful, it was hard to believe any violence could've occurred near this beauty spot.

"Look!" Wes peered into the sky where a raptor flew over their heads with a foot-long snake hanging from its talons. Jane shuddered as she tore her eyes away, fast.

They finished their short break, shouldered into their packs, and resumed the hike. After an hour on the ever-ascending trail, only once dropping down into a beautiful shaded valley from which they scaled steep switchbacks, they arrived at the high mountain lake. The group found comfortable spots to sit on fallen timber near the ruins of the tumbled-down homestead.

Wes gobbled down his lunch, then removed a collapsible fishing pole from his pack. The rest of them continued to eat, as he cast his line time after time.

"Don't fall in again," teased Jane. "And whoever put that fake spider in my lunch sack did not fool me." She drew the black plastic bug out and waved it around.

"Olivia must've done that, and she's not here to enjoy her own prank." Doug massaged the back of his neck.

Jane hid the plastic spider in her pocket. Would she be able to sneak it into someone's sleeping bag? She finished her apple and wrapped the core into her sack to pack out. "What's that through the trees on the east side of the lake?" Jane's right hand formed a salute across her forehead as she shaded her eyes.

"It's the cabin we saw from the amphitheater." Libby balled up her lunch sack and tossed the garbage into her open pack.

Jane hoisted herself onto a tall boulder. On the flat top she turned in all directions, with her hand once again shielding her eyes from the mid-day sun. She squinted down into the valley. "I think I can see where Quadtrini was killed from here. I wish I had some binoculars."

"I've got a pair." Libby swallowed the last of a juicy peach and cleaned her hands with wet wipes, before fishing out her compact, black binoculars.

Doug added, "Me too." The two of them clambered onto the rock to stand next to Jane. Libby was a head taller and Doug another head taller, forming stair steps like siblings close in age. They both peered through their binoculars for a moment, then Libby handed hers to Jane, who pressed the eyepieces against her cheeks and rotated the lens slightly right and then left. Sure enough, the view was clear all the way to the amphitheater.

"The person who came out of the cabin this morning could've been an eye-witness. I'm curious to know if Agent Marshall talked to him." Jane lowered the binoculars.

"He might be another suspect. After all, a local would be acquainted with Quadrini. What's the chance of one of the campers knowing him?" Doug hopped down from the boulder followed by Jane. Next came Libby, slithering down the rock and landing on her feet.

"Well, both the man and woman I heard talking outside the latrines knew him." Jane guessed the others were all thinking the same thing. "Let's go over to the cabin. Look. There's a path that winds around to it. We can just be friendly and see if anyone's home."

Wes stepped from the edge of the lake, snapped his pole down to its compact size, and shoved the contraption into his backpack. "Fish aren't biting. It's too hot in the sun. They're staying low in the water."

Doug nodded. "Okay, then, let's go over to the cabin."

As Libby gave a helpless, I-don't-care shrug, Jane

shot him a grateful glance. Doug took the lead on the footpath. In short order, they halted in front of the yellow-logged cabin, but all was quiet. Jane strained to listen for the German shepherd barking, but only the wind whistled in the pines. Standing at the edge of the path, they could see over the tree tops to the amphitheater below.

"The crime scene's in clear sight of this window. But what could anyone see in the dark of the night?" Doug threw his arms wide.

"Night vision goggles." Jane twirled the blue, ribbed strap of her backpack in her fingers. "If they had night vision goggles, they could've seen." Making up her mind, she darted up the steps and rapped on the door with a loud, rat-a-tat-tat. As she tried to come up with an excuse to disturb the person within, her heart started to pound a little more than usual, but no one answered the door, even after she knocked several more times.

All of a sudden, a bang hit the glass in the window overlooking the front porch.

Jane bounded back, her heart in her throat.

Behind the window pane, the German shepherd lunged at her with teeth bared, emitting a series of loud, vicious barks that clouded the glass.

"No one's here but the guard dog. Give it up." Wes flapped one hand.

Jane tried not to let her frustration show. "Okay. Coming." She stepped off the porch with leaden feet, then trudged with her friends to the trail joining the labyrinth of paths leading down to the amphitheater. The group was quieter on the hike back. The time was late afternoon when they arrived at the benches surrounding the giant fire pit.

Libby scuffed her feet on the hard ground, her eyes darting all over. "Let's not hang around here. I want to get back to our tents." Wes stood by her side.

But Doug edged over to the crime scene tape. "The investigators marked the ground with stakes where they found the evidence. See there? That's where Olivia's glasses were under the body." He knelt down and rocked back on his feet.

Jane stood next to him. "Doug, what do you think of the murder? As a former police officer, you know, your professional opinion."

Doug rubbed a hand across his brow. "Quadtrini was facing the shooter. Judging by the entrance wound, I think he was shot from fairly close range…by a standard caliber—"

"I don't feel so good." Libby forced her hands out, as if shaky on her feet, and tripped backward, collapsing onto the bench.

Jane stepped over to squeeze her friend's shoulder, as she glanced in Doug's direction. "What's 'caliber' mean?"

"The size of the barrel. Olivia's Derringer's a standard size. I only saw one bullet hole, but her double barrel is a single shot, a .38 Special. Mine's a standard, too."

"My Ruger is, too." Wes appeared deep in thought.

Doug scratched his head. "And so was Ben Malkon's. Forensics will figure it out."

Jane found his words interesting, but had no idea what he was talking about. "The investigators will be able to tell he was *not* shot by one of us, right?"

"Yes. Once they recover the bullet, they'll be able

to identify the gun. If he was shot by a semi-automatic, they'd recover the casings, and they can tell from those, too." Doug's hands flew around in the air. "But I didn't see any casings here this morning. And then, there's a chance the bullet might not be recovered. Sometimes the bullet passes through the body, especially if it doesn't hit a bone. They'd never be able to find the slug in these woods. If that's the case, they might not rule out our guns."

Jane furrowed her forehead. "Could that small rain squall have washed away evidence, like maybe the gun residue on someone's clothes and hands?"

"That could happen, yes." Doug caressed his bristling red mustache.

Libby was starting to look even more ill. She twiddled her rings around and around on her fingers and blinked rapidly. "Let's get out of here."

Wes patted Libby's hands as he said to Jane, "I meant to ask earlier, what did the ranger say when you told them about the people talking at the latrines?"

Jane shrugged. "Nothing. The ranger phoned Agent Marshall and left him a message."

"Can we leave now?" Libby's face was positively green.

"Just a sec." Doug stood up near a yellow flag poking out of the ground. "So, the murderer stands right here." He raised both arms into the air, joined his hands together with his index fingers pointed out and his other fingers folded back. He lowered his outstretched arms as if to shoot. "The murderer takes aim. Just like this. And pulls the trigger."

Jane could visualize it. She cringed as she imagined the pistol going off and Quadtrini falling to the ground. She felt an odd prickling at the back of her neck.

Chapter 4

Flickering LED candles in a plastic candelabra and a vase of flowering weeds in water graced the red and white checkered tablecloth on the picnic table. Soft jazz played from an iPod.

"Olivia, you were supposed to stay at the ranger station." Doug drew in a loud breath.

"I got bored and came back, Douglas. Don't you like what I did?" Olivia gestured at the table, like Vanna next to the Wheel of Fortune board.

"What's this gadget?" Wes lifted a small black box the size of a man's wallet from the picnic bench.

Doug threw Olivia a stern look, but answered, "It's a solar cellphone charger, and there are multiple outlets if anyone needs to charge your phones. I'll plug Olivia's iPod in so we can listen to music all evening without the battery running down." He located the cord that fit into the iPod and plugged it in. Jane extracted her cellphone from her pocket to charge, too.

Olivia smoothed the tablecloth and refolded one of the matching cloth napkins. "I'm making beef stroganoff for dinner since it's our turn to cook."

"Thanks for taking two meal assignments. Lunch and dinner." Jane laughed at the red Solo cups with wine glass stems set at each place. "You're sure glamping it."

"Talk about glamping...I've never heard of such a

fancy meal while camping. Everybody always tops us." Libby groaned, slipping off her stiff, laced hiking boots. "How many miles total did we hike today, between our hike to the amphitheater this morning and now this last one?" She wiped her forehead with a wet wipe, and her face started to resume its natural color.

Jane clucked her tongue. "Only about six or so total. The hike this morning was pretty short."

Olivia opened her eyes wide. "When I was reading over by the ranger station, I saw that man in glasses, the one in the red pullover, talking with a woman."

"Ben Malkon," breathed Jane. "Did you get a good look at the woman? Was she his wife? The one with the kids, I think."

"No. She was hefty and muscular. You wouldn't want to meet her in a dark alley." Olivia wiggled her eyebrows up and down, eyes still wide. "She looked mean."

Wes glanced at Jane. "She might be the same woman you overheard at the latrines."

Jane toyed with her red Solo cup. "I wish we knew who's who at this campground. Next time you see them, sneak a picture."

"The police have everyone's names. Let it go, Jane." Doug's forehead wrinkled while he rooted around in his cooler. He stacked jars and packets on the table next to a box of wine.

Jane's chin jutted out in defiance. "No one can stop me from taking pictures of the scenery. And if someone's in the background, it's not my fault."

A dangerous light glinted in Doug's eyes, as he eased out the spout on the wine box. "We might need to send you to bed without supper."

"Not me, I'm being good. And I could use some of that." Libby held out her Solo cup with the wine glass stem for Doug to fill.

Jane snagged a small square of cheese off a plate of appetizers and chewed with exaggerated bites, then slowly licked her lips, while Olivia chuckled.

As the group stood around to watch, Olivia sautéed onions and garlic in Jane's cast iron skillet on the campfire. She added beef strips to the pan. "We purchased the beef vacuum packed from an outfitter. All I need to do is warm it up," she explained, plopping in more squares of butter and a handful of chopped mushrooms. The savory aroma made Jane's mouth salivate.

Doug stationed himself over a pot on the camp stove waiting for the water to boil. Finally, he threw in a bag of egg noodles. Then he handed Olivia a container of beef broth to add to the large skillet. When the noodles were ready, he drained the water and Olivia poured the fragrant meat and mushrooms on top of the noodles, folded in sour cream, then let the creation rest on the warm burner for a few minutes.

After ladling their servings onto blue enameled camp plates, they reclined at the picnic table for the blessing over the meal.

"We would've brought the good silver, but we didn't want to polish it," Olivia joked.

The beef was tender, and they were quiet while enjoying the delicious chow. "I can't even make something this good in my own kitchen at home," whined Libby. "What's for dessert? Cherries jubilee?"

"How about S'mores? We can't go camping without them." Olivia winked. "Remember the time I fell backward off the cement edge of your fire pit when we were making S'mores at your house, Jane?"

"You did a somersault right off the patio edge, and you never even dropped your S'more." Jane laughed at the memory. "Hee, hee."

Doug grinned. "Oh no. Don't get her started. She won't stop giggling."

Olivia's eyes danced. "I saw one of those tear-drop campers on the other side of the campground. Before it gets dark, I'd like to have a closer look at it. Does anyone want to walk over there with me? We can toast the marshmallows when we get back."

"I'd love, love, love that. Let's go." Jane was sitting at the picnic table on top of her legs, bent at the knees, heels tucked under her bottom, but popped up, unfolding her legs as she rose.

Doug pointed at her. "How can you sit on your feet like that? It would kill my hips and knees."

"It's so comfortable." Jane pushed her bare feet into her flip flops. "But I'll be glad to give my legs a stretch after that filling dinner."

"Olivia, how's your ankle? Can you walk that far?" Doug stood.

"It's just a few yards down the road." Olivia tested her weight on her ankle. "I can make it, Douglas."

The Powells decided to come along. The friends left the campsite behind as they strolled at a slow pace along the dusty gravel. All the campsites were empty, and the markers at each site were devoid of the paper reservation slips showing the spot was taken. The other campers had pulled up their tent stakes and left, except for campsite number eight, where the campers appeared to be enjoying a long stay in their tear-drop trailer, white with red trim. A generator for electricity hummed a low melody. White paper lanterns waved from the camper's awning in the soft breeze. An atomic-patterned rug covered the dirt under two white, wooden rocking chairs in which two elderly folks were sitting, sleeping cocker spaniels at their slippered feet. Jane remembered them from the federal agent's gathering earlier that day.

Olivia introduced herself, then everyone else. The old woman said, "I'm Gloria and this is my husband Ted." The spaniels thumped their tails on the ground in a friendly way at the sound of her voice. "These are our dogs, Desi and Lucy."

"I love your camper." Olivia waved toward the trailer. "Can I see inside?"

Jane pulled up short at her friend's audacity, but the man rose out of his rocker. He extended his arm in a welcome. "We're pretty proud of our camper. I'd be glad to show it to you."

So Olivia shook off Doug's hand holding her arm and ran to the door. A busy hummingbird feeder hung near the window. There was only room for one visitor at a time, so Olivia went inside, with the host standing in the doorway.

She popped out after a moment. "It's just too cute. It has a u-shaped bench and dinette table. There's a sink and a two-burner stove. And she has *I Love Lucy* decorations all over. I want one!"

Gloria rocked forward in her chair. "We're regulars here. We stay at this campground every year for two weeks, always in site number eight..."

"How many years have you been coming?" Doug always showed polite interest.

Ted gave a vacant look. "I can't remember."

"It's our ninth year. The first time we camped here was just after our last grandbaby was born. You remember that, Ted."

"So, you probably knew the campground host?" Jane searched the lined faces of the elderly couple.

Gloria answered, "Yes, we knew Mike. So did that couple in site number five. They also come every year, but we never talk to them much. They stick to themselves, not very neighborly."

Her husband added, "Oh, yeah. Can't remember their names."

"So sad about Quadtrini's death, isn't it? Can you tell us anything about him?" pressed Jane.

Gloria rocked back in her chair, which emitted a loud creak. "He's been hosting this campground for a few years. Ever since he quit his job as a forest ranger. Never married. He turned into a bit of a grouchy, old man over time."

"We noticed that, too. But did you see anything out of the ordinary?" Jane's cheeks flushed warm as she held her breath.

Gloria stared at Wes. "We did see him arguing with a camper last night."

Wes scowled, and Jane's stomach plummeted. She asked in a small voice, "Did you tell the police about that?"

"We sure did," answered Gloria. "He was arguing with a woman in a gray sweatshirt. Might've been the lady from site number six, but I didn't get a good look at her face."

Jane could feel the group collectively let out a sigh of relief. Libby lowered herself to sit on the rug near

Gloria's feet, closing her eyes. The elderly woman grasped Libby's dainty hand in her own arthritic, veined one. "Now, now. Are you all right, honey?"

A big tear ran down Libby's pale cheek. "I don't know why I'm so emotional."

"It is upsetting, dear. I know how you feel." Ted's eyes were watery, too.

Wes tugged Libby by the hand to help her up. "We'll be on our way. We have marshmallows to toast."

They said their goodbyes to the nice older couple and traipsed along the short length of gravel road to Jane's campsite. Wes kept his arm over his wife's shoulder, and by the time they returned, Libby appeared to have recovered. She capsized into a chair next to Wes in front of the fire pit.

A beautiful sunset created a pink and blue watercolor background on the other side of the tall pine trees, and soft jazz played from the iPod on the glamorous picnic table. Wes whittled the ends of fallen branches to give them clean wood on which to skewer the marshmallows. After dropping a few into the flames by mistake, they tore into the package of graham crackers.

"I sliced some strawberries and bananas to add to the S'mores." Olivia opened containers of fruit as they assembled the gooey, chocolatey treats.

Jane smacked her lips. "I've never had S'mores with fruit in them before. These are great."

"I saw some recipes for gourmet S'mores made with caramel sauce, coconut shavings, even lime curd for a key lime S'more." Olivia wiped her mouth on her linen napkin. Jane didn't know what to say to that, since she'd never heard of lime curd.

Full darkness soon overtook the wide sky as they sat near the blazing, crackling flames. "Who has a ghost story to tell around the campfire?" Olivia gathered the dirty napkins as everyone gave her a blank look. "Well, I have one." She told the legend of the Abraham Lincoln funeral train draped in black mourning. The train traveled with the president's body seventeen hundred miles from Washington, D.C. to Illinois. Afterward, railroad workers reported sightings of a phantom ghost train with black crepe flowing from the last car.

Distant gunshots cracked and boomed from the firing range.

Libby let out a small scream.

Jane's spine shivered up and down.

"Who's at the range?" Wes's wide eyes darted around.

"Yes, who could it be? It's dark, and there aren't any campers left at the park besides us and those old folks." Jane shrank within herself.

Doug answered, "People need to practice at night, and the range is open to the public, not just for the campers. Someone probably drove in from town."

"It's hard to believe the range is still open after all that's happened." Libby clicked her tongue on the roof of her mouth. "We don't need to tell ghost stories, because we had a real life scare here last night."

"You're right. We should change the subject," Wes growled as he took Libby's hand. Beads of sweat stood out on his brow. "I can tell you a few things about this campground. There was an old mining town built on this site, a wild-west kind of town. People lived here

45

until the 1940s or so. You can still see the remains of some of the cement blocks from one of the buildings."

"Is that why there's a firing range near here?" Doug added wood from a bundle stacked to one side and stoked the fire to a blaze.

"Yes. When the old townsite was taken over by the Forest Service, the range wasn't included as part of the park. It's operated privately. Campers with gun permits can bring firearms into the park, but I don't know of any Forest Service that runs a pistol range."

"Oh, for some reason I was under the impression it was inside the park." Jane trembled as the night closed in and the temperature dropped.

Olivia flipped open her campground map. "You can walk over to the range from the campground, but it says here it's about a mile out." She refolded the map.

"It's a good thing we got a lot of exercise today, because I think I ate too much." Jane licked the melted chocolate off her sticky fingers.

"I agree." Olivia patted her flat stomach.

Jane gave her a sideways glance, then struck her marshmallow stick with force over the edge of the fire grate with a loud *cra-a-ack*!

Wes popped up out of his seat.

"What'd you do that for?" Libby gave Jane a stern look.

"Sorry. I wanted to get rid of the sticks so we don't attract any bear. There's marshmallow stuck to them." Jane held each end of another stick in her hands and cracked the branch over her bent knee, then threw the piece of wood into the fire. "Is everyone done with their sticks?" When they all nodded, she gathered the rest and shoved them under the flames.

"What did everyone bring for our potluck breakfast tomorrow? I brought some milk and those little cereal boxes that come in a variety pack. I checked my cooler. The ice is almost melted, but the milk's still cold." Jane looked around at the others. "And by the way, I found the fake ice cube with the fly in it. Whoever put that in my cooler didn't prank me."

Doug groaned. "That was me. I really thought that was a good joke. How did you catch on?"

"It was obvious." But Jane was holding the plastic cube back to use at a future cocktail party.

Olivia gazed at Jane with a knowing look. "We brought cinnamon rolls."

Wes added, "Instant oatmeal for us. Plus dried fruit to stir into it."

"This is hilarious. We are a gourmet dining club, but no one planned anything that needs to be cooked, unless you count boiling water for instant oatmeal. And everyone brought something different. It will be fun having a smorgasbord to choose from."

"I'm still full from dinner. It's hard to give thought to the next meal." Olivia yawned and stretched.

"We're breaking camp right after breakfast and heading to Denver." Libby stood up from her chair. "So, it's for the best that we have a quick meal with little clean up."

Jane gave a dejected sigh, having hoped to get one more hike in.

"I guess it's time to head to bed." Doug poured a bucket of water on the dying fire until all the red embers stopped glowing. Jane made sure everything edible was packed into the bear-proof box, and they said their goodnights.

Once Jane was settled in her tent, the evening wind kicked up, and the tall lodge pole pine trees swayed, their branches knocking together. The flimsy canvas walls billowed inward and outward, when a particularly violent gust came through. Sharp reports of bark snapping made her sit up and listen.

Was someone walking around?

The killer looking for the trail to return to the scene of the crime?

Oh, why did Olivia have to tell a ghost story on top of everything else?

Her blood ran cold as she forced herself to lie down. Turning this way and that, she was bound tightly in her twisted-up sleeping bag, and her skin felt slick with sweat.

She peeled herself out of the bag, floundered around for her keys, then gathered the flannel in her arms. She stumbled out of the tent, leaving the opening flapping in the wind, and dashed to her car, but dropped the keys on the ground. Picking them up in a death grip, she unlocked the door and catapulted inside.

But before closing the car door, she got a whiff of a strong odor of rotting garbage. She slammed the door lock down with the palm of her hand, then gripped her flashlight tight, but didn't turn it on. The hair stood up on the back of her neck, like someone was breathing down it. Sure enough, she heard the whoosh of a loud breath as a clumsy, but fast-moving, black bear emerged from the woods into the moonlit campsite.

The bear scampered around the front of her car, sniffed at the tablecloth, stopped at the fire pit, and then scrambled into the trees. Two pint-sized bear cubs, cute as could be, ran after their mama past the car window and out of view.

All of this had taken only a few moments, and Jane let out the breath she'd been holding. Tingling took a fast trip up her spine. She'd have an awesome tale to share in the morning.

Finally able to calm her heart, she lowered the driver's seat as far as it would go, wrestled her sleeping bag up like a pair of bib overalls, drew the bag in tight around her neck, and fell asleep.

****

She awoke before everyone else. After peering around the campsite from the safety of her car, she climbed out and started the coffee on her camp stove, then ripped the tablecloth off the table. The stinky bear had had her nose on that cloth.

Next, she set out the variety of cereal boxes, milk, bowls, and spoons. Soon the other sleepyheads gathered around for coffee and to add their contributions to the potluck.

"I saw the mama bear and two cubs last night." Jane grinned, as she thumped the brown, splintered top of the picnic table. "Right here." She described her bear encounter, as Wes boiled water for oatmeal.

"You should've woke us up," Olivia complained.

"To tell the truth, it happened too fast. And I wasn't about to get out of the car."

"The car?" Libby tilted her head. Then Jane had to explain her flight in the night.

"Scared-y." Olivia poked Jane's arm.

"Well, this oatmeal hits the spot for me. More coffee, though, please." Wes held out his blue speckled tin cup, as Jane emptied the dregs into it and the others chose what they wanted to eat.

"I found the spider in my sleeping bag," mentioned Olivia, with a wicked smile. Doug looked amused. He was probably planning to keep the spider to prank someone else and continue the joke.

"There's a chapel service at the amphitheater this morning," Jane told the group.

"We're not going back down there." Libby jerked her head from side-to-side. "We're already packed up. The car's loaded, and we're leaving when Wes finishes his oatmeal." She gave him an impatient glare, so he set his coffee mug down and got up.

"I'm done."

The others rose from their chairs and followed the pair to Wes's truck, then stood around as they climbed inside. Jane waved as the Powells steered out of their campsite. "See you in two weeks if not before!"

Their next club event was planned for the upcoming Fourth of July weekend. Cheryl and Bruce Breewood, original to the dinner club, were flying from Oregon to join the group. Jane's heart lightened at the thought of seeing her best friend, Cheryl, at the reunion. This camping trip was coming to an end, but at least she had something more to look forward to.

The remaining three started to break camp. Olivia scowled at her tent instructions. "I'm not sure how to take this tent down. The directions don't make sense in reverse."

"It's easy." Doug yanked the poles out from their sleeves, and the tent collapsed.

Jane packed her scant gear, while Olivia was still trying to figure out how to get their castle of a tent to fit inside its bag. Jane's camping supplies were stowed in her hatchback long before the Ladners were ready to leave. Finally, she helped Doug stash their cots in the trunk of his car.

Olivia brushed her hands together, as Doug slammed the trunk shut. "We'll walk down to the chapel service with you, Jane."

They covered the ground one more time to the amphitheater. In addition to the three of them, only the elderly couple was in attendance. A minister, wearing jeans and a checkered shirt, gave a brief sermon. He mentioned the death of Mike Quadtrini and that he understood their hearts ached over the situation. He prayed they would trust God to give them strength as they continued in their walk with Him.

After they trekked to their cars, Doug and Olivia drove away. Jane had been ready before them, but was the last to leave. With the minister's reminder still in her thoughts, her chest felt heavy. This much-anticipated campout was at an end. In spite of her efforts to make the best of it, the murder would overshadow their memories of the trip.

Without a doubt, Quadtrini suffered a far worse fate than a spoiled weekend. And a killer was out there somewhere, thinking he or she had gotten away with murder. Had the culprit remained in the park, lurking in the woods?

She gave herself a shake and clambered into her car to follow her friends out of the park, but a red compact drove ahead of her and got in between them. All three cars slowed at the temporary gravel road around the sinkhole, where a dusty road crew was busy shoveling, working on a Sunday morning.

Once on the crowded highway, Jane became separated from Olivia and Doug's white SUV as she joined the weekend traffic wending its way down the mountains to the city. She exited off the highway to look for a coffee shop. After speeding up on the narrow frontage road to pass a red car traveling much too slowly, she hit the brakes hard to swerve into a parking lot where she spotted the sign, "Latte Loco." She ordered a chai latte with soy milk at the take-out window, not wanting to enter the café smelling like campfire, but most likely others waiting for their drinks were also returning from a camping trip, too.

She pointed her car east toward Denver and enjoyed the beautiful scenery of forest and river along the frontage road parallel to I-70. Instead of returning to the highway, she veered onto a little used, two-lane county road that wound through the valley between the tall mountains. Fast running waterfalls bubbled over the tumbled-down boulders off the side of the road, colorful kayakers navigated the river cutting its way through the cliffs, and groups of muscled, young rock climbers clung to the sheer mountain walls by their hooks and ropes. She was traveling at less than highway speed on this road known mostly to kayakers and rock climbers, but the drive was less stressful than the highway, or at least it should have been.

Coming around a bend, she drove right up to a little red compact going about thirty miles an hour. Could this be the same car she'd passed before? Jeez, how did this goofball get in front of her again? She shouldn't have stopped for a latte.

She sped past the compact at the next opportunity, but then had to slow down as the road developed sharp switchbacks. When she glanced in her rearview mirror, the red car was riding her bumper. She picked up her speed, but the road twisted, causing her to hit the brakes again and again.

She kept glancing in the mirror. The car was so close she could see the driver's face—she was one of the campers from Yellow Mountain Campground—one of the women among the gatherers at the amphitheater. The big sunglasses covering her eyes didn't disguise her appearance. Could the driver be the woman whose voice she'd heard outside the latrine? Maybe the same woman in the gray sweatshirt who was arguing with the campground host?

Jane drove too fast for the narrow, winding road, the car's racing engine matching her speeding pulse. Her blood pressure went to the deep end, and her stomach clenched as she skirted the edge of the road with no guardrail. She jammed on her brakes to slow down, but the car behind rammed into her rear bumper, jolting her forward.

Chapter 5

Jane's car swerved to the right, then left, crossing over the center line. She jerked back to the right, and a driveway appeared out of nowhere, so she aimed the car through the tight entrance ringed by pine trees. She bumped along the pot-holed, dirt driveway, her head hitting the roof of the car. Bouncing to a stop, she stared into the rearview mirror, her heart thumping and her breathing ragged.

But the red car hadn't followed her up the driveway.

Her hands shook on the wheel as she crept her car forward until she came to a house where the driveway circled. After turning around and inching the car back to the county road, she sat with her foot on the brake while several cars whizzed by. Should she backtrack to busy Interstate 70 or keep going east on this somewhat deserted and winding county road? What if that crazy woman was waiting for her up ahead? Several more cars sped past and then none, as she sat there and the minutes ticked by.

Perhaps the woman was just mad Jane had passed her and then slowed down. Hitting the brakes couldn't be helped on the mountain road, but maybe this was nothing more than road rage.

She gripped the steering wheel, took a deep breath, and turned east onto the county road heading toward

Denver.

****

Exhausted from the tension of driving, she walked through the door, knelt down on her knees, and held her cheek out so Nick, the brown and white beagle, and Nora, the schnauzer mix, could give her pooch smooches. She squeezed her lips together in defense of errant tongue licks. The dog sitter had stayed until morning, but left a note on the counter explaining the puppies had been well behaved over the weekend.

Jane took over an hour to unload her camping gear and put everything away. She erected her tent in the driveway, swept it, and made sure the fabric was aired out, clean and dry, then folded the tent carefully into its sack. She aired her sleeping bag on the back patio railing, hosed and scoured out her cooler and water container, and ran the camping dishes, utensils, and the blue-enameled coffee pot through her dishwasher. She threw her camping clothes into the washing machine, then climbed into the shower to wash herself.

The dogs followed her from bathroom to kitchen to living room. While letting her hair air dry, she packed the clean camp dishes into her camping bin. She hadn't camped in years, but still had the routine down. Whew! Camping was a lot of work.

She wandered into the garage and examined the rear bumper of her car. A significant dent was overlaid with a smear of red paint. Trying to stir up a memory of the vehicles parked at the campsite, she could only recall the tear-drop camper and nothing more. She'd forgotten whether she'd seen a red car.

Hair almost dry, she went in the house to style it with the blow dryer in front of the bathroom mirror.

She flipped her fingers through her coiffure and applied makeup for the first time in three days. Then, she waited at the door, sneaking peeks out the window every few minutes.

Finally, her boyfriend, Dale Capricorn, rang the doorbell and strolled inside to give her a warm and lingering kiss. "I rushed over as soon as I got your text." His big brown eyes, under thick eyebrows, and his deep dimples heated the pit of her stomach.

She held his hand and led him out the patio door, so they could sit together in the swing facing the distant view of the Front Range Mountains. He put his strong arm around her narrow shoulder. "Tell me, how was the camping trip?"

"Where to begin?" In an excited voice, she recounted finding the campground host's body. "When I was driving home, I recognized someone behind me from the campground, and she forced me off the road!"

Dale withdrew his arm from her shoulder and reached his hands into her lap to pry her clenched fists apart. "Are you okay?"

"I wasn't hurt or anything. I pulled off on a side road and turned around. When I got back to the county road, she was gone. But I do have a big dent in my bumper."

"Let's look at your car." He held onto her until they entered the garage to examine her car's tail end. He knelt down to run his hand over the dent, then they returned to the patio to sit side-by-side in the swing. "You should report it to the police."

Jane sighed and leaned her head on his shoulder, her nose against the warmth of his throat. She breathed in a hint of musk. "How can I be sure it had to do with the campground host's death? What if it was road rage?"

"Let the police sort that out."

"All right, I'll call the Forest Service tomorrow and tell them." She drew her head back to look Dale in the eyes. "That's not the only strange part. Libby's reaction seemed too over-the-top. We were all upset, but Libby more than anyone else. It's Olivia who's the suspect."

He gave her an incredulous stare. "Not Olivia! Why her?"

"Her reading glasses were found near the body, and she had burned a pair of disposable gloves in the fire. The Special Agent seems to find that suspicious. Plus, she's a sharpshooter and has a concealed carry permit. Can you believe it?"

"Hmmm." Dale's eyebrows knitted together as he looked across the back yard. Western gray squirrels had built a messy nest out of pine needles and debris in one of the thick blue spruce trees. Nick and Nora were crouched under the shaking pine, looking up with hopeful expressions. He shrugged. "Why do you care so much about Olivia? She's the one who always has a snarky comment and hurts your feelings."

"After Cheryl moved away, Olivia became my closest friend, somehow." Jane didn't mention almost all her friends ditched her in the aftermath of her forced singlehood after her last husband died. "She's always there for me, and she's funny, too."

"Yeah, well, once the forensics people get done analyzing the bullet, everyone will be cleared. You'll see." Dale's eyes landed on hers.

Her shoulders sagged as she crossed her arms. "Let's hope so. I don't have a lot of confidence in the police." The dogs bounced up and raced at the fence as a squirrel scampered along the top. "Tell me how your weekend went."

"Let me take you out to dinner and I will."

While Dale called the dogs into the house and locked the patio door, Jane crossed over to the closet for a light sweater. They continued out the front way, and Dale opened the car door and helped her settle in the seat, then he drove to the local steakhouse.

After giving the waiter their usual orders, Jane said, "You were going to tell me about your busy weekend. How was your business meeting? Did you land a new contract or something?"

"No. I went out to dinner with Polly. She wants to open another restaurant."

Jane's stomach dropped and started to hurt, like she'd been punched in the gut. "You had dinner with Polly?"

"Yes." He flashed her a smile, but it didn't work.

"You took your wife out on a date rather than go on a weekend trip with me?" She tried to keep her voice steady, but her tone had risen a few octaves. After setting her knife and fork down across her dinner plate, she threw her crisp, white napkin on top.

"She's not my wife, she's my ex-wife, and it wasn't like that. It was business." Dale was an electrician by trade and ran his own electrical company, but he also owned two restaurants with his ex.

"You didn't tell me about it beforehand."

"I knew you wouldn't like it."

"Just my point. You hid it from me."

"I'm telling you now." His eyes shifted around the restaurant, and his feet were aimed toward the door.

"And you're making a bigger deal out of this than it was."

Jane tapped her index finger on the table top, her nail making clicking sounds, until the nail broke. "I am not. You could've met Polly to talk about business any time. Not this weekend. Not at dinner."

He had on a stubborn look, and his chin was set.

She snapped, "I'm finished here. Please take me home."

Dale touched his napkin to his lips, folded the cloth and laid it on the table, then signaled to the wait staff for the check. "You're mad."

"No. No. Well, maybe I am. Why shouldn't I be?" Jane was indeed irritated with him, but she had a red-hot hate for Polly, who was also the reason why Jane's last boyfriend, Everett, a gourmet chef at her restaurant, had taken a different job in Vail and moved away.

They drove home in complete silence. Dale did not apologize, and Jane didn't strike up another conversation. He dropped her off without walking her to the door.

****

The alarm clock on her cellphone dinged as the summer sun started to rise at five-thirty on Monday morning. Jane padded barefoot into the kitchen to pour a cup of coffee from the pot that automatically brewed on a timer. As she looked from her pristine kitchen out the tall windows at the ball of yellow coloring the sky, she found it hard to believe she'd been drinking coffee only yesterday morning at the campground. The weekend she'd anticipated so much was a bust all around. She wanted to call Dale, but refrained. She wasn't going to give in.

After twenty minutes spent reading her devotional, she applied make-up, climbed into a pair of black slacks and pulled a salmon-colored top over her head, then wound a patterned scarf around her neck. She ran a comb through her straight, dark brown hair that touched her shoulders.

Maybe she needed some new clothes. Polly always dressed stylishly. Perhaps a new pair of shoes, at least. New shoes always helped her self-esteem. Coming off a grubby weekend of camping was not a confidence booster.

After stopping for a latte on the way into work, she left behind the mountain memories and entered once again into the professional, urban scene of downtown Denver.

"Good morning, Evelyn." She stopped at her secretary's desk to recount the gory details of her camping trip.

"Another murder?" The efficient, young legal secretary shook her head. "I'll come by your office later, and we can discuss it some more."

Jane gave her the thumbs up before advancing to her paralegal office, a little bigger than a walk-in closet, filled with black notebooks of exhibits and cardboard boxes of documents. There was a lot of work to be done, but there was time for a quick call. She dialed the number, and after a few rings someone picked up. Jane asked, "May I speak to Marshal Marshall?"

"You mean Agent Marshall?"

"Oops. Yes. Sorry, that's who I meant." She was always going to think of him as Marshal Marshall. Well, at least she was unlikely to forget his name, especially since it was similar to her own.

"Agent Marshall here." His deep voice rang out suddenly, and she startled, the phone almost slipping out of her fingers.

"Hello. It's Jane Marsh, one of the campers at Yellow Mountain Campground this past weekend. Someone tried to run me off the road on my way home Sunday." She went on to describe the woman, with short dark hair and sunglasses. "Can you identify her from your list of campers? She was alone, if that helps."

"I'll look into it."

"And she was driving a red car. Red paint is on my rear bumper if you need it for evidence." She bit her lip and fidgeted with the tangled phone cord.

"I appreciate the information."

"Is the report for the shooting incident available yet to the public?"

"No. We're still investigating. By the way, I've learned you were the subject of a prior investigation yourself."

Jane heard a rushing in her ears. "What?" She tried not to shriek.

"Well, anyway, thanks for calling and letting us know what happened." He disconnected.

With a shaky hand, Jane replaced the phone in its cradle.

Naturally, he had found out about her past. Her first husband, Craig, died when he fell off a cruise ship on their twenty-fifth anniversary, and her second husband, Hugh, was swept off a cliff in Ireland into the sea while taking a selfie photo of the two of them. She had become a suspect in both deaths after posting the selfie as her Facebook profile picture. That photo was her best ever. How was she to know it would go viral?

Anyway, she should be used to those comments by now. Taking a few deep breaths to calm herself, she opened the folder on her desk to begin work for the day.

Later that morning, Evelyn entered Jane's office, sank into the side chair next to the desk, and stretched her long legs out in front of her. "I know you're going to investigate this murder."

Jane reeled away from her computer screen with a sheepish laugh. "I am?"

"Your friend Olivia's a suspect, right?"

"It's looking that way."

"I know how much you care about your dinner club." Evelyn's eyes flicked to the right and back to Jane's. "Now that your sons are married and all."

Jane put her chin in her hand with her elbow leaning on her desk. When she'd auditioned for the dinner club, she was feeling the effects of the empty nest stage of life. Her acceptance to the exclusive club had turned into an obsession, and once she was admitted, the group had become like family. And that family was under suspicion, including herself.

"Okay. So, I am going to investigate." Jane narrowed her eyes as she scratched her head with the end of a pen. "I called the Forest Service about the red car that rammed into me. They didn't seem to be very concerned."

"Why not call the State Patrol traffic division?"

"Because I didn't get the license plate number or even the make of the car. So the State Patrol won't be able to do anything about it. But I thought at least the Forest Service would take an interest as part of the murder investigation." She retrieved a yellow legal pad from her cabinet of supplies, and put pen to paper.

"What are you writing?"

"I'm making a list."

Evelyn chucked her gently on the shoulder. "I don't suppose you have much confidence in the police...from past experience."

"You're so right." Jane swirled her hands around in the air, taking in the framed diploma on her wall and her reference books crowding the shelves. "And I know how to investigate, after all. There's a lot I can find out on my own."

"Be careful. Don't forget the trouble you got yourself into before."

"I won't."

Evelyn drew in her feet and stood up. She left Jane's office, shutting the door.

When Jane finished brainstorming, she threw down her pen. The list was long, and she'd drawn next to each task a small, neat square, ready to check off when completed.

It was time to get serious.

Make a few check marks on her list.

Find out a thing or two the police probably wouldn't bother about.

She snagged her personal laptop out of her tote bag. After locating the website for the National Park Service, she scanned a press release with a brief announcement of the shooting. The report didn't name the victim pending notification of next of kin, and there was no other news.

She hit the backspace button twice.

Scrolling through a page on the history of Yellow Mountain Campground, much of which she'd already learned from Wes, she paused upon reading the campground had once been closed by an environmental agency. Someone had found asbestos in cement artifacts left from an old building. Asbestos caused cancer.

She performed a drumroll on the desktop with her yellow, pointy pencil. The public had a right of access to information, so she made an inquiry regarding the camp closure under a "Freedom of Information" request.

Next, she searched for the medical examiner's office closest to the park and called the number. "Can you tell me when the autopsy report will be available for Michael Quadtrini? His date of death was two days ago, on June twentieth."

"That report will be ready by the end of the week."

"Really? That soon."

"We don't have the need for many autopsies here in this county."

"Would you fax me a copy when it's done?"

"How are you related to the deceased?"

"I'm not, but the report is a public record, right?"

"Yes, I believe so. No one has placed a hold on it." The helpful assistant gave Jane her email address. Jane shot off a quick email to her requesting a faxed copy as soon as the report was available and providing her fax number.

With a satisfied smile, she ticked off a couple of the items from her list. The autopsy would indicate whether the bullet was found in the body. If so, the gun would be identified and her friends exonerated. The solution could be as simple as that.

However, nothing was ever that easy.

Chapter 6

"Have you solved the murder yet?" Olivia asked.

"Funny. Ha, ha. It's only Monday. Give me more time." Jane smiled. "Thanks for coming downtown to meet me for lunch today. It's hard to get into the work mode on the first day back."

Olivia and Libby, together with Jane, were sitting at a café table on the outdoor patio at one of the trendy restaurants in historical Larimer Square, poking forks into their salad vegetables and greens.

"But I did request the autopsy report before I headed over here."

Libby swallowed hard. "Why'd you do that?"

"There might be a clue there. Maybe the type of bullet that killed him or something. I've been thinking about you, Libby. How're you doing? You were pretty upset."

"Well…" Libby gazed across the street, as pedestrians surged along the busy sidewalk in front of the antique shops. "Um. Well…there's something I didn't tell the police. I can't sleep, it's weighing on my mind so much. I'm just hoping they make an arrest so I never need to tell them."

"Tell them what?" Olivia gave Libby's arm a shove.

Libby took another gulp. "I knew Mike Quadtrini years ago. He and I dated in college."

Olivia's eyebrows hovered near the umbrella over their table, and Jane sucked in her breath. Time froze as they waited for Libby to continue.

"He was in the ROTC. I never could resist a man in uniform." A hint of a smile flitted across her face. "I heard later he got out of the military and became a park ranger. I thought he'd still be in the park service. I had no idea he was the host at Yellow Mountain Campground."

Jane cleared her throat. "Does Wes know you two dated?"

"No. I was going to tell him, but he had cross words with Mike right away." Libby fixed her eyes on her hands in her lap. "Mike never said anything to me at the campground. Never even acted like he recognized me. Maybe he didn't after all this time. Yet, I wondered if he was being so mean because of me. After all, I was the one who broke up with him. But that happened so long ago, it couldn't have mattered anymore." Libby sighed as she picked up her fork and stabbed a cherry tomato. "I was too scared to tell the investigators."

"They asked me if I knew Quadtrini before the camping trip." Olivia dabbed the corner of her mouth with a cloth napkin.

"Me too." Jane inclined her head.

Libby gave up with the tomato, as her fork clattered onto her glass plate. Her eyes looked about ready to overflow. "I was waiting for them to ask me, but they never did. So, I didn't actually lie to anyone. But my conscious is bothering me, and I wanted to come clean with you guys. I'm scared."

Olivia cut in, "I'll tell Doug. He'll know what to do. He always told me people don't even have to answer questions put by the police. And they certainly shouldn't volunteer anything if they haven't been asked."

Jane patted Libby on the shoulder. "Olivia's right. If the police should question you again, and come out and ask if you knew him, you need to be prepared with what you're going to say, if anything."

"That's good advice, guys. You will talk to Doug, won't you?" Libby's eyes cleared, and she appeared more relaxed.

"Absolutely." Olivia sipped her Pinot Grigio.

Jane held a hand up to her forehead, then tossed back her hair. "What was Mike Quadtrini like?"

Libby's face darkened once more, and she answered through clenched teeth, "It was years ago that I went out with him!"

Jane drew back, giving Olivia a sideways look. A bright red bloomed on Libby's cheeks as her shaky hands flew to her face. "Sorry. I feel like I'm in the hot seat, and I just don't want to think about it—"

"You're the one who brought it up. And you'd better be ready for those questions. Just saying." Olivia jabbed her fork in Libby's direction, then speared a piece of lettuce from her plate.

"And you were the one worried about being in the hot seat a few short days ago, remember?" Libby shot back.

"True, true." Olivia sighed. "I'm probably still their target, too." Her teeth crunched down on the crisp greens.

Jane thumped the café table with a pinkie finger in her closed fist. "We need to solve this murder. That's all there is to it."

Olivia raised her wine glass in the air. "A toast to solving the murder." Jane made her fingers unclench as she picked up her water glass. Libby gave a stiff smile and raised her drink, then they all clinked their glasses together.

Libby glanced around the table. "I believe Jane can solve it, if anyone can. But in the meantime, I need to prepare myself, like you said. Olivia, if Doug thinks I should keep quiet about it, then I will. But if he thinks I need to tell the police, will he go with me to the station?"

"I'm sure he'd be glad to."

Libby frowned. "That means I'll have to tell Wes, too. I just don't want to upset him further." She paused, but then blurted out, "It was Wes who screamed in the night."

Olivia laughed. "You're kidding, right?"

"No. Not even kinda."

Jane covered her mouth with outstretched fingers. "Something was upsetting him. What was it?"

"The gunshots. He has PTSD, you know, Post-Traumatic Stress Disorder, from his time in the war."

"Oh. I didn't know." Jane's hands fell to her lap. "But Wes brought a pistol of his own on the camping trip."

"Yes. He's had the gun since his discharge from the military. He takes it camping for protection, but I can't remember the last time he fired it. He keeps that Ruger clean and oiled, though."

"We should have camped somewhere without a firing range nearby." Olivia raised only one eyebrow this time.

"He knew the range was there, but he'd never say

anything or complain." In spite of the warm day, Libby shivered for a moment. "He was tossing and turning and talking in his sleep that night. All I could do was lie next to him and watch. Then, we heard the shot. The noise wasn't loud, and it sounded far away, but he jumped off the air mattress and screamed. It was horrible."

Jane blinked back a tear as she imagined what Wes was going through, and Libby, too. "I'm surprised you stayed the next night at the campground after that. I'm glad you did, though."

Libby picked at her sleeve. "You know I wanted to leave, but Wes doesn't want to let the PTSD take over his life. Plus, we saw the look on your face when I said I wanted to get going."

"Really? Well, thanks for staying." Jane felt a pang of guilt.

Libby's feet were entwined around her chair legs. "Anyway, we told the investigators the shot was fired around four-thirty in the morning."

"That had to be when Quadtrini was killed." Olivia squinted, as if in thought.

Libby shrugged. "Not necessarily. There could've been more than one shot fired in that wilderness. How do we know that shot was the one?"

Olivia agreed. "You're right. Those investigators questioned me thoroughly about our time at the shooting range, then our hike to the amphitheater. Like maybe he was shot later in the morning, not in the night. They implied we were lying, that we didn't lose our way, but got to the amphitheater before everyone else and killed him, then circled back after you found him."

"Ridiculous. Quadtrini *was* shot in the middle of the night. I heard someone outside my tent right around the time Wes screamed." Jane sat forward, remembering the rustling noise, convinced now the sound was made by a person.

"You didn't mention that before. Probably your imagination." Olivia threw her a doubtful look.

Libby didn't notice. "After we heard the shot, we laid awake until sunrise. We talked it out, and I could tell he was doing better after that. And he agreed to go to therapy. I've told him many times to look into counseling through the VA."

"Good idea." Olivia nodded in sympathy, then there was silence for a moment.

Jane broke into their thoughts. "I have some news, too."

Olivia acted out a fake swoon. "Don't tell me you dated Quadtrini, as well. Or were you two engaged?"

Libby gave a nervous laugh, and Jane rolled her eyes, but her voice came out quiet and small. "On the way home yesterday, I was run off the road by a woman from the campground, the one I overheard. The woman who said Quadtrini had caused her trouble." At least, Jane was now convinced in her own mind that the woman was one and the same person. Her friends gasped as Jane went on. "I'll bet she's the one those old folks saw arguing with Quadtrini. I think she's the murderer."

Libby breathed, "Ooohhh," as Olivia asked, "Why didn't you tell us this right off the bat?"

"I'm telling you now." Jane propped her elbows on the table and formed her fingers into a steeple. "I wonder what Quadtrini did to her. If I can find out her name and phone number, I can call her and ask."

Olivia's voice rose. "You can't confront a suspect on your own. Don't even think about it."

"Okay. Okay." But Jane's chin ascended into the air, leaving some room for doubt.

Olivia clicked her tongue. "Tsk. If you meet up with her, I'll need to go with you. But you're focusing on the woman. What about the man you overheard? You have his name already. Ben Malkon."

"Yes, indeed." Jane chewed on a fingernail. "I'm doing a deep dive query on both Ben Malkon and Michael Quadtrini."

"What's that mean?" Libby appeared perplexed.

"Internet searches. Public records searches, like getting the autopsy report, the campground closure records. Maybe a few searches that aren't public, too."

"Good." Olivia's eyes met Jane's in a moment of understanding. "We're all in this together, my friends."

"I'll let you know what I find out."

Chapter 7

Did Ben Malkon and Michael Quadtrini have anything in common?

Jane played that question over and over in her mind all afternoon, as she finished drafting a pleading in a traffic accident case her firm was defending.

Did they know each other from years ago, like Libby knew Quadtrini? Were they related, even, or did they meet at some point by chance? Having in mind the accident case she was working on, she wondered if Malkon and Quadtrini could've been involved in an auto accident, for example.

That night after work, Jane climbed into comfortable stretchy pants, microwaved leftover enchiladas, and set her dinner plate on the granite-topped kitchen island. She plunked dog food into the dogs' bowls, so the puppies would not beg for her supper, then slid onto a counter stool. After forking a steaming morsel into her mouth, she opened her laptop to search the internet. Driving records in Colorado were not a matter of public record as they used to be. What to do?

She logged into the state website to search the dockets, because court records were still public.

Bingo. There it was.

Benjamin Malkon, as next friend of Marcus Malkon, a deceased minor vs. Michael Quadtrini—a wrongful death lawsuit filed in Denver District Court. This blew everything wide open…

She closed her laptop since the case was not recent enough for more information to be available online. After wiping her mouth, she wadded up her paper napkin and slam dunked it into the trash can. Her mind buzzing with the new clue, she went about her routine, hardly paying attention as she cleaned up her supper and loaded the dishwasher, then let the dogs outside in the back yard for their nightly ritual.

Her work satchel contained her yellow pad, so she went to get it. Looking over her to-do list, she added a note to review the old case file at the courthouse. She drew a star next to the task. That should be the very next thing. Then, she checked off her list that she'd requested the autopsy report and searched the internet for Quadtrini and Malkon. Grabbing a manila folder from a drawer, she wrote "murder" across the top and shoved the yellow pad into the folder.

Her cellphone pinged with a text from her son, Caleb, who asked if she wanted to meet for coffee the next day. She replied *yes* and suggested ten in the morning at a coffee shop near the courthouse. Tomorrow after meeting Caleb, she would take a look at the court records.

She was about to put her phone away, but checked her voice mail, then other text messages, but there was nothing from Dale Capricorn. Her breath came out in short spurts as she rapped out a text message to him that she was sorry and asked if they could meet—but what if Dale suggested getting together at Polly's restaurant? Bile rose in her throat. She backspaced and typed in a message that she never wanted to hear from him again.

Her hand hovered over the phone screen. She came to her senses and deleted the text message. Better sleep on it.

She might as well post some of her camping photographs on Facebook, so she opened her camera application. Her heart lifted a little as she scrolled through the photos of the campground. There were pictures of her one-man tent in a cozy spot snuggled between the pine trees and the old picnic table, the trout Wes caught, and dinner club members sitting in their collapsible camping chairs around the campfire on Friday night. The photos skipped to Saturday and the hike to the homestead and mountain lake, Libby eating a peach with juice dripping down her chin, the mysterious cabin, the gourmet dinner of beef stroganoff, Olivia losing a marshmallow in the fire, and Doug biting into a gooey S'more. She went back to the beginning to look for the best ones.

Should she post the shot of her tent in the beautiful, secluded campsite?

Halting at one of the pictures, she could see Doug and Olivia's spacious tent with its poles like elegant pillars on either side of the opening and a welcome doormat below the flap. Who takes all that stuff camping anyway? Trust Olivia to have every possible convenience in the wilderness.

She pinched the screen to enlarge the photo. Standing behind the Ladners' tent, almost obscured, was the man wearing the red jacket... Jane pinched the photo even larger. The picture contained Ben Malkon, and a woman was next to him—the woman in the car that hit Jane.

The woman was hefty with broad shoulders. Her

worried expression had a hint of anger. But then, in the far corner of the photo was yet another person. As much as she enlarged the image, Jane could not see the third person's face. Most of the body was outside of view. She scrolled through all the photos several times, but did not find any others like that one.

She posted the revealing photo on Facebook and tagged her friends with a comment, "Look who's in the photo behind the Ladners' tent."

****

Early the next day, Jane met her son at a breezy coffee cart tucked in a back street behind the Denver City and County Building. "Good morning Caleb. Let me get your drink. Let's see. A caramel latte, half caf?" Jane set her purse on the bistro table and fished inside for her wallet.

"Sure, Mom."

She paid for their drinks with a gift card, and they sat at the table in the warm sun. Caleb had graduated from law school and was studying for the bar exam. He often looked for an excuse to take a break.

"How's Erin?" Jane peered at her son over the top of her colorfully striped sunglasses. Erin and Caleb had been married a little over a year.

"Busy. Since she started teaching summer school classes, she hasn't had much extra time. How's everything going with you?"

Jane repeated the story of the campground host's murder. Then she gave him the reassurance she didn't feel herself. "I'm sure they'll catch the killer soon, because it had to have been one of the other campers, and the investigators seized everyone's guns. So, they'll figure out the weapon and all of that."

"That's a real zonk on the head, but you're staying out of the investigation, right?" Caleb gave her a stern look.

She paused for a moment, trying to reason out what he'd said. His T-shirt read, "People change, now I'm a lamp." Not mentioning her plans after their coffee break, she switched the subject. "Have you heard from your brother?"

"No. I should give him a call today. Have you?"

"Not lately. Luke and Brittany were out of town themselves this weekend, but I'll try to Skype with them soon, and I'll let you know how they're doing." She took a deep drink of her latte, then checked the time on her cell. "I can't visit long because I need to run into the courthouse before I go back to work."

She gathered together her purse and files, but Caleb remained seated. There were a couple of moments of silence. "What's wrong?"

"Why do you think something's wrong?"

When her boys were young, she'd told them mothers have eyes in the back of their heads, so they always knew what their children were up to. They didn't believe her at first, but to prove it, she stood facing the kitchen window in front of the sink and asked them to hold up their fingers behind her. Then she spied in the window's reflection Luke holding up one finger and Caleb holding up two. When she gave them the correct numbers, they swept her hair all around the back of her head searching for the eyes they were convinced existed.

"The eyes in the back of a mother's head are invisible, but they still see everything. Out with it. Is the studying getting to you?" She sank onto her chair.

"No. That's not it. I got a job offer from the DA in Durango."

Jane's heart soared. "Before you passed the bar." Then, a pain shot across her chest. Durango was a mountain town far away in the southwestern part of the state.

"Yes. I'd start as a law clerk, then once the bar results come out, I'd be a junior prosecutor. But Erin doesn't want to leave Denver. We just bought the loft, and she loves her job here." Caleb's brows wrinkled, and he ran a jerky hand through his hair. "We've never argued about anything until now."

Jane let out a low whistle. "That's a dilemma. It's hard to turn down an opportunity, but at what price?"

"I told her it'd only be for a few years, and we'd come back to visit all the time, but..."

"That's a day's drive, what six or seven hours to the Four Corners?"

He dropped his head and closed his eyes. "Yes. You're both right. It's too far."

"I didn't say that. You need to weigh the pros and cons. Sit down with Erin and make a list of reasons to go and reasons to stay."

"Thanks, Mom. That's a good idea."

"You two want to come over for dinner one night?" Jane felt an empty weekend without Dale looming ahead.

"How about instead we go out to eat at the food trucks? I'll check with Erin and see what night is best."

"What food trucks?" Jane knew Caleb and Erin didn't really care for her usual comfort food from her Midwestern upbringing. In spite of being in the gourmet dinner club, for family meals she fell back on her hamburger casseroles made with mushroom soup and smothered in plain, regular, cheddar cheese. The kids preferred kale and Swiss chard or Mangostee—whatever those were. They wouldn't be caught dead cooking with canned soup. The old adage about nothing being better than Mom's home cooking did not apply to them.

"Gourmet food vans park outside the breweries downtown. They serve French, Mexican, Asian Fusion, you name it."

"Those things used to be called 'roach coaches.' It's hard to believe they're the new trend. Just let me know when and where, and I'll be there."

"Ask Dale, too."

Jane hadn't told anyone about the argument with her boyfriend. "He's been busy lately. I'm not sure he'll be able to make it." Busy with Polly, no doubt. Anger made her cheeks burn as she sprang out of her seat. "I have to get going."

"My turn to ask. Everything okay with you?"

"Sure, hon." She forced a smile and squeezed his shoulder. "Love you."

Leaving Caleb with his studies and latte, she hurried around the corner to the court house, raced down the stairs to the basement where the archived files were kept, and gave the clerk the docket number. Once the folder was in her hands, she scanned the thick volume and made a copy of several pages at the copy machine.

The pleadings alleged Quadtrini was negligent in striking a vehicle driven by Ben Malkon, causing the death of his son.

Chapter 8

Brittany's youthful, sun-kissed, smiling face appeared on Jane's computer screen. "Hi, Mom."

Once home from work on Tuesday night, Jane had sent a message to her son, Luke: *ready to Skype?* Then, she'd placed the video-call and Brittany answered.

"Hi, daughter-in-law. Tell me what you've been up to." Jane scooted closer to her laptop, with the dogs sleeping at her feet, and enlarged the video screen. Luke was rummaging in the refrigerator in the background.

Brittany caught Jane up with her news about school and work. A soldier in the Army, Luke was not going to be deployed again until next year. All good news. "How was your camping trip with your gourmet dinner club last weekend? Did you try the recipe I gave you for huevos rancheros?"

"Yes. It was a hit. But I need to tell you what happened to the campground host." Jane recounted the story, including the clues she'd uncovered, and waited for Brittany's active mind to come up with a suggestion. Her daughter-in-law was a big help with solving a murder in the past.

Brittany screwed up her eyes. "You absolutely need to track down Ben Malkon. Do you know where he lives?"

"No." Jane marshalled her thoughts. "Wait.

79

Usually the plaintiff's address is included in the court file. I might have it."

"If you know the neighborhood where he lives, you might find him on 'Nextdoor.' It's a social network for neighborhoods, where people share information about housepainters and dog sitters and garage sales, like that."

"How does the app work? Don't you have to live in the neighborhood to join?"

"You're supposed to, but there's no way to keep anyone out."

"That's deceitful."

"Any social media site has the potential for fraud."

As Jane went to retrieve her yellow legal pad, she said over her shoulder to the laptop screen, "You always come up with good ideas. I'll write it on my list. Thanks."

She was soon back, scribbling a note.

Luke flopped down next to Brittany to join in the video chat. "I talked to Caleb this afternoon, and he told me about the job in Durango. He should take it."

Buttoning up her lips for a moment, she waited for the pang to shoot through her. "I know it's a good opportunity, but they've got to decide for themselves."

Brittany's eyes held Jane's for a moment. "You could move out here near us, Mom."

"That's sweet, but I have my job here." Then she hesitated. "I will think about it, though." She went on to explain the latest hipster craze with food trucks, and they chatted a long while about other news before disconnecting. She rose from the leather couch where she'd been Skyping and nearly tripped over Nora lying at her feet. The schnauzer bounded up and barked, her front paws lifting a few inches off the floor with every woof.

Paging through the legal documents again, she located an address for Malkon, but the information was several years old now. After querying the county assessor's website, she learned Ben Malkon still owned the home in the Highlands Ranch neighborhood. She searched the internet for the Nextdoor Neighbor website and then sent a request to join, not using her real name. In a few moments, she was accepted as a member, so she scrolled through the postings for Malkon. He appeared in an entry in May with a comment about the traffic on his street. That way she verified he lived in the house he owned; it wasn't a rental. She wrote the address on her yellow tablet.

Jane stuffed the pleadings into her murder folder, then went to her closet. Black pants, black pull-over with a hood, dark sunglasses, black baseball cap. What else? Jane folded each item into a duffle bag, black of course, and zipped the bag shut. She believed in being prepared.

****

After clocking out from work on Wednesday, she slid into the office restroom with the duffel bag and changed into her surveillance outfit, then made rapid strides to her car to motor down to Highlands Ranch.

The internet map wasn't quite accurate; Malkon's street wasn't where the map showed it should be. She drove around and around, past the same houses over and over again. Would someone with a neighborhood watch group report her? Dressed in black, she probably looked like a cat burglar.

Stopping at a four-way intersection, she searched

her phone apps for a different map and directions. A car tooted its horn from behind, so she turned into a parking lot for a soccer field and shoved the gearshift into park. She searched again for a phone app and downloaded it. A woman's elegant voice provided directions for each turning, but she drove past the same houses as before.

An hour had gone by, and the sky was fully dark now.

As it worked out, she happened upon the street after several random turns. Close observation was best under cover of darkness, anyway. Nosing her car to the curb across the street from a spacious, cheerful, yellow two-story, with a wide front porch and a three-stall garage, she heard children's laughter from a nearby back yard.

"Jane! Dick!"

She ducked down in her seat so fast her hat hit the seat back and flipped off her head to the floor. What in the world? And who was Dick?

An overweight man in slippers stepped off a porch at a house down the block and called out, "Dick! Jane!" Two young children ran around the corner and skipped up the steps into the house.

This was a nice, safe, family community, where children named Dick and Jane lived, not the place a killer would live. She was the one who stuck out as an intruder. Maybe she should have worn soccer-mom clothes. She plopped the hat onto her head and remained scooted down low in the seat. The street lights were farther along the block at the corner, and Malkon hadn't turned on his porch light. The house was in darkness with no movement, nothing to see.

Time ticked by. She fiddled with the radio, but turned the station off. Her murder folder was in her satchel on the floor, so she scanned the pages before throwing them down on the seat. Opening her cellphone, she scrolled through text messages, but there was nothing recent. She typed in a new text to Dale. *Don't bother to call me. Polly can have you.* Well, she'd slept on it. But she backspaced, backspaced, and changed the words to *call me.*

After another uneventful thirty minutes, she started the ignition and cruised home.

****

A little before noon the next day, she searched the park service website for an updated news release, but did not find a new posting. However, another query on Quadtrini's name resulted in a funeral announcement. Quadtrini had been cremated, and the short paragraph revealed his birth and death dates and the name of the mortuary. There was a link to the Parks and Wildlife's website on campground hosts, so she followed the thread. Quadtrini's photograph popped up with the other hosts. Prophetically, the quote under his name read, "No place more peaceful and comforting exists than in the Rocky Mountains, where I'll always live, or die trying."

A shiver ran up her spine.

Some warm sunshine would be nice.

Time for a break.

Since it was her lunch hour, she exited the office building to stroll on the sunny side of the street and enjoy the bustle of downtown. Passing a window in a building on Larimer Street, she read a large, color poster announcing, "Krav Maga—Self Defense

Training Headquarters." The woman in the picture had a fierce expression and muscular shoulders and arms. Jane slipped inside for a brochure.

A young woman with black and magenta hair, nose and lip piercings, and tattoos sat behind a desk. "Can I help you?"

"Am I too old for this training?"

"No. We have lots of older people. Even in their sixties, like you."

"I'm not sixty," Jane squawked.

"Oh. I mean, you're not too old at all. It's for everybody."

Jane furrowed her eyebrows as she studied the description. The self-defense training guaranteed a good workout, like boxing and judo combined. This was something she could do, rather than take shooting lessons, as Doug suggested.

"Would you like to join a free, introductory class? There's one starting right now."

"I'm not dressed for it."

"You won't be doing anything too strenuous. It's just an intro. They mostly explain what it's about and show you a couple of defensive moves."

Jane glanced at her watch. There was time. Well anyway, she would make the time. She hadn't gotten very far in her inquiries, but who knew? She'd need those defensive moves if the investigation turned dangerous.

Chapter 9

"Hiyah! Eeee-yah!" yelled the instructor.

"Ow, that hurt!" shouted Jane, in her black, tailored slacks, with the long sleeves of her silk blouse rolled up. Punching the instructor's arm had sent an electric-like shock up her own arm, now hanging limply by her side. He was wearing safety guards, totally unnecessary for Jane's ineffectual attack.

"Target the body's most vulnerable points, such as the eyes, the neck, the throat. Hitting the arm is not going to neutralize your opponent."

"My aim was off." A scowl on her face, she rubbed her shoulder, then resumed the Krav Maga offensive stance.

Her instructor pounded his fist into his palm. "You need to understand your surroundings and identify potential threats before an attack occurs. But if you must, you will use your body as a weapon."

After he demonstrated a few more jabs, the introductory lesson was over. Jane waited in line at the front desk to sign up for more classes, then strode into the women's shower room to clean up. She looped her pink scarf around her neck and checked that her pink, dangling earrings were still in place, then hurried to her office.

She paused by her secretary's desk to tell her about the self-defense class, ending with, "Evelyn, you might want to try Krav Maga with me."

"I'll wait to see how you do."

"You'll never join, then." Jane laughed. She was sore, but felt stronger, taller even. She'd learned Krav Maga used the judo ranking system, starting with the white belt and proceeding up level to black. Could she possibly hope to earn at least the first belt, white?

****

That night, her doorbell rang. The dogs raced down the hall to the entryway, barking and growling, pretending they were watch dogs. Jane stood on tiptoe to peer through the peep hole, but the image on the other side was too distorted to see anything. Was the visitor Dale? Or one of those dangerous strangers the Krav Maga instructor warned everyone about?

She opened the door a crack and poked her nose around the corner, ready to use her body as a weapon.

"Agent Marshall?"

"Mrs. Marsh?"

"Can I help you?" She eased the door open an inch farther.

"I talked to the woman who ran into the back of your car on the county highway."

Jane waved him in. "Would you like some coffee? Or hot tea?" She ushered him down the hall, past the guest bedroom at the front of the house, past the dining room, and into the great room—the kitchen and family room combined. "I have a pot of coffee brewed already."

"I'll take coffee, then."

She poured a new cup and topped hers off. "What's the name of the woman?"

He surveyed her over the rim of his cup and didn't

answer the question. "She admitted to bumping the tail end of your vehicle, but said you disappeared down a side road, and she didn't feel comfortable following you to exchange insurance information—"

"Humph. *She* didn't feel comfortable." Jane slapped the table with the palm of her right hand. "And she did more than tap the bumper."

"She claimed you were following her, you passed her several times, and after you went around her the last time, you slammed on your brakes."

Jane took a long breath. "I think I did pass her more than once, but I had to slow down because the road went into a sharp curve."

"The woman said you were driving aggressively."

"Me?" Jane's voice hit a high note. "Listen, she rammed into the back of my car. I know enough about car accidents to know it was her fault. Would you like to see my rear end? I mean, the damage to my car?"

His expression remained blank. "I'm not investigating the traffic accident. But since you reported it to me, I thought I'd stop by to talk to you about it."

Jane slouched down on the kitchen counter stool, but peered sideways at the agent. "I called you because she must be involved in the murder. Why else would she crash into me?"

"We haven't found a link between her and Quadtrini. However, I do have another question for you."

She drew her head back and lowered her chin down. "Yes?"

"You were investigated in the deaths of your two husbands."

Jane sucked in her breath. "I was never charged

with anything. They were accidents, horrible accidents. It was a coincidence they both fell into the sea and drowned. Many wives lose husbands to such deaths."

"It's not like you live near water and had seafaring husbands. How likely is that to happen to someone living in a land-locked state such as Colorado? Such coincidences are rare."

She narrowed her eyes and pinched her lips into a tight bow.

"I don't believe you had anything to do with your husbands' deaths, though."

"You don't? Why not?" Jane stared at the floor.

"You don't seem the type. But the clincher was the Facebook profile picture. A killer wouldn't post a photo taken right before shoving her husband over a cliff."

She wished she had thought it through before posting the selfie, but it was too late now to take it back. Anyway, the selfie was the best picture Hugh had taken of her. When she looked up, she caught a glimpse of his lips twitching. "What's your question, exactly?"

"That was it. Just being thorough about asking." He took another sip of coffee before returning the cup to the counter and standing up.

Jane unfolded herself from her seat. "Thanks for talking to that woman. For what it's worth, I believe she's connected to the murder. She ran into me as a warning. She thinks I overheard something important outside the latrine. I didn't, but I've found out Malkon has a motive."

"What?"

Jane planted both fists on her hips. "Mike Quadtrini killed his son in a car accident."

"How do you know about that?"

"Malkon sued Quadtrini, and I came across the court records recently." Jane couldn't look him in the eye as a few moments of tense silence passed.

"If you see the woman again, which is unlikely, call me." He slid a card from a compartment in his wallet.

"I have your card already. You gave everyone cards at the campground Sunday." She crossed her arms over her chest.

"Where'd you get those bruises?" Marshall gave her a piercing look.

"What bruises?"

"There." He stared at the back of her arms.

She lifted her right elbow. Black and blue marks decorated the back of her arm. She raised her left elbow and found matching colors. "I was at a Krav Maga class today. I'm sore, but I didn't know I was bruised, too."

"You're taking Krav Maga?"

"I've only had an introductory class." Her arms fell back to her sides as she peered at him from lowered eyes.

He scrunched his face as he considered her, then forced his wallet into his pocket. Jane led him down the hall to the front of the house. After closing the door behind him, she scurried on shaky legs over to the fluffy couch, grabbed a sofa pillow, and hugged the softness against her stomach. She could not escape her past.

Her phone pinged. There was a text message, but she didn't bother to open it. She punched in the number. "Dale?"

"Hi, babe."

Her forehead muscles relaxed, and she took a long,

cleansing breath. "One of the officers investigating Quadtrini's death stopped by my house. He just left."

"What did he want?"

"Can you come over? I'd feel better if you did."

"Sure. On my way."

Jane rushed into the bedroom to run a comb through her hair and check her appearance. She looked white, so brushed a rosy blush on her cheeks. Might as well freshen her whole face. After scrubbing her skin clean, she applied fresh mascara and blusher, then eyeshadow, and a smudge of lipstick. What would Polly wear if Dale was on his way over? She changed into her most flattering jeans and a long-sleeved top, which hid the bruises, but showed off her small waist, and took one last look in the mirror as the doorbell rang.

When he strode through the door, she flew into his arms. He ran his fingers through her hair, as he cupped her face to meet his.

They never got around to talking about Polly. It was as if their argument hadn't happened.

****

When Jane arrived at the office Friday, Evelyn suggested they take a bike ride over their lunch hour. Jane worked hard all morning in anticipation and finished her projects at record speed.

Once clocked out, she grabbed her water bottle and stowed her cellphone into her pocket. Just as she was leaving to meet Evelyn at the bike racks outside their office building, the mail clerk handed her a fax from the county coroner, so she thrust the autopsy report in her pocket, too, and hurried down the elevator. Evelyn was outside already, rolling up her right pant leg and securing the fabric with a band to keep her pants from getting caught in the bicycle sprockets.

"I just got the autopsy report for the man who was killed. We can take a break to read it at the Cherry Creek Mall before we turn around to head back."

"Let me have it. I'll read the report while you unlock your bike." Evelyn flipped the pages to the end. "It says the death was by cardiac arrest caused by a gunshot wound."

"We knew that. What else?" Jane twisted the combination of the bike lock.

Evelyn read out loud, "'Gunpowder particles are present on the skin and clothing surrounding the wound. The wound track is through the skin and soft tissue of the chest and heart with the bullet exiting out the back slightly higher than the entrance wound. The path of the bullet was at an angle, missing the ribs and spine. No bullet or bullet jacket is found. The ballistics findings show the weapon was fired from an intermediate range, not consistent with a close range of fire wound, making it impossible for decedent to have shot himself. Therefore, the manner of death is homicide.'"

"I never considered anything else." After unlocking it, Jane wrapped the bike chain around the post under her bicycle seat. "Anyway, the bottom line is, the bullet wasn't found in the body."

"So, where did it go?"

"He would've been standing when shot, I think, so the bullet could've gone right into the woods. If the investigators didn't recover it, then none of my friends are cleared."

"So, no one is off the hook, yet." Evelyn clicked her tongue and shook her head. "Unless the police can tell who fired their guns. Forensic evidence and all that."

"My friends were shooting at the gun range, along with others from the campground, so a lot of guns had been fired that day. Not only that, but the killer probably had time to get rid of his clothing and wash up to hide the gun residue."

"Even if the bullet isn't found, aren't there casings left at the scene?"

Jane chewed on her lips. "I don't even know what those are, but several people have brought that up, too. I can ask Doug, since he used to be a policeman." She peered over the back of Evelyn's shoulder. "What does the report say about time of death?"

They scanned the pages until they found the answer…that he died between three and six in the morning, but because of the fluctuating temperatures from the cold night and the smoldering logs in the fire pit, determination was inexact.

Evelyn handed the report to Jane, who wedged the pages under her water bottle and cellphone in the bike basket. The two cycled over to the bike lane on Lawrence Street heading to the Cherry Creek trail.

While pedaling away, up and down hills, under the overpasses, up a steep incline to Speer Boulevard, and past the country club near the Cherry Creek Mall, Jane kept thinking again and again, *no bullet was found, no bullet was found, no bullet was found.*

Once the ride was over, they locked their bikes into the rack and returned to their desks. Jane placed the autopsy report in her murder folder. There must be a reason Ben Malkon hadn't been arrested. Because they didn't recover the bullet? Or was there another explanation? What was it?

She checked the forestry website for an updated news release. Quadtrini was now identified by name and the Forest Service bio was included. There must be someone else to question. She returned to the mortuary's website and called the phone number posted. Maybe she'd uncover the identity of one of his relatives.

"I'm inquiring about Michael Quadtrini's ashes. Have they been interred anywhere? Your website doesn't say."

"No one picked up the ashes. We're storing them for now, but if they aren't claimed, we'll dispose of them."

Jane cringed. "Who arranged for his cremation?"

"His estate is being handled by an attorney in town. We sent a bill with a note to let us know what to do with the ashes, but haven't heard back. The bill was paid, though."

"Can I have the name of the attorney, please?"

"Sure."

Jane wrote down her name and number and made haste to place the call. "I'm inquiring about Michael Quadtrini's estate. I understand you're the one handling it."

"Yes. I was appointed Public Administrator to pay his final bills and dispose of his belongings, since there's no family."

No family. What a sad situation. Jane had a sudden thought. "I didn't know him well, but I don't want his ashes to end up in the garbage, uh, not to be blunt. It'd be nice to spread them in the mountains. He did love the Rocky Mountains."

"How did you know him?"

"Just from camping at Yellow Mountain."

"A permit is required from the Chief Ranger's Office to scatter ashes in the parks. There's no charge for the permit, and the mortuary can get one. If you'd like me to, I can make arrangements with the funeral home for someone there to accompany you."

"That'd be nice. Thank you."

"Thank you for volunteering to do it. The funeral director will call you."

Jane disconnected and was about to get back to work, but the mortician returned her call right away. "When would you like to scatter the remains?" He had a well-modulated, radio-broadcaster type voice.

Jane ran a finger over her desk calendar. "The only time I have this week is Saturday morning. After that I'm pretty busy until after the Fourth of July weekend."

"I have this Saturday free, too, if you'd like to do it then."

"Can you get the permit that fast?"

"Yes. We request permits all the time."

"Well, let me think about it." Jane wavered. Did she want to spend a Saturday doing this?

"Is there a problem?"

She made up her mind. "No, not at all. Should we meet at Yellow Mountain Campground Saturday morning?"

"Yes. See you there."

They confirmed the time to meet and disconnected.

A busy hour passed, then Dale called. She had time for a break and settled in for a chat. They got around to discussing the murder investigation, and after Jane shut her office door for privacy, she told him about the autopsy report she'd received before lunch. She held back mentioning her plans to scatter Quadtrini's remains. Wouldn't he and everyone else think it odd she'd wish to honor the memory of someone she didn't know?

But there was something else she'd been meaning to tell Dale. "Libby told me Wes has PTSD from his time in the war. It explains why he was so strange at the campground."

"Strange?"

"He got upset whenever we heard the gunshots from the firing range."

"When did you find out he had PTSD?"

"Libby told us at lunch on Monday. You're a veteran yourself. What do you think?"

"I've heard even the sound of a car engine backfiring can trigger a flashback. You don't think Wes's anger flared up to the point he could've shot the campground host?" His voice sounded worried.

Jane's nervous eyes darted around her office. "No. Wes is not capable of that. He's the most helpful, kindest person. But I'm concerned if the crime investigators find out, they might suspect him. They already suspect Olivia."

"Do you want to go out to dinner tonight? You can ask Libby and Wes to meet us. I haven't seen them in a long time, and we can find out how Wes is doing."

"Good idea. Thanks for thinking of it, Dale."

Once off the phone, Jane texted Libby to meet for dinner that night. Libby replied they were available, and they decided on the Wine and Cheese Bar at the shopping center.

****

Jane was the first to arrive, so she snagged a high-top table at the window. Shoppers hurried by, bags in hand, apparently without concern.

But everyone had secrets, feelings they kept to themselves, as they went about their business. Shame like a drunk the day after a bender, guilt like an uninsured driver speeding through a stop light, or fear like a single dad whose daughter started to date. Or ratchet it up, fear like a young soldier in a war zone.

How could she bring Wes's PTSD into the conversation? Was it rude to ask about it? Too personal? Something veterans were ashamed of? Upsetting to talk about? What was the right thing for a caring friend to do?

Dale glided in the door at the same time as Libby and Wes, and they joined her at the table. She gave Dale a quick peck on the cheek. The waiter stopped for their wine selections and an order for two cheese platters.

"How've you been?" Jane gazed from Libby to Wes.

"Doing fine." Libby smiled and squeezed her husband's fingers. "Have you heard anything new about the murder?"

Jane repeated the information regarding the autopsy report and ended with the car accident in which Malkon's son was killed. Libby's smile faded. "That's heartbreaking for both families." They fell silent, as the waiter placed their wine glasses in front of them and a cheese platter in the center of the pub table.

"I started counseling with the VA for my PTSD." Wes adjusted the fork lying on his napkin. Jane was about to reach for a piece of cheese, but let her hand drop to her lap, glad Wes was the one to broach the subject.

"What kind of counseling?" Dale leaned in.

"It's called cognitive therapy. We talk about what makes me upset and how to replace those feelings with positive emotions. The therapist says I'll learn ways to cope with anger and guilt." Wes exchanged a glance with his wife.

"But why would you feel guilty? You couldn't help what happened to you." Jane wrinkled her brows. "You've got nothing to feel guilty for."

"You don't know anything about it."

"What do you mean?"

"You were at home, safe…probably shopping at the mall like all those people." He jerked his head toward the window overlooking the store-lined street. "You were what? In elementary school? You were playing with dolls, then."

"My friends' older brothers were in the war."

"Brothers! So what?"

"I knew when they didn't come home."

"It's not the same." Wes's eyes raged. It was as if a mask were stripped from his face. "Not like your buddy standing next to you, stepping on a mine. Blown up into the air. Blown to bits, gone."

"Don't, don't tell me." Jane put her hands over her ears.

"You're ignorant. It's nothing like something happening to a brother of someone you knew years ago. Someone you didn't even bother to keep in touch with, I'll bet."

Jane's insides churned, as Wes's pain stirred up her own. Her mind conjured up the vision of Craig, straddling the ship railing, laughing at his daring perch, suddenly slumping and tumbling over into the water. Hugh's hands stretching out to her as the powerful gust of wind carried him over the cliff's edge. Her friends abandoning her when they heard the news...even her best friend, Cheryl, ended up moving away.

But this wasn't about her. It was about Wes.

"You're right." Her voice quivered. "I can't know what you're feeling."

Wes groaned, as he rubbed a hand over his forehead and down his stricken face. "I'm sorry, Jane. It's my problem, not yours."

"You're not in this alone, honey." Libby gripped his fingers, but her eyes darted to Jane, then Dale. "Part of his therapy is to talk about the symptoms and what triggers them, to teach him how to react to the stress."

Dale held up a hand. "You can call me any time. We can meet to talk."

"Thanks, Dale. Libby told me you were in the military, too." Wes blew out his cheeks.

"I was. I know it's not easy to talk about things that bring on bad memories. It takes time. A lot of time."

"One of his assignments is to organize the photos he took during the war." Libby jiggled her husband's hand.

"It's hard to look at the pictures of my friends. Especially the ones who didn't make it home." Wes worked his jaw back and forth. "But it is helping. It's a way of honoring my buddies. Acknowledging we were trying to do good and not harm, trying to help, and doing our duty to our country." He turned toward the window, his profile the same shape as the young, untroubled boy he once was.

"We're proud of you, Wes." Jane felt a tear escape.

"Have you shown anyone the album?" Dale asked.

"Just Libby. It's not that many pages right now, but I'll show you the scrapbook when I'm done."

"The photos help me to understand what he went through." Libby held Wes's hand tighter. "I already know what causes the bad memories. Hearing the gunshots from the firing range, for one."

"Why did you agree to camp at a place with a firing range next door?" Dale tilted his head in question.

"I don't want to be the guy everyone has to accommodate." Wes stuck out his lower lip. "But now I wish I had said something. I sure didn't like the way I felt at the campground, but then again, that's what put me over the edge and forced me to seek counseling."

"Something good's come out of this whole thing, then." Jane gave him a smile. He nodded, but his eyes did not meet hers.

Chapter 10

Nick and Nora thumped their tails on the floor, whined, and pounced with their front paws on Jane's knees. The time was early Saturday morning. The sun shone in a robin's egg blue sky, so she decided the dogs needed to go for a walk. And what better place than on the paths at Yellow Mountain Campground?

She shoved her feet into her well-worn hiking boots, then poured a full coffee carafe into a thermos, snatched two bottled waters from the fridge, disentangled the dogs' leashes and harnesses from the basket by the door, and stashed the dogs' collapsible water bowl inside a backpack. After opening the car door to let the dogs leap into the backseat, she climbed inside and reversed out of the driveway.

The drive up the mountain was uneventful, with Nick and Nora only panting at little at the windows, smearing their wet noses against the glass.

Since she had a yearly park pass posted in her windshield, the park ranger waved her through to the day-use end of the park. Jane hastened over to the black hearse parked among the jeeps and SUVs. A short, thin man in a stiff, black suit coat and black slacks emerged. Black hiking shoes peeped out from under his pressed pant cuffs. "Are you Jane Marsh?"

"Yes."

"Nice to meet you. I'm Cole Bradley." He was the

same man with the nice voice. He extended his hand for her to shake. "I got the permit."

"Thanks for taking care of that and meeting me here."

"No problem." He extracted two silver cylinders from the backseat, plus a bottle of water.

"Where's the urn?" Jane gave a little shudder.

"We use these to scatter the ashes." He handed her one of the cylinders.

"This is heavy." She almost dropped it.

"There's two to three pounds in each of these. Do you want me to carry yours?"

"No, I can do it. I wasn't expecting it to be so heavy, that's all." Jane slid the tube into her backpack. "Would you mind if I bring my dogs with us? They're little and they're friendly, but I can leave them in the car since we're not going very far. I thought just to the fishing pond."

"I don't mind at all. I love dogs."

"Wonderful." She stepped to her vehicle and snapped leashes to collars before the puppies bounded out the car door, excited about a place with new smells and sounds and sights. Cole bent down to pet them, and they wagged their tails at the attention. The sky was blue at home, but in this high mountain spot it was overcast. Jane wasn't worried, because the forecast didn't call for rain until afternoon, and the time was still mid-morning.

"This way to the trail." She led the man to the path—the distance was a half mile to the fishing pond—enough of a journey for the puppies' short legs. Halfway along the trail, she offered the pups a drink from their collapsible water bowl, but they were too worked up sniffing at the trees and brush to pause for more than a few laps. "So, Quadtrini had no family, then?" The Public Administrator had already told her this, but it didn't hurt to dig around some more.

"We were told no family. You were friends, right? You must've known that."

"I didn't know him well. I'd only met him while camping." Jane didn't elaborate. "How come he was cremated?"

"He left a will, but the executor he'd named died years ago. That's why a Public Administrator was appointed. That happens more often than you'd think."

Jane and Cole climbed the dusty, steep switchbacks, neither saying anything more, the dogs at their heels. The trek was slow, due to the pups' stops at every stump and rock. When they arrived at the pond, no one else was around. "I brought some flowers from my garden." Jane set her backpack on the ground and knelt down beside it, unzipping the pocket and extracting a bunch of daisies, which still looked fresh. "Should we scatter the ashes in the water?"

"There are rules about water. You have to be so far out from shore, we'd need a boat. And we have to step off the trail to scatter on the ground. How about over there?" Cole jerked his head in the direction of a rock outcropping about a hundred yards away.

"Okay."

Bearing the cylinders, the two plodded through the underbrush. She secured the dogs' leashes around a thin aspen trunk and left her backpack next to them, before climbing up a tall rock with toehold-like steps. Jane asked, "Did you happen to know him?"

"No. I didn't. I'm sorry."

"Oh. This is a small community, so I thought you might. Can you say something anyway, before we do this?"

Cole cleared his throat. "These beautiful mountains were a favorite place for Michael Quadtrini. In casting the ashes of Michael, we dedicate this spot to his memory." He turned to Jane. "Did you want to say something, too?"

"Yes." She shifted her feet. "We recognize the presence of God in this place. We hope Mike is now at peace."

"Now for the scattering." Cole untwisted his cylinder and let the ashes slide out. They cascaded to the ground and some floated on the air. Jane opened her tube and did the same. Next, she tossed the flowers on top of the ashes. At the sight of the daisies flying from Jane's grasp, the dogs barked and hurtled toward them, bending the aspen and excoriating the leaves in their mad dash. They jumped up, pouncing against the rock with their front paws. Their small hind feet stomped the ashes and flowers and aspen leaves into the ground.

Horrified, Jane admonished them. "Nick! Nora! Get down." She hopped from the rock and untangled their leashes from the thin tree now bowed to the ground. "Well, dust to dust and all that." She gave a weak laugh.

But Cole didn't crack a smile. She eyed the trampled mess as he clambered from the rock with a stony face. After they stepped well away, he poured water from a bottle over Jane's hands first, then his own, and handed her a hand towel. She grasped the cloth with an awkward motion, then passed it back.

They hotfooted it along the trail to return to the

parking lot. The pups were exhausted, and after lapping up some water from the portable dog dish, they settled into the back seat with a plop. Jane shook Cole's hand and sighed with relief when he left in his black limo.

As the hour was still fairly early, but the dogs were tired, Jane decided to take a short stroll on her own. She made sure the windows were cracked, the sun roof was open a few inches, and the car was in a shady, cool spot, before scratching the dogs on their heads and locking up. She glanced over her shoulder a few times, but she wouldn't be gone long, and the temperature was cool in the shade with a breeze blowing through the sun roof and out the gap in the windows.

She trotted at a brisk pace down the gravel road. The campground was now full once again, since it was the tail end of June and the height of camping season. Happy families were gathered around picnic tables and fire pits. How many were aware of the murder the week before?

The residents of at least one campsite were aware. The tear-drop trailer was still parked in site number eight. Jane strolled past the buzzing generator up to the camper door and knocked. Hummingbirds whirled close to her face as they drank from the feeder attached to the awning. She was about to knock again, when the door opened a crack, and Gloria's hangdog face looked out. Her mouth opened, but no words came.

Jane gave her a tentative smile. "How're you doing? I see you're still here."

Gloria lowered her head and appeared to shrink back.

"What's the matter? Are you okay? Where's Ted?" Jane's hands flew to her throat.

Gloria choked back a sob. "You'd better come in." She opened the door all the way.

Jane stepped into the trailer and right into the 1950s. Aluminum-framed windows were cut into the pink walls with white and pink checked, fluffy curtains hanging on either side. White Formica countertops gleamed, and pink appliances didn't show a dent or stain. A tin cookie jar with Lucy's and Ethel's images from the chocolate factory sat on the small counter under a tin sign that read, *I Love Lucy*. A salt shaker of Lucy in her grape-stomping outfit was nestled against a pepper shaker in the shape of a wine barrel.

"Do you want anything to drink? I have iced tea in the fridge." Gloria sank onto a pink cushion on the bench at the table next to her two elderly spaniels, whose eyes gazed up at Jane and noses sniffed the air.

"Let me get it." Jane yanked open the miniature square door on the refrigerator and plucked out the pint-sized pitcher of tea. She peeked into the cabinet above the tiny sink. A set of vintage, Tupperware glasses in pretty, pastel colors were lined up in a row. She poured the tea into two of the glasses, pink and yellow, and carried them two steps over to the table. "Now, tell me what's wrong."

"They've arrested Ted!" Gloria's hand shook as she picked up, then set down, her glass, almost missing the table top.

"No." Jane slapped her hand on the sparkling, white, speckled Formica. "Why?"

"It's a long story."

"Tell me."

"The night Mike was shot, Ted thought he heard a bear, so he went outside. I waited at the door here, but I lost sight of him, so I went out, too. I looked around. He was gone." She clutched at her cardigan sweater. "You see, Ted's been diagnosed with Alzheimer's. I shouldn't've let him go, but he was determined." Gloria's nervous hands next grasped a pink dishtowel. She sponged the condensation off the bottom of her glass and folded the towel into a tight triangle.

"If he has Alzheimer's, why'd you let him go outside by himself?" Jane couldn't keep from asking.

"The doctors say he's just got the early signs. Some days are better than others, and he'd been doing so much better that day."

"Okay. Go on." Jane glanced out of the corner of her eyes at the elderly woman. "Where did Ted go?"

"I don't know. I was so worried he'd gotten himself lost in the forest. I walked into the woods a little ways and called for him, but the sky was dark, and I couldn't see him anywhere. I went back to the camper and put on my robe, then went over to the campground host site."

Jane held her breath. "To Mike Quadtrini's?"

"Yes. But Mike wasn't there. I called his name a couple of times, and I knocked hard on his camper door. I even opened the door and poked my head inside, but the camper was empty. I walked all over his site and saw no one around. I didn't know what to do. I got a little panicky, so I went over to site five to try to get someone to help me." The dogs snuggled closer to Gloria, and one burrowed its nose under her shaking hand. "I called out, 'help, help.' A woman came out of the tent, and I told her my Ted might be lost in the woods, and I didn't know what to do. Then, the woman tells me her husband wasn't there, that he'd gone to the latrines."

"Was this Ben Malkon's campsite? I don't know his wife's name, but Ben wore a red jacket, and he has glasses."

"Yes. That's right. It was his site, but he wasn't there."

"What did you do?"

"Well, the woman waited with me for a long while for her husband to get back. She told me she couldn't leave because her kids were asleep, and I told her the campground host wasn't at his trailer, either. And we ran out of things to say. We just stood and listened for Ben to come back, but he never did." Gloria patted one of her dogs on the head and took another small sip of tea.

"Malkon never came back?" Jane's heart thumped.

"No. But Ted came walking up the gravel road. I was so relieved. I thanked the kind woman for waiting with me, and then I took Ted to our camper. I asked him what happened, but he couldn't remember anything." Gloria's pale blue eyes were so wide the whites showed around the irises. "At the time I just thought he was lost and found his way back. I got him into the camper and locked the door up tight. Then I watched until he fell asleep."

"What time was this, do you know?"

"About five in the morning or thereabouts."

"Is that why he was arrested? Just because he was in the woods without an alibi?" Jane sucked in her breath, because it did sound bad.

"Mike's gun was missing from his campsite. The police said Ted was confused, took Mike's gun, and thought he was shooting a bear, but he shot Mike instead." Gloria stared at Jane with watery eyes.

"No way." Jane took a big swallow of tea, then sucked on an ice cube. She crunched down on the ice and said around a full mouth, "Don't worry. He would've had gun residue on his hands or the gun would've been found with his fingerprints on it or something."

Gloria's eyes pinged around the mini camper.

"What do the police have on him?" Jane grasped Gloria's elbow.

"They found Mike's gun in the woods, and it did have Ted's fingerprints on it."

Jane tried to keep the shocked expression off her face.

The older woman's lips trembled. "It could be explained. Ted could've found the gun, picked it up to look at it, and dropped it in the woods."

"Yes. Yes, of course. I agree." But Jane was shaking her head side-to-side.

Gloria went on. "Anyway, I called our son right away. I gave Jack that Marshall's phone number, and he was going to call and find out what's happening." Gloria's hand shook as she withdrew Agent Marshall's business card out of the pocket of her cardigan.

"Why don't you call your son now and find out if he knows anything yet? Jack, is it?"

"Yes. I will. My cellphone's in the car where I charge it." Gloria rose from her seat, and Jane followed her out. Gloria retrieved a flip-type cellphone from the phone charger. They scooted over to the picnic table to sit on the bench. Gloria punched in numbers. "Hello, Jack?"

Jane wasn't shy about eavesdropping on the one-sided conversation.

Gloria held the phone with one hand and picked at the surface of the table with the other. "Oh, that's good. I'm so relieved. Thank you so much, dear. I'll see you soon."

"What's the good news?" Jane leaned forward across the table with a hopeful grin.

"Jack said Ted's not arrested, just being questioned, that's all. He's going to bring Ted here and help us pack up the camper, and we're going home. He said it's all circumstantial evidence, that they can't prove Ted killed Mike. Since the bullet wasn't found, he said, they don't even know if Mike was shot with his gun or another gun."

"Right." Jane narrowed her eyes. "It's going to work out, you'll see."

"Do you really think so?" Gloria snapped the cellphone shut and dropped the phone onto the table.

"Certainly. When is your son supposed to get here?"

"By this afternoon."

"Do you want me to stay with you until then?" Jane would need to get her dogs from the car.

"You're really kind to offer, but I'll be fine now I know Ted's not arrested." Gloria dabbed at her cheeks with her sweater sleeve. "I'm almost done packing. Most everything is put away inside the camper."

Jane glanced toward the tear-drop. "You had more stuff out?"

"Oh, yes. I have a whole collection of Lucy things." Gloria smiled, but her smile did not light up her eyes like it usually did. "You could do something for me. Can you reach the hummingbird feeder?"

"I'll get it." Jane sprang up to unhook the feeder, then poured the clear nectar out in the stream on the other side of the trees. Dark clouds overtook the sky as she helped Gloria unload the picnic table and store the tablecloth in one of the diminutive cabinets. Gloria rolled up the outdoor rug, and Jane stuffed it under the bench in the trailer. They folded the camp rocking chairs, which went in a storage area in a miniscule closet. Gloria cranked the awning closed, while Jane helped guide the poles into position in a compartment on the side of the camper. They both washed up the iced tea glasses in the sink.

Gloria gave Jane a hug and thanked her, as Jane assured her one more time everything would work out. After they exchanged cellphone numbers, Jane waved goodbye, then walked with brisk steps toward the parking lot, wondering how Nick and Nora had been doing by themselves in the car. She took a quick look at the time on her cellphone and picked up her pace even more.

Scurrying past the campsites, Jane was reminded again of the camping fiasco of last weekend. Originally her good friend Cheryl and her husband Bruce were going to join the campout, but decided to shorten their visit to only the week of the Fourth of July. Jane begrudged Cheryl a little bit for not taking part in the camping trip, too, but considering the murder, it was probably for the best.

Just then, someone grabbed her shoulder and spun her around. Heart in her throat, she did a double take as she stared into the eyes of a muscular woman with short, brown hair—the driver of the red compact. "I want to know what you're doing back at the campground." The woman's fingers dug into Jane's shoulder.

"Tell me why you forced me off the road." Jane returned her glare and jerked away. Why didn't she go for another Krav Maga lesson last week?

"It was an accident. You slammed on your brakes, and I couldn't avoid it." The woman smirked, and her eyes glimmered.

"I don't believe you. It was intentional." Jane took a step backward to face her opponent square-on. She was at least twenty pounds heavier than petite Jane. Was her voice familiar? Jane took a stab in the dark. "I heard you talking to Ben Malkon about Mike Quadtrini outside the latrine."

Out of nowhere came drops of rain, splashing onto their heads. A crack of lightning lit the sky, and they both looked up. The woman's gaze returned to Jane. She hadn't denied she was the one outside the latrines with Ben Malkon. Jane's hunch must be right.

"Tell me why you're here. Are you following me?"

Jane gave out a bark of laughter. "Ha...no." Was this woman nuts? But she was looking Jane up and down, as if Jane were the crazy one.

As rain pelted down in jumbo-sized, ice-cold splashes, a man's voice shouted out, "Connie!" The woman recoiled, then darted away toward the nearest campsite.

At first Jane could only stand there, getting wetter by the second, but after a few heartbeats she ran after her. The woman had run into the campsite, and instead of getting under shelter, she'd kept going and disappeared into the trees.

Jane hung back near the picnic table, glancing

around for the man who shouted Connie's name, but saw no one. So, she wandered into the pines, her eyes searching and ears straining for any sound. Where did the woman go? Jane stared this way and that. The raindrops pitter-pattered the leaves, but not many reached her under the forest canopy. A fresh, earthy smell rose up as the soft splats of water made their way down to the dirt.

A squirrel twittered. Something rustled in the trees. Was the black bear still around with her cubs? The hair stood up on her arms.

Ker-rack!

Jane hit the ground, flat. The lightning was close, and she was probably in an electrical field. She rose to crouch on the balls of her feet. Another loud *kaboom* sounded near. Standing up, she pivoted one-eighty to point her body in the direction she'd come, then sprinted back to the campsite. Tempted to look around, she paused at the picnic table, but couldn't bring herself to peek inside the tent's window, and it was not a good idea to tarry among the tall trees. After skirting the tent, she stopped at the site marker displaying a reservation sticker. The name holding the reservation was O'Hennessey.

Another boom caused her to miss a step, and she went down on one knee, ripping a hole in her hiking pants on the sharp gravel rocks. She bolted upright and clutched her knee, now bleeding. Her heart was in her throat as she hobbled as fast as she could to the parking lot. Were the dogs all right in the storm?

But there they were, paws on the door, heads poking through the small space left by the open window, tails wagging, and glad to see her. Out from under the trees Jane dodged the raindrops, unlocked the door and dove inside, clicking the locks into place. As the dogs lunged into the front seat and licked her face, she took a deep calming breath, then slid the sun roof closed. The seats were damp from the rain. The pups bounded into the back seat again. The rain pelted down harder and harder, so she drove her vehicle out from under the trees to the middle of the parking lot, where they were safer from lightning strikes.

The rain reverberated on the roof of her car. Her knee was only bleeding a little, and her slacks seemed to have suffered the most damage. The dogs hopped from seat to seat and nudged under her chin with their noses. To wait for the storm to pass, she lifted her work satchel from the floor at the front passenger seat and withdrew her murder investigation folder. After finding a pen in her purse, she wrote the name, "Connie O'Hennessey," in her notebook, making sure to note the correct spelling. Was that really the woman's name or was Jane letting her imagination put the names together?

She poured herself a good measure from the thermos and took a sip, but the stale coffee was not appealing. After a few moments of chewing on the end of her pen, she tucked her tablet away and patted the dogs' heads, as they'd once again leapt into the front.

After a few minutes more, the rain let up and the sun's rays shone down between the trees rimming the parking lot. "Nick, Nora. Get into the back seat, now." Obedient for once, they jumped into the rear. She turned out of the parking area, her car tires parting the puddles that formed in low spots in the road and halted at the ranger station.

"Excuse me, uh, could you help me?"

"That was some rain squall, wasn't it?" The ranger's shaved head, topped with a brown cap, poked out the booth's window. They both gazed up at the sky, which was turning bluer by the moment.

"I'm supposed to meet my friend here. Connie O'Hennessey. But I drove around and can't figure out which campsite she's in." Jane gave the ranger what she hoped was a wide-eyed look and an innocent smile.

She squirmed as he stared at her for a moment, then narrowed his eyes at his paperwork. It seemed she was not going to get help after all. Then he shuffled through the papers and read out loud, "George and Connie O'Hennessey, site six."

"Thanks so much." Jane shot him a grateful glance. She turned her car around as if going to site six, then drove at a slow speed through the park, slicing the puddles in half once again. She steered past O'Hennessey's site, leaving behind the deserted-looking tent with no one about. She didn't find another exit, so had to escape out the driveway near the ranger station, hoping he wouldn't wonder what she was doing.

She turned her car toward the nearest town to find a coffee shop. Since the sun shined in earnest once more, she again locked the pups in the car in a shady, cool spot with a breeze and the sun roof open and the windows cracked. She rushed inside an independent coffee café and bookstore. Passing a section on local Colorado history and sights, probably for the tourists, she stopped short upon seeing the title, "A History of Yellow Mountain Campground—the good and bad years."

She snatched the small paperback and thumbed through it, then made the impulse purchase along with her skinny, two-pump mocha latte. The clerk mentioned, "That book was written by one of our locals here in town. In fact, she's sitting right over there." The clerk nodded his head in the direction of an elderly woman with a knit cap perched on her short gray hair. "If you want her to sign it, she will."

"Thanks." Jane paid for the book and latte and darted past other display racks and full tables over to where the gray-haired woman sat reading. "Excuse me."

"Oh, I see you've bought one of my books." The author smiled at Jane, and her gray eyes had a friendly look.

"Would you please sign it for me?" Jane glanced sideways at the book cover. "Uh, Ms. Wimple."

The woman opened the book to the first page. "What's your name, dear?"

"Jane." She chewed on her lip for a moment as the woman wrote a brief sentence and signed her name with a flourish, "Eleanora Wimple." Jane asked, "Did you know Michael Quadtrini?"

Eleanora's gray eyes looked into Jane's with interest. "Yes. So sad about his death. You knew him, too, then?"

"No. But I was camping there when he was shot."

"Oh, really?" She gave Jane a probing gaze.

"I didn't have anything to do with it. I don't even own a gun." Jane splayed out her fingers.

After Eleanora's lengthy hesitation, during which time Jane examined her nails and adjusted her sleeves, the author patted the seat of the wooden chair next to her. "Here, sit down."

Jane perched on the edge of the chair. "I'm sorry I don't have much time. My dogs are waiting for me in the car. I already left them alone once this morning, and I don't want to be gone long."

"What kind of dogs?" The woman was not about to be rushed.

"One's a beagle. The vet told me the other's a schnauzer mix because she's got the face and also the bark, but she's a little smaller and lighter than a normal schnauzer."

"I have a couple of hounds at home." Eleanora added a few words to her signature inside the cover and handed the book to Jane.

"About Quadtrini?"

"I tried to interview him for the book, but he wouldn't talk to me. Cantankerous for a young man."

"Young? I think he was around my age."

"Yes, he probably was." Eleanora's gray eyes smiled. "The campground hosts over at Rifle Falls knew him pretty well. Gene and Holly Toavne. You might want to talk to them."

"Gee, I wish I'd known about them before." Jane puckered her lips. What if they had wanted to spread his ashes? Maybe there were others who would've liked to have come along, too. "Do you know who lives in the cabin above the amphitheater?"

"Uh, that would be the man who runs the weather station. He's a bit of a hermit." Eleanora chuckled. "Quadtrini and he made a pair, both of them being loners. They didn't like each other at all."

Jane raised one eyebrow. "Why do you say that?"

Eleanora gazed around the room. "This is a small

town. It was well known."

"What happened between them exactly?"

"Well, since it's not a secret, I might as well tell you. They got into a fist fight at least once, maybe even a couple of times. Ed Koopmer tried to get Quadtrini dismissed as the campground host."

"Ed Koopmer, huh?" Jane sucked in her breath. She had another witness's name now. "Why?"

"Maybe you should ask Koopmer about it."

"I'd rather you just told me."

Eleanora gave her a steady look. "Rumor was that Quadtrini had a drinking problem. He'd have a bit too much, run across Koopmer, they'd have words."

Jane leaned in on her elbows. "Did he hate Quadtrini enough to kill him?"

"That seems farfetched."

"Who do you suspect, then?"

Drawing back, Eleanora answered, "Nobody around here." As she crossed her arms across her ample bosom, her eyes took on a guarded look.

Jane got up from her seat, clutching the book in one hand and her coffee in the other. "Thank you so much for the information. And for signing my book, too."

Eleanora inclined her head and focused once more on the book she was reading. Jane retreated to her car, but the dogs weren't even staring out the windows this time. They were curled up together, sound asleep, in the cool, shady driver's seat. Rapping her knuckle on the window, Jane smiled as their heads shot up, then they took to their feet and shook as she unlocked the door and climbed in, nudging them over.

She set her coffee in the cup holder and fastened

her seat belt. "Time to head home, you two."

Before putting the car in gear, she took a glance inside the book cover. Eleanora Wimple had written, "Hope you enjoy this Colorado lore," and then under her name she added, "Dogs help you get through the good and bad years."

Jane smiled. Yes, her fur kids did help through the good and the bad, the busy and the lonely days. She wondered what the bad years were at Yellow Mountain Campground. She shoved the book into the sack, looking forward to reading it.

But once home, there wasn't a spare moment to read her new book, since it was time to get ready for the dinner invitation she'd received at the last minute.

Chapter 11

After a shower, she creamed a tanning lotion on her legs, then carefully rinsed the lotion off her hands. She went into the closet to choose a flattering, date-worthy outfit.

What to wear that would be exciting and fun?

Like Everett.

Jane blushed at the thought of her former boyfriend's intense attraction to her, making her feel young and pursued. She hadn't seen him since he moved to Vail last year. He was handsome in a rugged way with his small, blue eyes, square jaw, and shoulder length hair, often hidden under a chef's toque. He was always ready to cook her a wonderful meal, even after working all day at the restaurant. Naturally, he was knowledgeable about wine and the trendy new recipes, making dining a fun experience.

Why not go all out for this date? After all, she had stiff competition.

Peering into the mirror, she carefully made up her face and glued on false eyelashes. She twisted hot rollers into her hair, and after the rollers cooled, she drew them out and ran a comb through the waves. She shoved her feet into new, strappy-heeled sandals and tottered around the bedroom. They didn't hurt her feet too much. The shoes were the perfect accessory to pair with the short denim skirt and lantern-sleeved top she'd decided to wear.

Ready early, she sat on the back deck with a teensy glass of white wine to watch the sun traveling over the peaks along the Front Range. Birds attacked the feeders and splashed in the bird bath, while Nick and Nora ignored them. Because she would have a glass at dinner, she probably shouldn't have poured herself a drink, but the wine was relaxing in the warmth of the sun.

She hadn't had a chance to tell anyone about Connie O'Hennessey's aggressive behavior at the campground earlier that day. Safe in her own back yard, she questioned whether it'd even happened.

Everett's face swam in front of her eyes. What would he have to say about her news if she had a chance to tell him?

The doorbell rang, and Dale stepped into the hall to give her a warm kiss.

"I'm glad you asked me out, Dale." Jane banished all thoughts of Everett. After all, Everett had packed up and moved to Vail, and Dale was here. Jane always had a hard time with change.

"You might want a jacket for later," he suggested.

"All right." She didn't want to cover up her carefully chosen clothes, so she slung her white denim jacket over her arm.

"You look really nice, Jane. Did you shop the glam?"

"Your slang sounds like Caleb's." She laughed.

Once they'd made sure the dogs were settled on the couch, Dale and Jane headed out. She swung her bare legs inside the car, and he shut the door after her. He navigated to the highway, then turned south.

"I'm sorry I was so jealous. I trust you to keep your relationship with Polly strictly business." Jane reached over to rub the back of his neck as he drove.

"I'm sorry, too. I'm glad we went out with Libby and Wes last night, but you and I didn't get to talk much."

"Well, we have the whole night to ourselves this time. And remember, you're coming with me to the cabin in Estes Park next weekend."

He gave her a slow wink. "Wouldn't miss it."

Jane's stomach fluttered. "Where are we going to eat?"

"Polly's restaurant."

"What?" Jane sputtered, her stomach sinking, the warm buzz gone. She withdrew her hand from his neck and clutched the arm rest.

His right hand left the steering wheel and came down on hers, squeezing her fingers. When she didn't respond, he pressed her fingers again. "You have no reason to be concerned."

"So you say." As she gazed out the front windshield, her eyes narrowed. At least she would look her best when meeting her rival. She'd been planning to tell him about running into Connie O'Hennessey and the police questioning Ted, but kept quiet and let Dale talk on the drive south. Her mind mulled over clever retorts, but she didn't say them out loud.

Polly greeted them at the door with an insincere smile and seated them at the best table near the fireplace. She handed out the large menus. Jane couldn't read hers in the dim light from the fire. Polly returned with a bottle of Merlot. "I want to know what you think of this new wine we've added to our wine list, Dale."

After Polly poured the wine, Jane took a sip and rolled the liquid around on her tongue. Without waiting for Dale's opinion, she announced, "It's obtuse and a little breezy."

With a raised eyebrow, Polly acknowledged her for the first time. "Really, you think so?"

Jane flushed hot as she set her glass down on the table, because she'd just made it up. "Uh, I think I smell black currant, perhaps?"

Polly turned away as the waiter appeared. After they ordered, Jane took another sip. "I don't know anything about wine tasting. What are the three components again?"

Dale answered, "Balance, depth, and complexity."

"Oh." She wasn't sure what that meant.

They munched on their salads while Dale told her about a new construction developer, who was considering contracting with his company for the electrical work—a big contract that would keep his electricians busy until the end of the year.

Polly once again appeared at Dale's elbow, much to her annoyance. Jane said with false cheer, "Polly, I found your car keys in my salad. I put them in your office on your desk for you." The other diners must have taken that moment to pause in their conversations, because Jane's voice carried across a quiet room. Polly glared at the surrounding tables, and her customers all gaped at her. Without another word, she stomped away.

Jane laughed at her own joke, but Dale had a stern look on his face. Oh dear, another disagreement, and so soon after the first one. The ex-wife would always be a sore spot. The conversation lagged even more after that.

They talked about work and the weather on the drive home, then Dale did not come inside after dropping Jane off at her house.

Once she'd closed the front door and kicked off her sandals, she blinked back a few tears. The hour was late, but she texted Olivia anyway. Her friend called her right away. "If neither Polly nor Dale can take a bit of teasing, then that's their problem."

"I guess, but I wish I could take it back. I thought it'd be funny, but I can never tell a joke. And I suppose I wanted to take a jab at Polly. Dale might find an excuse not to go to the cabin with the dinner club."

"He'll cool off by then and won't want to miss out on the fun."

"Do you really think so?" Jane had a catch in her throat. She'd fantasized about her old boyfriend, Everett, but now that she was in danger of losing Dale, she preferred him. She had a weighed-down lump in her chest.

"Yes. Forget about it."

Jane carried her phone into the closet to drop her sandals onto the shoe rack. "All right. I'll try. Hey, I finally got Quadtrini's autopsy report, and I have a couple of questions for Doug."

"Do you want to talk to him now? He's right here."

"Sure." She heard her friend pass the phone to her husband, and Doug came on the line.

"Hello, Jane. I've put the phone on speaker."

Jane shuffled on bare feet into her bedroom and perched on the edge of the bed. "I have a question for you. The autopsy shows the bullet was not found in the body. So, no bullet, but what about casings? Aren't bullet casings usually left at the scene?"

"Yes. If the shooter used a semi-automatic, but not if the gun was a revolver. All of us in the club had revolvers."

"So, there's a chance *no* evidence was found to clear any of us." She had a catch in her throat.

"There's a lot that goes into crime scene investigation. I was never one of those special scene investigators, so I don't know everything about it. But they'll turn up the evidence, don't worry."

Jane explained Ted had been taken in for questioning and she'd learned the names of O'Hennessey and Koopmer. Both Olivia and Doug sounded shocked as they discussed her confrontation with the woman. Olivia ended with, "We'll see you tomorrow at the concert, and we can talk more then."

"Thanks. See you tomorrow." Jane was cheered a little, looking forward to the outdoor concert the club planned to attend the next day. She scrubbed off her carefully applied makeup, removed the false eyelashes, and brushed her teeth. Next, she climbed into her pajamas and shoved her arms into a light robe, tying the belt snugly around her. After settling on the sofa with her laptop, Jane patted the seat and Nick sprang up next to her, thumping his tail.

Finally, having a few moments to investigate further, she searched several internet sites, but was unable to find Connie O'Hennessey or Ed Koopmer on any social media.

What was O'Hennessey's connection to Quadtrini? And how did O'Hennessey and Malkon know each other? Malkon would have the answers to those questions.

Too late at night to drive down to Highlands Ranch

for more surveillance. And besides, she didn't learn anything the first time. Not being lucky enough to get her hands on his phone number, she couldn't call him.

She would have to think of an excuse to knock on his door.

Chapter 12

Jane rapped her knuckles on the screen door's wooden frame.

A moment later, Gloria, in a bright magenta sweater, peered through the dingy, gray iron mesh. "Hello, Jane." Her voice was shaky as she gestured Jane inside.

"How're you doing?" She hugged the elderly woman for a moment or two.

"We're all right. I'm glad you called me after church this morning to get together." Gloria wobbled into the living room and brushed aside a stack of Sunday newspapers on a sofa covered with so many afghans Jane couldn't tell the color of the upholstery.

"Have the police questioned Ted any more or have they given up on that theory?"

"They haven't contacted us since they released Ted yesterday. Our son told us to call him right away if the police show up again."

"Where is Ted?" Jane set her purse on the coffee table.

"He's outside. He's having a fight with the squirrels because they keep getting into the birdseed." Gloria tugged the thick, dark curtains open, and light poured into the room with dust motes dancing on the beams.

Both women gazed out the window. Ted stood in

the middle of the cluttered yard, his hands resting on top of a rake, his chin on his hands. The women sidled away from the window to take seats. Jane wedged her bottom between a couch cushion and a napping cocker spaniel.

"Well," Jane began as she scrunched the spaniel's ears. He woke up and nudged her to keep going.

Pop, pop—POP! Yip!

Gloria's eyes widened and her eyebrows shot up. Jane bounded to the window as Gloria limped after her. Ted aimed a rifle into the trees at the end of the yard. Gloria thumped on the window. "Ted. Stop that."

Her husband swiveled an angry face toward the house, the rifle swinging around with him. Jane ducked and dragged Gloria with her, both of them tumbling to the floor, as a shot hit the window with a *craackk*!

"My God, Gloria. What's he doing?" Jane screamed.

"He's shooting the squirrels."

"He shot at us!"

"It's only a BB gun. It didn't even break the window." Gloria sat up, rubbing her hip.

"You okay?" Jane rose high enough to peek over the window sill.

Gloria inched herself to a stand. "No bones broken. I'll go get Ted. Don't worry." Gloria hitched her way out the back door and disappeared into the yard.

Jane crawled to the couch to retrieve her purse with a plan to escape, but on her way across the floor, sirens sounded as if they were approaching. She climbed to her feet and vaulted to the front door, yanking it open as a police cruiser sped up the driveway.

"What's going on here? We have a report of a gun

being fired." The officer hopped out of the patrol car.

"It's just a BB gun, not a real one. It didn't even break the window." Jane smiled, sure it was more of a grimace.

"It's illegal to shoot pellet guns or BB guns in the city."

"Oh. I didn't know."

"What did you do with the gun?"

"It wasn't me." Jane waved her hands around.

"Right. We have a good idea who it was. Where is he?"

She hesitated a moment, then gestured for them to come inside. "Follow me." She scooted down the hallway to the door at the rear of the house.

The officer spoke into the walkie clip on his shirt collar. "Come around through the gate. He's in the back yard."

Jane flew once more to the window as the officer stepped out the back door. In less than a few seconds, two policemen had Ted surrounded, with Gloria standing nearby, hugging her sweater around her stocky body.

Should she go comfort Gloria or would it be best to stay out of the way?

Her hesitation made the decision, because the officers led Ted and Gloria back inside, as Jane pressed against the wall like a shy teenager at a party.

"We don't want to get another call from one of your neighbors. No more shooting the squirrels."

"Yes, officer. I won't." Ted hung his head, his hands clenched and unclenched, then clenched again. Gloria plucked at his sleeve. They looked helpless, so Jane scrambled out of the corner to walk the officers to the door, while the elderly couple sat in a daze on the sofa.

"How'd you get here so fast, anyway?"

"The neighbors complain frequently about this guy. I think they have us on speed dial."

Once the policemen left, she returned to the old folks. "You should give your son a call. Jack, isn't it? Maybe he'd like to come and get the BB gun." Jane dipped her head, trying to catch Gloria's eye.

"Yes. That's a good idea." Gloria grabbed her phone from the sofa table.

"Well, I'll be on my way, then." Jane threw her purse strap over her shoulder.

"Yes, dear. Maybe you could come back another time." Gloria's watery blue eyes appeared anxious, but resolute.

Jane nodded. "I'll call you." She pivoted on her heel and left at a half-trot. Steering out of the neighborhood, Jane gunned the car's engine when she reached the highway. Could Ted have shot Quadtrini after all?

****

Later that afternoon, the dinner group met at the outdoor jazz concert at Denver City Park. They'd packed bottles of wine and picnic baskets, then gathered across the lake from the pavilion where a jazz band performed. People playing Frisbee dodged hibachi grills and picnic blankets spread on the ground. Others played hacky sack and others bocce ball. Few actually paid attention to the music.

The club formed a circle with their collapsible camp chairs to share snacks of cheese, crackers, and fruit.

As Doug and Olivia had already heard the news, Jane told the Powells the police had taken Ted in for questioning and all about her encounter with O'Hennessey.

"You never told us what you were doing at the campground, Jane." Doug tugged on his mustache.

"I took the dogs for a hike." She was about to explain that she'd spread Quadtrini's ashes before running into O'Hennessey, but something made her hold her tongue.

Wes pursed his lips and whistled. "That woman has quite a nerve talking to you like that. But at least you have a name to match with a face now."

"But what if Ted's the killer? No motive, just a mistake. That would be very sad." Libby slathered brie onto a cracker and handed it to Wes. The band played a jazzy tune with a strong, lively beat.

"I hope it's not him." Jane poured wine into paper cups.

Wes changed the subject. "Thanks for making the reservations for next weekend at the cabin and organizing the meals, Olivia."

"Someone had to do it. Couldn't let a holiday weekend go to waste." Olivia tucked a strand of black hair behind an ear. "Is everyone ready?"

"I'm not yet, but I will be by then." Jane took a sip of wine as she contemplated her assigned meal at the cabin—breakfast on Saturday morning. She'd found a sweet and savory French toast recipe she could assemble the night before. She would only need to bake the dish in the oven an hour that morning.

"Uh oh. Look." Libby waved her hand in the direction of a white-haired woman dancing to the rhythm of the music, with a portable oxygen tank slung over her shoulder. Jane stifled a laugh, but stopped short as two uniformed officers skirted around the woman and aimed toward the dinner club members. "Are we going to get in trouble for having alcohol in the park?" Libby whispered.

"Everyone else has it." Jane felt her blood rush in her ears.

"Those are federal agents. What're they doing here?" Doug popped a piece of cheese in his mouth. He sliced another piece off a block and handed it to Olivia.

The officers marched straight up to the group. When they drew near, Jane recognized the same two who questioned them at the campground.

"Olivia Ladner?"

"Y-yes?" Olivia's voice wavered as she dropped the cheese. She set her wine glass on the ground, and the cup tipped over.

"We'd like you to come with us for questioning in connection with the murder of Michael Quadtrini."

As one of the agents took her by the elbow, Olivia rose from her chair in shock. Doug jumped to his feet. "I'm coming with her."

Jane stood also. "Doug, I'll take care of your chairs and picnic basket. I'll drop your stuff off at your house. I'm sure the officers won't detain you long." She stared at the agents with a deathly glare.

"Thanks, Jane." Doug trotted behind the officers as they escorted his wife out of the park. The crowd had been staring, but soon resumed their play.

"I can't believe what just happened." Libby's eyes bulged out.

The three of them looked from one to another for a

moment, then stood up to fold their chairs. No one felt like partying anymore, so they packed up. Jane put a cork in her wine bottle and gathered up her plates and utensils to stow in her basket, plus Olivia and Doug's.

Libby slung the bag with her folding chair over her shoulder. "How'd they know Olivia was here with us?"

"They might've showed up at her house, found them not home, and asked one of their neighbors if they knew where she was." Wes picked up a picnic basket with one hand while tossing his folding chair over his shoulder with the other.

"But how did they find us in this crowd?" Libby frowned and her eyes darted through the swarm of people.

Wes stopped to think. "They knew she was with Doug and he's pretty hard to miss with that red hair and mustache."

"What can we do to help them?" Jane pounded her fists into her waist.

Wes swung his head from side-to-side in slow motion. "I'll call Doug in a little while and try to find out what happened." The Powells walked with Jane to her car and helped her load the Ladners' picnic basket and camp chairs into her trunk, together with Jane's picnic supplies.

Libby gave her a quick hug before they departed. "I'm sure they'll release Olivia, and everything'll be fine."

But both Wes and Libby looked as worried as Jane felt.

First she motored home to Limestone Heights to drop off her things and check on her dogs. Once she took care of the puppies, she drove to the Ladners' house in Verano and parked her car in front to wait. She checked the text messages on her phone—nothing new there, no apology from Dale—and logged onto Facebook. Finding no interest in the postings, she scrolled through the photos on her phone. After exhausting every avenue of distraction, she chewed on a fingernail.

Finally, Doug and Olivia drove up. Jane hurtled out of her car and popped open the trunk to hand Doug his picnic basket.

"Was the questioning awful?" Jane began, but after looking at Olivia's tear-stained face, she held up a palm. "I won't keep you. I just wanted to make sure I returned your things."

Olivia unlocked the front door. "Thanks, Jane. Please come inside."

"Are you sure? We can talk later."

"Get in here." Olivia held the front door open. Jane sailed inside while Doug was left to deal with the picnic supplies. Soon, he joined them in the kitchen, where Olivia plugged in a tea kettle and snagged tea bags out of a cabinet. "The police had nothing new, just the same thing as before. They suspect me because they found my reading glasses with the body. That's all."

Doug plopped into a chair at the table with a heavy sigh. "Well, Agent Marshall also told us the trajectory of the angle of the bullet track fits Olivia's height. No bullets found in the body or casings at the scene, so they can't pinpoint the gun conclusively. Probably a standard caliber revolver."

"I wonder if that eliminates Ted because he's kinda tall, at least five or six inches taller than Olivia. Was Agent Marshall the one who did the questioning?" Jane seized a mug of steaming water from her friend's trembling hands.

Olivia shakily poured another mug for herself, then sank into the chair next to Doug's. She slid the basket of tea bags across the table to Jane. "Yes. He was waiting at the forestry office near the federal buildings downtown where they took me. I'm glad Doug followed me in our car, so I wasn't all by myself."

"I understand that." Jane chose a peppermint tea from the assortment. They each steeped their bags. Jane asked, "Did Marshall find out you're a good shot?"

That got a smile out of her friend. "No. There's no way he could find out unless he saw me shoot."

"Olivia, the others at the firing range probably noticed you hit the bullseye every time." Doug's cellphone rang, and he answered it. "Hi, Wes. We're home now." He withdrew outside to the patio to take the call, but returned after a few moments.

"I filled Wes in briefly, but I'll call him tomorrow to talk further."

Jane cleared her throat. "Did you speak to the investigators about Ben Malkon's lawsuit against Quadtrini? That Quadtrini killed his son is a huge motive, and Olivia has none."

Doug answered before his wife could get a word in. "Yes. They claimed he had an alibi. They could've just been saying that, and the story may not have been true."

"They can lie to you?" Jane's mouth turned down, and she crossed her arms over her chest.

"Oh yes. It's an effective tactic to get a confession." Doug probably knew this as a former police officer.

"But I don't have anything to confess. Oh, I wish I hadn't left my reading glasses on the picnic table. Why didn't I take them into the tent with me?" Olivia grabbed a fistful of her hair and squeezed her eyes shut.

"Don't beat yourself up. We're going to figure this out." Jane rubbed Olivia's arm.

Doug faced Jane directly and narrowed his eyes. "What've you done to investigate so far?"

"Not much, I'm afraid. I've already told you everything." Jane sat up straighter in her chair. "Except, I do have an address for Ben Malkon, but no phone number. There's no number for him on the internet."

Doug brightened. "An address is all we need. Is there anything else?"

"I have the name of the woman, remember? Connie O'Hennessey. Then, there's that man at the cabin, Ed Koopmer. And I've got a copy of the autopsy report. That's about it."

"I'd like to see the report."

"It's at home. I'll scan and email it to you tomorrow. The only other thing I've done, and it probably won't be any help, was to request information on the campground. The camp was shut down for asbestos remediation. It's a long shot the murder has anything to do with the camp closure, but I thought it might be interesting. The camp was reopened years ago, and that seemed to be the end of it."

"Good job, Jane. It's worth following every lead."

She slugged down a mouthful of the hot tea and gave him a stern look. "Can't you use your old police connections to find out more?"

He pinched the bridge of his nose. "No. For one thing, I don't know anyone at that federal agency. If I asked a friend on the force to call them, they would put two and two together and figure it's me asking. And I don't want them to know."

Silence prevailed for a moment. The sun disappeared behind a cloud, and the sky outside the window turned dark, casting the kitchen into gloom.

Doug punched the light switch on the wall and the room lit up like a stadium.

Jane blinked. "Think about this angle. Say Connie O'Hennessey has something to do with the asbestos problem. Maybe she's the whistleblower. She knew about the contamination somehow, alerted the government, and got the campground closed down. And because of that, Quadtrini may have threatened her."

"Whistleblowers are kept anonymous for that reason." Olivia's eyebrows furrowed.

"Thanks for shooting down my one idea." Jane frowned.

Doug turned to his wife. "You told me Libby knew Quadtrini from college."

She stirred a spoon around in her teacup, making tinkling music. "Yes. I don't think she's told the investigators or Wes yet. If she does go to the police, she'll want you to go with her, Doug."

"Tell me about it again." He closed his eyes and crossed his arms as Olivia recounted Libby's words.

"And there's something more." Jane shoved her sleeves up her arms. "Because of the gunshot noise, Wes had an episode of PTSD and couldn't sleep. He's started counseling now. If you are going to talk to Libby, keep that in mind about Wes."

"I'm glad you explained that." Doug pushed his cooled tea away. "You think the woman you overheard outside the latrine is the same one who ran you off the road?"

"Yes. Connie O'Hennessey. I think she's one and the same. She's puzzling, though." Jane tugged her cellphone out of her purse and scrolled through the photos. "Here's a snapshot of her."

Doug studied the photograph then returned the phone to Jane. "I saw that picture on your Facebook page. I'm going to check the pictures I took, too."

He extracted his phone from this pocket, as Olivia rifled through her purse for hers. Soon, they were both tapping their screens with their fingertips.

Olivia poked her phone into Doug's face. He nudged her hand back a few inches and then gripped the phone steady to peer at the photo. "It's almost the same picture."

"Yes. I snapped a shot after we put the tent up. The campsite was so pretty."

"What? I want to see." Jane studied the photo of Malkon and O'Hennessey, as Olivia angled her phone in her direction. Quadtrini was clearly the third person in Olivia's photograph.

"I'm going to talk to Malkon," Doug announced. "Do you want to go with me?"

Olivia said, "I do."

Jane waggled a finger at Doug. "You're the one always telling me to keep out of the way of the police. What if they find out you questioned Malkon?"

Doug huffed into his mustache. "You're not one to talk, Jane. You're always butting in."

"Am not." Jane screwed her mouth into a pout.

"Children, children." Olivia slammed her tea cup onto the table, then asked Jane, "You're coming along, right?"

"Yes. Count me in."

Chapter 13

I'm in jail!

Not certain she was fully awake, Jane stared at the text message and clutched her cellphone, but it squiggled out of her hands and landed on the bedside table. She snatched the phone and punched in Libby's number.

Her friend's voice sobbed into the phone. "The police brought Wes and me in for questioning. They showed up at our house first thing this morning. Wes is in the interrogation room now, and they just finished with me. I'm waiting in the hall for him to come out—"

"Oh my gosh. First Olivia, now you two. Why in the world?"

"They told me a witness saw me with the campground host, but as it turns out, they only saw a woman wearing a gray sweatshirt." Libby made gulping sounds into the phone.

Jane gasped. "And you have a gray hoodie—"

"Right. The police took it. But you know how many people have gray sweatshirts?"

"Everyone has one," breathed Jane.

"Oh, here comes Wes. I'll call you later."

"Okay. Call me back."

But Libby had already hung up.

Jane donned her robe and scooted into the kitchen. She didn't have to leave for work this Monday morning, since she'd taken the week off as a mini-vacation, of sorts. The original dinner club members, Cheryl and Bruce Breewood, were due to arrive in Colorado that day. They were staying a week and were joining the club at the cabin for the upcoming Fourth of July weekend. Jane planned to hang out with Cheryl whenever the Breewoods were not visiting their daughter. Plus use any opportunity during the week to investigate further.

Now was her chance.

She poured herself a cup of coffee, then skimmed down her to-do list, when she remembered to check the mail. She'd totally forgotten about it over the past few days. She threw on yoga pants and a T-shirt and hurried to the mailbox. Sure enough, the response to her request under the Freedom of Information Act was there, stuck between two advertisement flyers. She hightailed it into the house.

After tearing open the envelope, she read through the report. Eight years back, the Colorado Department of Public Health and Environment had confirmed the presence of asbestos in the cement artifacts left over from the old town near where the campground was now located. The Army Corps of Engineers monitored the air and determined the fibers were airborne. Until the contamination could be remediated, the Forest Service had mandated closure.

Jane raised her head from the report and drummed her fingers on the table. Inhalation of asbestos fibers could cause serious respiratory problems, including cancer. She'd seen the attorneys' commercials on television for people suffering from mesothelioma.

She bent her head once again. The man who

operated the weather station for the National Oceanic and Atmospheric Administration was relocated temporarily. It said Ed Koopmer recorded daily meteorological data, like temperature, precipitation and snowfall levels. Likely his cabin was the one they'd hiked to.

Did weather watchers also look out their windows with binoculars or did they only check their instruments? He must've had a clear view to the amphitheater where Quadtrini was shot.

She folded the asbestos report into the envelope and crammed the packet into her murder folder, just as Cheryl phoned to make plans for that afternoon.

They met at the corner of Sixteenth and Larimer in Denver to walk the Cherry Creek trail to Confluence Park and along the Platte River to the Children's Museum, just like they used to do over their lunch hour last year when Cheryl still worked in Denver.

"I'm thrilled you could meet me." Jane gave Cheryl a tight hug, then held her at arm's distance for a long look. "I've missed you. We have so much to catch up on."

Cheryl's chestnut-colored hair was swept into a bun at the crown of her head, and a bright, multi-colored, filmy scarf was knotted at her neck. Jane stubbed her own plain white tennis shoes on the pavement, as she glanced at Cheryl's chic, knee length shorts and stylish Skechers.

Jane adjusted her sunglasses. "So how's Megan doing? What's the news?"

"She's doing great. We went out to breakfast this morning, then went shopping. Megan needed new clothes, and she ran me ragged through the stores. I'm exhausted already. It's Bruce's turn now. They're having some father-daughter time, but they only went to a movie, so he gets to sit." Cheryl held up a hand to shade her eyes under the glare of the bright sun.

Jane chuckled. "That sounds about right. So, what are you doing the rest of the week?"

"Megan has a lot of things planned, but I'm going to be sure to see the new traveling exhibit at the Denver Art Museum. I'll have plenty of time for you, too." Cheryl smiled at Jane, who returned her grin. "And how're your sons and their wives?"

"Luke's home from his deployment with the Army."

"Oh, that's good. I'll bet Brittany's glad."

"Yes, we all are. And right now, Caleb is studying for the bar exam, and Erin's teaching summer school. But I'm a little concerned about those two. They're having a disagreement."

"Oh dear. Married couples argue the most about money or kids. I suppose money will be tight until Caleb gets a job."

"It's not that. He has a chance for a good job in Durango, but Erin doesn't want him to take the position. And I don't either." Jane stopped and turned to face her buddy. "What if both my boys live far away? It would kill me."

"What about me? We moved far from Megan." Cheryl gave Jane a stinging slap on the arm.

"Ouch, that hurt." Jane rubbed her arm up and down. "So, tell me, how do you deal with it?"

"Bruce and I aren't kid centric. You need to concentrate on your own life journey, Jane. Haven't you figured that out yet?" Her friend rolled her eyes.

Jane sighed. Cheryl was right. What was wrong with her? Why couldn't she get past the empty nest?

The familiar walking path took her down memory lane. Both boys grown, gone, married now; Cheryl had moved across country, and they didn't talk nearly as much as they used to; even Dale had left her, and probably he was back with Polly.

Cheryl must have read her thoughts. "Talking about leading your own life, how's Dale?"

"Talking about arguments, we had one about his ex-wife. He went out with her instead of going on the camping trip with the club. We haven't quite worked it out yet."

There was empathy in Cheryl's voice. "The man's a fool."

"I knew I could count on you to take my side." Jane forced a smile. They'd stopped near a park bench in Confluence Park where kayakers practiced in the water near REI. Cheryl led her over to the bench out of the sun, and they both sank down. Footsteps pounded up the trail as a runner, arms swinging wide, passed them a few yards away. Jane stretched her feet in front of her and crossed her arms over her chest. The trees formed a canopy of shade, giving them a respite from the heat.

Then Cheryl tapped her arm. "So, you're involved in yet another murder investigation. Your email didn't explain everything. There must be more to it. So tell me."

Jane caught her friend up with the investigation. "It's very sad that Mike Quadtrini had no relatives, so I met the funeral director Saturday morning, and we scattered his ashes at the campground." Jane knew she could confide in Cheryl, who would not think her odd.

"That was a nice thing to do, and really going out of your way for a stranger. He didn't sound like a nice person, either."

"Everyone should have someone to say goodbye."

"So, he had no relatives, but what about enemies?"

"I do have a couple of suspects. Ben Malkon, first, and Connie O'Hennessey, the woman who ran me off the road, second. Ben appears to be a family man. He has a wife and kids. I'd hate to think he's a killer, but he's my prime suspect."

"Wow. One of his kids killed in a car wreck. That's a big motive for murder. A parent just can't get over something like that…"

"I've read the death of a child is worse than the death of a spouse. I can't imagine." Jane's heart lurched, but she swallowed down that particular fear.

"What does O'Hennessey have to do with Quadtrini?" Cheryl gave her head a little shake, and the scarf around her neck fluttered.

"You got me there. I don't have a clue. But I ran into her when we scattered the ashes. She accused me of following her. I'm not sure what her problem is, and I'm probably all wrong about her because the police seem to suspect Olivia, not Connie. They questioned Olivia yesterday about her reading glasses. And they questioned Libby and Wes this morning. If Libby told the police she'd dated Quadtrini, she'll be a suspect, too. And I suppose, Wes, also."

"Don't read too much into the questioning. Police have to do that. They keep questioning the same people over and over, hoping they'll remember something more." Cheryl brushed her long bangs from her eyes.

"But why would Wes be a suspect? I can sorta understand Olivia and Libby."

"What?" Jane bristled.

"Come on. Olivia's glasses found with the body. Libby dated him. I'm not saying they did it, just that the police have a reason for questioning them. But what's Wes's motive?"

Jane slumped back onto the bench. "His PTSD and maybe jealousy—"

"I don't think PTSD can drive someone to murder."

"In most cases you're right, I'm sure, although killers have tried to use the condition as a defense."

"Hmmm. I haven't met your newest dinner club members yet. I'm looking forward to meeting them this weekend."

"When you do, you'll see that Wes would never hurt anyone." Jane touched her finger in her palm. "But the police don't know that."

"Are those all of your suspects?"

Jane drew a line between her brows. "There are a couple more. A man who lives in a cabin close to where Quadtrini was shot. And this old guy, Ted. He has early Alzheimer's, and the police think he may have confused Quadtrini with a bear and shot him." Her head fell to her chest. "And then, there's me."

"You?"

"My 'widow of the waves' reputation precedes me."

"Oh, that." Cheryl barked out a laugh. "No one could believe you're a killer."

Jane's eyes searched out her friend's for comfort, and Cheryl gave her a smile. "Let's keep walking." She bounded up from the bench, so Jane did the same.

Cheryl pumped her arms up and down as they resumed a quick pace along the path. "Tell me what you are going to do next."

Jane huffed alongside. "Doug wants to talk to Ben Malkon, and I'd like to, as well. But the police know about his history with Quadtrini already, yet they haven't arrested him."

"That only means they're still trying to gather more evidence."

Wondering what the police knew that she didn't, Jane was determined to find out.

In short order, the two companions returned to the Sixteenth Street Pedestrian Mall. Cheryl glanced at the clock on her cell. "We'd better hurry. It's almost time to meet Bruce."

Jane walked Cheryl to her car, then headed to her own to follow her friend north on the Valley Highway. Once at their destination, she trotted through the cigar lounge storefront, past the large humidor with its steamy, pungent aroma, and into the area for members only.

"Hello Bruce." She dropped her satchel in a chair to give her best friend's hubby a hug, her arms encircling his waist as he towered over her. "And hello to you, stranger." Jane gave Cheryl a finger wave. Cheryl had made better time and had beaten her there.

"Bruce has a bottle of wine in his locker. I'll get it." Cheryl vaulted up and ran to the humidor.

"Why do you still have a locker here, Bruce?" Jane jerked the paper wrapper off an energy bar.

He scooted over to make room at the table. "I belong to a cigar lounge in Portland now. It's a chain, so I keep lockers in both places." He blew a smoke ring, and the exhaust fan whisked the vapor up and out of sight.

Jane stuffed the uneaten energy bar into her purse as she lowered herself onto a chair. She would eat at home later. "Did you enjoy the movie with Megan?"

Before Bruce could answer, Olivia and Doug appeared at their side. Olivia plunked her hefty pink handbag on the table and slid onto the chair vacated by Cheryl. "Where's Dale?"

"I don't know." Jane frowned. Dale had not returned any of her text messages since he took her out to dinner at Polly's restaurant. Olivia raised one eyebrow in question, but Cheryl returned, waving a bottle of Syrah in one hand and a package of plastic wine glasses in the other.

She and Bruce hauled up extra chairs so everyone could sit close, then they chatted happily about their new jobs and the loft they'd purchased in Portland as everyone enjoyed a glass of wine. Soon the conversation came around to the murder investigation. Cheryl asked, "Did you hear about the report Jane got on the campground?"

"What's this?" Doug fixed his eyes on Jane.

"I have it with me." She fetched the envelope out of her tote bag. "Remember, I told you I was getting this information on the asbestos shut-down."

Doug leafed through the pages. "Ed Koopmer's name's in here as a witness. I'm going to take tomorrow off work, drive up there and talk to him. He's probably the guy from the cabin."

"I thought we were going to talk to Ben Malkon." Jane narrowed her eyes.

"Patience, patience," Olivia teased. "I know. Let's make a day of it. Drive up to the camp and on the way home stop at Highlands Ranch to talk to Malkon."

"We can come, too. We don't have plans with our daughter until tomorrow night." Cheryl glanced over at Bruce for his consent. He shrugged in acquiescence and blew another smoke ring.

"Will we fit in one car?" Jane peered around at the other four, counting heads.

Bruce tapped his cigar on the ashtray. "We're renting an Expedition. We can all fit."

Jane screwed up her face and scratched her head.

"What are you thinking, Jane?" Doug eyeballed her.

"I ran into a local writer at the coffee shop in the town near the campground. She knew Quadtrini. She said he and the man who ran the weather station did not get along. That's Koopmer. She also said Quadtrini had friends, the campground hosts at Rifle Falls. I wrote their names down." After rummaging through her satchel again, she plucked out her notes. "Gene and Holly Toavne. I don't know how it's spelled, but that's what the name sounded like. Toe-vein."

"Do we have time to stop there, too?" Olivia tugged her chair closer to the table.

Doug ran a hand over his mustache. "Rifle Falls is quite a bit farther west. We may need to make that another trip."

"What about your new club members, Libby and Wes? Do you think they'd want to come along?" Cheryl tapped her cigarillo on the ashtray, then left it balanced on the rim.

"You know they were taken in for questioning this

morning, right?" Jane glanced at Doug's and Olivia's faces as they nodded. "But I don't know what happened. I can't reach Libby on the phone."

"I'll call her right now." Olivia clicked her nails across her phone screen, then held the phone to her ear. "Nothing, just voice mail."

"I've left her a few messages. I hope they're all right." Jane's hands went to her throat. "But let's think this through. If all of us descend on Ed Koopmer, should we plan in advance what to ask him? And Ben Malkon, too."

"We were policemen, remember. We know how to question a witness." Bruce cracked open his mouth, and a trail of smoke swirled out. The two men both had a history in law enforcement with experience in interrogation.

"Will the police be upset if you guys question possible suspects? Can we trust them not to mention it?" Cheryl threw her husband a look, but he was scrutinizing Doug.

"I don't care if they do." Doug smoothed down his mustache. Bruce shrugged, so they made plans to meet at Doug and Olivia's house at nine the next morning.

Cheryl suggested, "Let's stop for lunch at a brew pub on the road back from Yellow Mountain Campground. There's one right on the way I've been wanting to try for a while."

"Sounds good. A toast to our success tomorrow." Doug held up his plastic wine goblet, and they bumped glasses.

"And what if we solve the crime? The weather watcher could be the murderer. He would've known Quadtrini well if they had been neighbors for several years." Olivia smiled, her eyes bright.

Jane had a sudden thought. Her friends were involved in her investigation now. If she had left things alone, they wouldn't have known the weather watcher did not get along with the dead man. They wouldn't have heard about Ben Malkon's suspicious statements outside the latrine and his motive from the car accident. Or about Connie O'Hennessey's threatening behavior. Were they headed into danger because of her?

****

On the drive home to Limestone Heights, Jane plugged her cellphone into Blue Tooth and spoke Libby's number into the auto dial function. There was still no answer. Just as she was wondering whether to try Wes's cell, her phone rang, and she hit the button to pick up the call.

Libby's voice wavered. "Jane, I got your voice messages. I know you've been trying to get ahold of me, and I'm sorry I didn't call you back earlier."

"Are you okay?" Jane exited the highway and turned into a gas station parking lot. She shoved the gearshift into park to idle.

Libby sighed into the phone. "Wes finally went out to the garage to tinker and decompress, so I can talk now. I told the police everything, that I knew Mike Quadtrini years ago. It turns out Wes knew about Mike all along. I'd forgotten I told him about dating Mike in college. I don't recall telling him, but he remembered. The police think Wes had a motive for murdering Mike."

"But Wes didn't go to the firing range. He wouldn't have had gun residue on his clothes like the others."

"But his Ruger had been fired, remember? They claimed he could have been the one to fire it. They said the gun residue was washed away when he fell in the pond. They think he jumped in on purpose."

Jane sucked in her breath and closed her eyes. "So what if you knew Quadtrini? I'm sure a lot of people knew him."

"The fact that neither of us told the police before now is suspicious. They even questioned Wes about his military experience and whether he has PTSD. They hinted his anger was over the top."

Jane's heart sank, not knowing what to say. She watched as a car turned into the gas station and another drove out. Dark blue clouds hovered over the mountain peaks on the horizon. The sun was setting, casting a glow from behind the mountain tops, streaking the sky with orange and pink.

Bright beams suddenly shone through her back window.

A police cruiser with revolving lights had driven up behind her. The policeman climbed out and marched up to her car door.

"Sorry, Libby, but I'm driving and can't talk. I'll call you when I get home." She heard the quaver in her words, which had gotten loud. After tapping her phone off, she rolled down her window. Her heart beat faster and she swallowed hard. Was she going to be hauled in for questioning, too?

"Are you okay, ma'am? Are you having car trouble?"

"No," she trilled. Steadying her voice, she continued, "I mean, I'm fine. I just pulled off the road to take a phone call."

"I'm glad you didn't talk on the phone while driving. I'm just checking to make sure you're okay." He had a head of gray hair and a nice smile, but a suspicious gleam to his eye. He turned to leave as Jane rolled up her window. She merged onto the highway while the police cruiser followed her. Her heart kept pounding in her chest as she glanced in her rearview mirror over and over again. After a few miles, the police car exited the highway, and she breathed a sigh of relief, speeding up for home.

The dogs licked her face as she bent down to greet them, then she plopped her tote bag on the counter. She was starved, but filled the dogs' bowls with their dinner first. Next, she checked her phone. Dale had not called.

She punched in Libby's number as she settled at the counter to eat a simple salad for dinner. "I'm calling you back. You were telling me the police suspect Wes? That's crazy."

"I know. It's absurd. But I'm doing better now. Even though the police have more reason to suspect us, it was actually good to come clean. To Wes, too. I don't have a reason to feel guilty for holding anything back now."

"If this is any comfort to you, remember even that old guy, Ted, was taken in for questioning. And Olivia, don't forget. You weren't the only ones."

"That's right." Libby let out a big sigh. "I suppose I shouldn't be glad, but that does make me feel better. So, everyone in the group has been taken in for questioning, except you…and Doug."

"I'm sure my turn will be next." Jane's stomach twisted at the thought, but she had nothing to hide, other than her own investigative efforts. "Oh, and I found out something more." She caught Libby up with the recent news that they had the weather watcher's name—a new witness identified. "The gang is driving to Yellow Mountain Campground tomorrow to talk to him. We're also going to stop and talk to Ben Malkon."

"I'd like to go, too."

Jane swallowed a bite of lettuce in a gulp. "Okay. We're all meeting at Olivia's house to drive up together. Bruce has an Expedition, so there's plenty of room to ride in one vehicle."

"I'll check with Wes, but I know he has a lot going on at work tomorrow. He might not come, but I'll be there."

"Sounds good." After disconnecting, she finished her salad, deposited her plate and fork in the sink, and swung open the patio door, while the dogs scurried outside for a potty break. They zoomed around the yard, sniffing the trees and along the fence line, as Jane stared out into the night.

Now Libby, too, was involved in tomorrow's plans. She only had herself to blame. Her and her big mouth. But she couldn't hold back from her friends.

After a few minutes, Jane called to her dogs, "Nick, Nora! Get in here." Once they scampered inside, she spent time getting ready for the next day and catching up with laundry. Before long, she climbed into her pajamas and slithered under the bedcovers. She'd brought the book with her, "A History of Yellow Mountain Campground—the good and bad years."

Expecting a dull read of historical facts and dates, the kind you get from a tour guide at a museum, Jane perked up when she reached the chapter entitled, "The Bad Years." Evidently Eleanora Wipple had made the same records request as Jane, since she quoted from the same asbestos report, but Wipple had uncovered an additional fact. A lawsuit had been filed against the U.S. Forestry Service for an alleged cover-up.

Jane unfolded herself out of bed and retrieved her laptop. Returning to her place under the blankets, she fluffed up her pillow, then re-positioned the computer on her lap. She searched the internet for the lawsuit and found it.

Litigation was initiated six years previously, but was dismissed within a year. Filed by a non-profit environmental group, the lawsuit alleged the Forestry Service knew about the asbestos contamination, but did not perform a timely study and had mismanaged public lands. A dismissal motion had been granted, and that was the end of the court docket.

But buried on page fifteen in the Complaint, right at the place she almost stopped reading, was the allegation that a Forest Service employee hid the discovery of asbestos in the materials left over from the old buildings constructed in the 1940s. The employee simply covered the site over with a bulldozer. Then, he hired an excavating firm to haul out some of the debris, disturbing the asbestos and releasing the fibers, creating a worse health hazard than if he had left the site alone. An employee of the excavating firm developed symptoms of lung disease—chest pain and spitting up blood.

Jane made a note of the environmental group's attorney's name and phone number.

Typing in the phrase "asbestos remediation" on her laptop search engine, she learned construction materials from the 1940s into the 1970s commonly contained asbestos. Warnings abounded that anyone working on a building constructed in that time period should have the materials tested before disturbing the structure.

She sent her research to her wireless printer.

****

The next morning, she drove to the Ladners' house with a nervous stomach, unable to eat a bite for breakfast. Libby was already there, and the Breewoods arrived moments later. They piled into Bruce's enormous rental car, but before setting out on the road to Yellow Mountain Campground, they needed coffee. Next, Bruce turned into a gas station to fill the car, having apologized for not being prepared.

"Let me chip in with gas money," offered Doug. "I know these big vehicles don't get the best mileage."

"I told you to get gas before we left Megan's," Cheryl nagged.

"I'll contribute, too." Jane sat in the farthest back seat with Libby.

After some serious negotiation, Bruce and Cheryl agreed to let the others treat them for lunch instead. Finally, they were on the road, chatting happily as if on a vacation road trip. In no time, Bruce pulled the ginormous vehicle into a parking spot in the day use area at Yellow Mountain Campground, and they all clambered out.

"Olivia, how are you planning to hike in those sandals?" Jane had prepared ahead by wearing her hiking boots with the frayed laces, but Olivia had orange, flat, strappy sandals on her feet—not the best footgear for a hike in the mountains, but adorable with her capris.

"I'm staying at the picnic area to read because my

ankle is still sore. Look." She swiveled her foot outward and up, revealing a dark blue bruise. "You guys go without me." She tugged an iPad out of her sizable handbag and propped a pair of orange reading glasses on her nose.

"You got new glasses." Libby pointed to her face.

"Had to. The police still have my purple ones."

"Are you going to be all right here by yourself?" Jane's eyes scanned the crowd.

"Of course."

"I insist someone stay here with you."

"Quit hovering." Olivia winced.

"Okay already." But Jane was hesitant to leave her friend alone after her confrontation with Connie O'Hennessey in this very place. If she reminded them, Doug might have second thoughts about investigating, so she kept silent.

However, it seemed he'd taken the investigation over when he rubbed his hands together, saying, "Let's be on our way."

Olivia parked herself at a picnic table. "Yes, you guys can take off. I'll be fine. I can always wait in the car, too. Just be quick. Don't stop to take pictures."

Bruce handed her the car keys. "I'll leave these with you."

As he trotted to the park's entrance booth, Doug threw his words over his shoulder, "Let me tell them to keep an eye on you." He spent a few moments with the ranger, gesturing to where Olivia had settled herself in.

Jane took in a deep breath of the fresh mountain air and shook off the feeling of foreboding. Certainly Olivia would be secure under the eyes of the park rangers. Anyway, this side of the park appeared safe enough with several small children playing in the picnic area as their parents sat nearby.

After Doug returned and Olivia opened her e-book, the hikers trekked along the pitted gravel road skirting several campsites, then veered onto the shorter route to the amphitheater from which they could reach the cabin. When they stopped to hydrate before climbing to the lookout point, Jane took a long pull on her water bottle. The sun was blinding in a cloudless blue sky. Yellow black-eyed Susans waved in the breeze next to Indian paintbrush and purple coneflowers.

"We'd better not take too long. We can't keep Olivia waiting." Libby patted her wrist watch, and Jane jumped to her feet.

As they went on their way, the hot sun continued to blaze down until they reached the cabin, where they stopped in a spot of shade to decide what to do.

"I'm going to knock on the door. I don't mind if anyone else asks questions, but let me have a first pass." Doug's eyes went from one to the other of them.

Bruce inclined his head, but before they could advance more than a few steps, a man in khaki pants and an Aussie-style, outback brim hat with earflaps stepped out of the door with a German shepherd by his side. He thumped down the steps and strode up to the group. "Are you lost?" His eyebrows were bunched up, and his eyes were not smiling.

Doug answered, "No. Actually, we hiked up from the campground to talk to you."

"If you wanted to see how the weather station works, you should have made an appointment." The man tucked his chin low and crossed his arms over his chest.

"The weather station sounds interesting, and I'd like to see it, but I wanted to first ask about Michael Quadtrini."

"Why ask me?" He faced them, feet planted wide.

"I figure you must've known him. We'll only take a few minutes of your time." Doug stroked his red, bristling mustache. "By the way, I'm Doug Ladner." He held his hand out to shake, so the man uncrossed his arms and took a step closer for a short hand grip.

"Ed Koopmer." He stepped back and crossed his arms again.

Doug introduced the others, while Ed's eyes narrowed and he remained reticent for a moment or two more. Jane started to sweat and was about to apologize for bothering him, when he sighed. "Let's sit down." He motioned to the porch, then mounted the steps with the guard dog trotting at his heels. The dog's ears were laid back on its skull. The three women lowered themselves onto a wooden bench, while the men perched their behinds against the porch railing. Ed said, "Why are you so concerned?"

Doug raised his shoulders, then let them fall. "We were camping here the weekend Quadtrini was shot. My wife's reading glasses were found with the body. Someone at the campground stole her glasses and planted them at the scene."

"I don't know anything about that."

"Do you know if Quadtrini had any enemies?" Doug fixed him with a look.

Ed unfolded his arms, dropping them to his sides as he gazed in the direction of the mountain lake. "Park visitors complained about him. He wasn't good with people, and I suppose working with the public took its toll." He swung his head around to look at his cabin with satisfaction. "I like being alone up here with my dog. I couldn't take dealing with all those folks myself. Only a few stragglers ever make it up here to ask about the weather station."

"Was there anyone in particular he argued with?"

"He was surly to just about everyone, so I couldn't say. He never had a lot of friends." Ed's cold eyes made him look unapproachable himself.

"You can't think of anyone?" Doug propped his fists on his hips, and his voice was hard.

Ed spoke in a slow manner, as if unwilling to part with many words. "Well, there was something a few years back. The Forest Service closed down the campground, and Mike was fit to be tied and worried about losing his job."

"Why? What happened?"

"Someone called the EPA and told them asbestos was uncovered in those old buildings near the firing range, and then a bunch of different federal agencies got involved. Mike found out who the person was that complained and confronted him. I guess he said he would have Mike's job."

Jane sat up straighter, and Cheryl gave her a thumbs up, apparently for having done a good job investigating. Even Doug glimpsed sideways at her before continuing. "This was a man, then?"

"Actually, I don't know if the person was a man or a woman."

"Okay, but why wouldn't Quadtrini want the camp cleaned up? He lived here. He had to breathe the air."

"You got me. He was stubborn."

"Did you see or hear anything the night he was

shot?"

Ed sucked in his cheeks. "I told the police a woman in a gray sweatshirt was talking to Mike in the amphitheater around dusk the night before. I could see them through my binoculars from the cabin." Ed nodded his head toward the window with the view of the amphitheater at the bottom of the gulley.

Doug's eyes lit up. "Did you see anything else?"

Ed's lips formed a straight line, and he leaned his shoulder against the doorframe. Once again he peered at the mountain scenery before giving his answer. "Mike gave the woman a shove, and she stumbled backward. I wasn't surprised he would treat a woman that way, but I wondered if he would lose his job this time. If she complained about him, that is. I certainly would have."

"Could you identify the woman?"

Ed's gaze darted to the three women on the porch bench, studying their faces. "She had the hood of her sweatshirt up, covering her hair. I couldn't see her face or the lower half of her body. I only noticed the gray sweatshirt."

Doug looked at Bruce. "Anything else you want to ask?"

"How'd you know it was a woman?" Bruce's eyes glinted.

Ed stared back at him. "I could see her hands through the binoculars, and she had on red nail polish."

Libby curled her fingers into fists and shoved her hands into her pockets. Her nail polish was red.

"I have a question." Jane piped up. "How did Quadtrini know the identity of the whistleblower?"

"I have no idea."

"Quadtrini wasn't killed at dusk when you saw him with the woman. He was shot in the night."

"Maybe they agreed to meet again later. I think we're done here. Right?" Ed wheeled around and started down the porch steps.

"No." Jane took off after him. "I heard you and Quadtrini got into a fist fight. What was that about?"

Ed's jaw dropped. "Who told you that?"

"This is a small community. Everyone knows."

"Well, whoever told you blew that way out of proportion."

"You tried to get him dismissed as the campground host."

"Me and everyone else. He was pretty bad with people. He had his issues." Ed gave her a filthy look. "I have nothing more to tell you."

Doug said in his polite way, "Thanks for your help." He held his hand out, and after a moment or two Ed shook it.

The friends began their descent down the hiking path. The dog padded after them for several hundred feet, then turned around to return to the cabin.

Before long, they arrived at the picnic area where Olivia was sunning herself. She had kicked off her sandals, folded up her capris, and stretched her legs out under the sun. She sat up straight, and shoved her feet into her sandals. "What'd you find out?"

Doug helped his wife gather her belongings. "We can talk in the car."

"Did you see anything interesting while you were waiting?" Jane held her breath.

"Nothing happened. The murderer did not pop out from behind the bushes and confess." Olivia rolled her eyes.

Jane sighed, but made no attempt to respond. She climbed into the far backseat with Libby.

On the drive down the mountains, they discussed everything they'd gleaned from Ed Koopmer. Then, before stopping for lunch, Jane told the others what she had learned from the book, "A History of Yellow Mountain Campground—the good and bad years."

"Do you think Michael Quadtrini was the employee who hid the asbestos with the bulldozer?" Olivia peered backward over the middle seat to ask Jane.

"If so, just think about it. Quadtrini was sued in a wrongful death action for killing Malkon's son, and now he's implicated in causing a person to get a lung disease, which could lead to another death. How likely is that?" Jane scrubbed a hand over her face.

"It shows a pattern of careless disregard for others." Bruce turned the car into a crowded parking lot.

They all poured over the menu at the brew pub, while Olivia used the ladies' room. When she returned, rubbing antibacterial gel over her hands, the others continued to discuss the clues.

"Let's think about the unknown whistleblower. Why would he kill Quadtrini? It seems like it would've been the other way around, since Quadtrini was mad about this person alerting the EPA." Jane snapped her menu shut.

"Good point." Libby picked at her fingernail polish. "But how about this? Do you think the whistleblower could've been the woman in the gray sweatshirt? Maybe he threatened her first, and she shot him in self-defense."

They were interrupted by the waiter who discussed the various brews with Bruce. Jane ordered a half club sandwich instead of her usual salad, and the waiter left to put their orders in.

"I don't think the murder has anything to do with the asbestos. That's over and done with, isn't it?" Cheryl had on a grim expression. "It was too long ago, now."

Jane puffed out her chest. "I disagree. The cover up could be the key to the whole mystery."

"But Malkon's a more likely suspect." Doug fingered his mustache. "It'll be interesting to talk to him, if we can catch him at home." Bruce agreed, and they rehashed the possibilities some more. The waiter brought their meals and they dug in.

After finishing, the group climbed back into the Breewoods' vehicle. Bruce punched Ben Malkon's address into the navigation system, then pointed the car in the direction of Highlands Ranch. The GPS misdirected them, and they drove around in circles. As they passed his street, Jane waved her left hand out the window. "Turn here." Bruce swung the Expedition around the corner at the last minute, and her shoulder hit the passenger door. "I think that's his house." She gestured toward the yellow, two story.

Doug gave her a high-five. "Good job. I didn't think we'd ever find it." They glided up to the curb at three in the afternoon.

"Do you want me to question the witness this time?" Bruce asked Doug. No one asked Jane. Doug agreed, so they trooped up to the house, and Bruce rang the bell.

They heard footfalls on the other side of the door before it swung open.

"I recognize you. You were at the campground when Mike Quadtrini was shot," Malkon's deep voice growled, his jaws clenched, and his hands formed into fists.

Chapter 14

They took a collective step backward. Doug's head dipped a fraction. "Yes. We were wondering if you'd be willing to talk to us about him. If we put our heads together, we might come up with some answers. Do you have just a minute or two?"

His jaw working, Ben hesitated, then stepped aside. "Come on in." They traipsed after him down a wide hallway, past walls loaded with family photos and a hall table with homey knick-knacks, to the back of the house where the hallway opened to a large, comfortable family room. Ben stretched out on a heavy recliner, as the group lowered themselves onto two sofas facing each other. Ceiling-to-floor, curtainless windows on either side of an over-sized fireplace made the space feel as if the room were part of the outdoors, where tall, leafy trees filled the back yard.

"You discovered my connection to Mike Quadtrini, I suppose." Ben's eyes slanted sideways.

Doug cut in with a frown. "We know about the accident."

"Mike t-boned my car, killing my son. I did hate him for a long time, but I let it go and moved on."

"We're so sorry for your loss." Jane scooted forward to the edge of her seat.

Bruce looked at Ben with a wary eye as he began to question him. "Why did you camp at Yellow

Mountain Campground, Ben? You had to know Quadtrini was the campground host."

"Obviously, that was no coincidence. I've been camping there for years. I always camp in site number five."

"Were you trying to provoke Quadtrini?" Bruce sat forward on the sofa.

Ben let out a long sigh and thrust the recliner downward, planting his feet on the floor, with elbows on knees and hands clasped together. "Yes, at first. After a time, though, I began to feel sorry for him. I realized how unhappy he was. Almost as much as me. We talked it out at length, and he cried bitterly and asked me to forgive him. He said even if I forgave him, he would never forgive himself, but he needed to ask my forgiveness anyway. Plus, he slid on the ice. It was an accident. Couldn't be helped." Ben blinked several times.

Jane tensed, as Bruce said quietly, "You were seen talking to Quadtrini at the campground the day before he was shot."

"Certainly I was going to talk to him. We know each other pretty well, now. I mean, we knew each other well." Ben focused on his hands, tenting his fingers. "I didn't shoot him. The police questioned me over and over again. I didn't do it, though, so I'm not worried."

Bruce appeared to believe him. "Do you have any idea who did shoot him?"

"No." Ben looked up, and his eyes scanned his visitors. "Really. I don't know."

Bruce took a deep breath. "Gloria, the elderly lady with the tear-drop trailer, told Jane her husband went missing the night Quadtrini was shot, and she asked your wife for help in finding him, but you were gone from your site, too."

"Ah-ha! So, I'm not the only person who left his tent that night."

"Her husband, Ted, has Alzheimer's. He wandered off and had nothing to do with the murder." Jane pointed out, "He returned before you did."

Ben gave her a hard look. His low voice rumbled, "I went to the latrine, that's all, and I can prove it, since one of the other campers saw me there." His eyes burned into hers.

Jane glanced away. "I heard you talking about Quadtrini with a woman near the latrines the morning his body was found."

Bruce asked him, "Who were you talking to?"

"That was a private conversation." Ben's shoulders stiffened, and his face hardened, as he directed his question to Jane. "Haven't I seen you somewhere before?"

Her fingers touched her chest. "Me? Well, we were all at the campground."

"No. I've seen you right here in this neighborhood driving down our street."

"I'm not sure how you could have seen me." Jane lifted one shoulder in denial, but her eyes darted around.

"Humph! My wife's going to be home shortly with the kids. I need to get busy with dinner." He shot up from his chair, and everyone else rose after him.

"Thank you for your time." Bruce offered his hand, and Ben shook it with a firm grip, looking him directly in the eye. He walked them through to the front porch.

After they piled into the Expedition and slammed the doors with loud bangs, Olivia stabbed her index finger in the direction of his house. "It was him. He's the killer."

"I don't think so. He seemed genuine." Bruce's hands spun the steering wheel as they turned the corner out of the neighborhood.

"How can you know?" Libby's arms hung over the seat in front of her. She balanced forward, straining the seat belt.

"Body language, for one. He didn't show any indication of telling a lie." Bruce drummed the wheel.

Doug chewed on his mustache with his lower teeth. "There weren't any 'tells.' Like wringing his hands or acting uncomfortable or anxious."

"Or leaning away, crossing his arms, fidgeting, talking over us," Bruce added.

Jane probably did all those things herself all the time. "Can you really tell by that?"

"Not with certainty." Doug darted a look over his shoulder at Jane in the back seat.

Bruce smirked. "Come on, Doug. You can tell when a suspect is guilty."

Cheryl screwed her mouth up in a pucker. "I wonder about the lawsuit he filed against Quadtrini. Was there a trial or did he settle?"

Jane had an opinion. "Most likely settled. Insurance companies will settle, even if the accident couldn't be helped. It's hard to go to trial in a case involving the death of a child, and many times the insurance company doesn't want to take the risk."

They hashed over the clues on the hour drive from Highlands Ranch to the Ladners' house in Verano, then discussed the upcoming Fourth of July trip to the Estes Park cabin.

The friends soon arrived at the Ladners' home, and Olivia clambered out of the car. "Does anyone want to come in? We can order pizza delivery."

Cheryl gave Olivia a hug goodbye. "Thanks anyway, but we're meeting Megan. We need to hurry or we'll be late." Her fingertips brushed her husband's arm.

"I should get home myself." Libby waved, walking to her car.

"Me too." Jane checked the time on her cell. "But thanks for asking. I'll see all of you Friday at the cabin." As the others drove away, Jane unlocked her car and climbed in. The Ladners went into their house, as Jane steered her car down the street and around the corner.

Her phone rang from her purse and rolled over to her Blue Tooth connection. The caller was Dale. The phone rang a few times as she considered whether to answer while driving. She was both a little excited and a little scared, wondering if he was still mad at her for teasing Polly at the restaurant. She decided to answer just as the phone stopped ringing. Why didn't she pick up on the first ring? Disappointed, she took the next exit and motored into a gas station parking lot.

Her heart fluttered when she dialed, and he answered the phone. "Hi, Dale. I was driving when you called, so I pulled over to call you back."

"Hi, hon. Are you doing anything tonight?"

She took a deep breath. It certainly seemed he was no longer mad at her. "No. I'm on my way home."

"Long day at work?"

"Remember, I have the week off."

"Oh yeah."

"Why haven't you called me before this?"

There was a loud rap on Jane's car window. She jumped in her seat and hit the car horn with a toot. Jerking her head to the left, her eyes landed on the same police officer who questioned her at this same gas station the day before. His eyebrows were knitted together, and he had a questioning look on his face.

Pointing to her cell, she mouthed, "I'm on the phone." Returning to her conversation, she went on, "I'll be back at my house in about twenty minutes, if you want to meet me there."

"Okay, see you soon."

She disconnected to hurry off, but the officer remained stationed on the other side of her car window. Her heart plummeted. Maybe he was there to haul her into the police station for her turn to be grilled.

Rolling the window down, she said in a breathless voice, "I'm fine. Just taking a phone call." Without mirth, she smiled. "Remember, it's good to pull over."

"Okay, ma'am." He stepped a few paces back and waved her on.

She took a deep breath as the officer retreated to his police cruiser. When she turned out of the filling station, he followed her onto the highway once again. She breathed another long sigh of relief when he veered off on the next exit, and she continued on her way to Limestone Heights.

Olivia had given her an idea. Pizza delivery was on the menu.

Chapter 15

"So, you've been investigating without me?" Dale teased, as he fed bits of sausage to Nick and Nora begging on either side of his chair with their noses pointed up at him.

Jane told him about the group's outing that day. "We already knew Ben Malkon had a motive, since Quadtrini killed his son in a car accident." She placed her half-eaten pizza slice on her plate and took a sip of Dr. Pepper. "But after talking to him, Bruce and Doug don't think he did it."

"Do you think he's the murderer?"

"I don't know. Yet." She tapped a finger to her chin. "There's something about the camp having been shut down that's nagging at the back of my mind."

"Okay. What about that?"

"I wish I knew who the whistleblower was." Putting her chin in her hand, Jane pulled a face. "The police seem to be focusing on the dinner club."

"How's that possible?" Dale didn't pay attention as Nora nipped a bite of pizza from his hand.

"They suspect Libby because she'd known Quadtrini and was wearing a gray hoodie, like the lady seen arguing with him. Olivia, because her glasses were found with the body and her knuckles were all cut up and she'd twisted her ankle. Wes, because they think he went off the deep end from PTSD and jealousy. All of this is utterly ridiculous."

"Lucky for Cheryl and Bruce they weren't on the camping trip or the police would find something suspicious about them, too."

"And you, too." She jabbed her elbow in his side. Would he bring up anything about their last time together? Should she? "So, Dale—"

"I'm full. I really like your pizza delivery service." He patted his flat belly.

"Yes. There's not a lot of restaurants out here, but we do have a good pizza place." She wiped her fingers on a napkin, then rubbed the napkin across her lips.

After stacking the plates together, she carried them to the sink to scrap over the garbage disposal. Dale boxed up the leftover pizza. The puppies' hopeful eyes trailed him to the refrigerator, where he shoved the pizza box onto a shelf.

"Let's take the dogs for a walk." Dale snagged their leashes out of the basket by the door. The dogs' eyes filled with intense longing and their back ends waggled. As Dale snapped the leashes onto their collars, Jane thrust her feet into flip-flops. They trekked with the dogs over to the Community Center and through the short woods to the pond.

Now was the time for a serious talk. Jane began, "So, Dale—"

He interrupted her. "I'm worried about Wes. He called me after the police questioned him. He's had a flare of his PTSD." Dale paused at the point on the path where a glimpse of Long's Peak was within view.

"Oh, no." Her heart sank to her stomach. "Libby didn't mention it today."

"Maybe he didn't tell her. We met at the cigar

lounge on our lunch hour and talked it over."

Jane stopped to slide her foot out of the flip-flop, brush pebbles off the bottom of her sole, and shove her foot back in. "Libby can usually tell, I think. So what did he say?"

"He had severe flashbacks. He'll probably get worse before he gets better, as he confronts his issues."

"Tell me, Dale, do you have some stress related to your time in the military?"

"Not like Wes. And you know, not everyone who's seen combat has post-traumatic stress."

"What are the symptoms?"

"Nightmares. Remembering the friends who didn't make it. You have a feeling in the back of your mind something bad is about to happen. Some disaster is just around the corner. These feelings cut you off from people."

"You never had any of that?"

"Nah." Dale took her hand in his, since the dogs had settled down and were no longer straining at their leashes.

"You never feel cut off from people? Have difficulties with relationships?" Jane squeezed his hand.

"Well, my time in the service may have had something to do with my failed marriage."

The couple turned their backs to the view of Long's Peak and emerged out of the woods at the Community Center.

"Really?" Jane gave him a sidelong glance. Good, now was their chance to talk about their argument.

"Yeah. I felt responsible for the divorce. I kinda gave up on the marriage instead of sticking it out to make it work."

"Is that why you've stayed friends with your ex-wife?"

"Not really. Mostly we stayed in touch because Polly hadn't paid back the money she owes me for the restaurant, and I'm not about to give up my investment."

They'd reached the front door, and Dale let the dogs run in first, then trailed in behind. After disentangling the puppies from their leashes, they ambled out onto the back patio to enjoy the beautiful evening.

She paused and cleared her throat. "So, Dale…"

"Hmm?" His eyes raked her up and down. She had a tingling in the pit of her stomach when he gave her a light kiss on the lips.

Should she ask him about their disagreement? Was it worth bringing up when they seemed to be getting along? Was it better to talk it out or let it go? He may have denied it, but did he have PTSD, too?

He kissed her again, longer this time.

"Are you still coming with the dinner club to Estes Park this weekend?" she finally managed to ask.

"Definitely. I'll meet you there Saturday afternoon. Remember, I can't make it Friday."

"I remember. Just making sure you remember." She gave him a slow smile.

"I wouldn't miss it." He yanked her even closer and put his arms around her. She leaned her head against his shoulder as the wind chimes played a melancholy tune. His hand reached under her chin as he pulled her face to his once more.

****

The next day, she awoke at her usual time, not

accustomed to having a day off in the middle of the week. Since she had nothing planned that morning, she rifled through her murder folder for the lawsuit paperwork filed against the Forestry Service over the asbestos contamination. Locating the phone number, she dialed the environmental group's attorney, only to find out he'd left that firm and moved to another. Once she put her hands on his new number, she called and left a message. While she was in the shower, the attorney returned her call, so after she dressed, she made short order to phone him back. Jane introduced herself and got right to the point. She asked him about Quadtrini.

"Why do you want to know?" He had a suspicious, but crisp, professional voice.

She took a quick breath. "I'm gathering background information for a project."

"Well, I do remember the lawsuit, but that was a long time ago." He must've bought into her lame reason.

"Six years."

"That long? I'd need to pull the file and review it before I answer any questions." He paused, and across the line she heard clicks on a keyboard. "I have about a half hour free around ten, if you'd like to come in. That will give me a chance to look at the file."

"Yes. That would work perfectly. Thanks." Jane then texted Caleb to see if he could meet a little after ten-thirty. If she was going to take a trip into downtown, she might as well make a morning of it.

After parking in her usual spot in the garage under her office building, she hot-footed it down Seventeenth Street to the attorney's office a block away. Once seated across from him at his desk, Jane said, "Thanks so much for meeting me. Did you get a chance to look at your file?"

His eyes peered through the wire-rimmed glasses balanced on his nose, in a no-nonsense, get-down-to business way. "Yes. Michael Quadtrini was the Forest Service employee who worked there at the time of the asbestos contamination. That's what you wanted to know, right?"

"Uh-huh." Jane put her fingertips together. "Since Quadtrini was the park ranger, I thought he'd be named in the suit, but he wasn't."

"None of the rangers were named individually. I did hear later he became the campground host there after he left the Forest Service. You might want to go talk to him. For your project." Evidently, he didn't know about the murder.

Jane chewed the inside of her cheek. "Do you have the name of the injured worker exposed to the asbestos fibers? Since he wasn't a party, he isn't named in the court documents."

He folded his arms across his chest. "I can't give you the name. Privacy, you know."

"Can you tell me if his name was O'Hennessey?"

He adjusted his glasses. "No, that wasn't his name."

"What happened to him? Did he die?" She held her breath, waiting for the answer.

The attorney shook his head in the negative. "Last we knew, he was still alive. This can be a lingering disease." The attorney's eyes flicked down to his paperwork on his desk. "And my client had no liability whatsoever."

"Without a doubt." Jane inclined her head.

"The case was strictly an environmental action and not a personal injury claim. He had a separate worker's comp suit for that."

"I understand, but I won't be able to find the worker's compensation claim without his name."

"I can't help you there." He slapped his file shut with a loud smack.

"I heard a whistleblower alerted the EPA and started the whole investigation." Jane gave him a hopeful look, but his mouth was buttoned into a tight-lipped grimace. "Isn't there anything else you can tell me?"

"No, sorry. You understand why I can't divulge the name of the whistleblower." He looked at his watch.

"Right. Well, thanks for taking the time to talk to me. I appreciate it." Jane stumbled up from her seat.

"You're welcome and good luck with your project."

She arrived at her usual coffee shop a few minutes early. After retrieving her murder folder out of her satchel, she crossed this task off her to-do list. The meeting had not yielded any clues as to the murderer, but at least she had not left that stone unturned.

Soon afterward, Caleb strolled through the door and stepped into line to place their orders. She rose to meet him at the pickup counter, where the barista deposited her soy milk chai latte and his caramel half-caf. She put her investigation aside, as they sat at a table to enjoy their drinks and catch up on family news.

"Did you and Erin decide about Durango?"

"No." He frowned. "I'm discovering how stubborn she is."

"Best to keep your wife happy." Jane took the lid off her cup and blew on the hot drink.

"Actually, she said I should take the job." He swallowed a gulp of his coffee.

"What? Are you going to?" The air whooshed out of her lungs, and it was hard to take another breath.

"We still haven't decided. She wants what's best for me, but I know she won't be happy if we move."

"And you want what's best for her. Ah, *The Gift of the Magi* all over again."

"Whazup with that?"

"The story about a young couple, each wanting what was best for the other. They both sacrificed their own prized possessions to buy the other a Christmas present. Let me tell you, it didn't turn out well. Do the pros and cons thing, write out the reasons to go and to stay."

"We did that. The pros won, and Erin said I should accept the job. I knew you'd take her side. Luke always complains to me that you take Brittany's side, too."

"I'm not taking anyone's side." She tried to keep her voice light. "Do the pros and cons chart over again. I'm sure you forgot a few of the cons."

He laughed. "Okay. Good idea."

She stared out the window. When would the sadness of the empty nest go away? Cheryl was right. The time had come to think about her own life journey. Once the murder was solved, the dinner club could get back to their routine, and perhaps she could relax and not be so on edge about Dale. "Don't forget I'm going up to Estes Park with the dinner club this weekend. I'll be back Sunday night."

"Do you have a dog sitter lined up?"

"Yes. The teenager in the house behind mine worked out well when I left the dogs with her to go camping."

"Have you heard anything more about the murder of the campground host?"

"Nothing conclusive." She opened her mouth to tell him about the club's efforts the day before, but stopped when Caleb glanced at his cellphone.

"I need to get back to my studies. Can you believe this is July first?"

"Yes. And the bar exam is in a few weeks. You'll be ready. Don't worry. Anyway, I need to get going, too. Talk to you soon."

Caleb rushed off, so Jane picked up her bag and tossed her empty latte cup. It was probably for the best not to discuss the investigation with her son, whom she knew worried about her. She didn't want to be a worry to anyone. No, she wanted to be able to take care of herself. So, instead of heading to her car, she proceeded to the Krav Maga studio.

"Can I join a lesson? I signed up for them, but haven't taken any yet, except for the introductory one."

"Yes. We're starting in fifteen minutes and there's room."

"Great." Jane hurried into the changing room and dug a T-shirt and yoga pants out of her satchel. It didn't take long for her to switch clothing, and soon afterward other students arrived, too. The class started by stretching, then went into jumping jacks and pushups. After a few minutes of those, Jane was glistening in sweat, and her T-shirt was damp. She glanced around at the other students, and several of them were sweating, too. The instructor demonstrated open-palm heel strikes, and they practiced on punching bags.

After the class, Jane took a shower and changed into her street clothes. The lessons were empowering. Maybe she'd lose a little off her hips, too. The rest of the students had departed, and she had the large mirror all to herself. She launched into the Krav Maga stance and faced the glass. She only looked like a startled chicken. But what was that underneath her upper arms? A slight waddle? Ack! She looked in the mirror, and the person she saw this time could've scared Rocky Balboa. Better, much better.

She checked text messages as she plodded to her car. There was one from Cheryl: *I'm on my way to the art museum. Bruce and Megan didn't want to go. Can you meet me there?*

Jane was quick to reply. *Yes. Count me in. I can be there in ten minutes.*

She smiled in deep satisfaction. Her best friend had already spent the first two days of her holiday in Colorado with her, so this was a bonus. Cheryl's visit was the reason Jane took the whole week off work, but she didn't expect to see her every day. She strolled along the Sixteenth Street Pedestrian Mall to the Denver Art Museum in the Golden Triangle neighborhood. Having arrived first, Jane plopped onto the grass to bask in the sun under the giant red Lao Tzu sculpture. Someone kicked her foot, and she sat up. Cheryl stood over her.

Jane bounded to her feet, and they both crossed the grounds to enter the museum. Cheryl led her to the traveling exhibit of bold, large-scale southwestern paintings. After getting their fill, they wound their way into the museum restaurant and ordered drinks.

"That was awe inspiring. Thanks for meeting me here." Cheryl sipped on a Merlot. "So, have you talked to Dale?"

"Yes. He came over last night after we got back from questioning Ben Malkon." Jane fiddled with her glass of Chardonnay.

"And?"

"We never got around to talking about our problems." Jane knitted her eyebrows together. "It was as if the argument never happened."

"You need to nip that in the bud. Communication is the key to a good relationship, you know that. Call him up and tell him you want to talk. Hit it head-on, so you can resolve the issue. Otherwise, it'll keep coming up. Maybe that's why his marriage to Polly didn't work out."

"You're probably right. And I don't want to argue at the cabin." Jane cringed. That would not be a good thing.

Cheryl sniffed. "He'd better be nice to you or he'll hear from me."

Jane rolled her shoulders and massaged the back of her neck. Yup, she'd better talk to Dale sooner than later.

A text pinged, and both women reached for their phones, but the message wasn't for Jane this time. Cheryl's fingers scrolled down her screen. "Megan just phoned Bruce, and she'll be at our hotel in half an hour." She took a last swig of her wine. "I'd better be on my way."

"You go on. I'll pay the bill. My treat." Jane tugged her wallet from her purse.

"Thanks, Jane. I'll be busy all day tomorrow, so

I'll see you Friday at the cabin." Cheryl gave her a quick hug goodbye and trotted out the door.

Jane motioned for the waiter, then punched Dale's number into her phone. She left a message on his voice mail. "We've got to talk."

She strode out of the café and down the pedestrian mall to her car. On the drive home she stopped at a meat market in Limestone Heights and purchased a porterhouse steak. Her cellphone rang as she turned out of the store parking lot. After the call went to Blue Tooth, Jane answered, "Hello, Dale."

"What's the matter? You said we need to talk?"

"I did. Tonight. Can you come to my house for dinner?"

"Yes."

"Okay, then. Be there by five. You don't need to bring anything, I've got it covered." She hung up.

Chapter 16

But when Dale knocked on her door, he held a bouquet of twelve red roses. He stepped in the entryway, wrapped his arms around her, roses held at her back, and gave her a lingering kiss. "You aren't breaking up with me, are you?"

Jane stumbled, knees weak. "No way," she breathed, then shook herself. "Except we need to talk about our relationship."

He appeared pale as he followed her down the entry hall to the great room. Jane had changed out of her jeans into a body-hugging tank dress with a scoop neck, a scoop back, and no sleeves. Her legs were bare and so were her feet. She turned around to find him eyeing her posterior. She considered it too big, but the opposite sex never seemed to mind.

"Sit down."

Dale slid onto a counter stool, while she poked the roses into a vase. Next, she poured Dale a glass of wine, using one of her largest goblets.

"You can watch me finish dinner." She chopped garlic, thyme, and rosemary sprigs, as her knife wielding hand went up and down. Swiveling away from Dale, she sautéed the herbs in her heavy cast iron skillet until the garlic yielded its fragrance, then added the porterhouse, flipping the meat once to brown on both sides. She passed the skillet into the oven. "It won't take long, just a few minutes."

She took a deep drink from her own wine glass. "About Polly. I don't ever want you to take me to her restaurant again."

Dale gulped. "If that's what you want. But then, I'll have to go by myself."

Jane batted her eyes and gave him a look.

"The only time I go is when I take you. That is, except for the once when you were camping. That time I went by myself, but I couldn't wait."

She arched an eyebrow, and put a hand on her waist.

Dale continued. "I asked Polly to sign bank loan papers. That way she could pay me off and owe the bank instead of me."

"So, there's no reason for you to go there anymore?" Jane smiled.

"Well, not exactly. I'll need to go once in a while. I retained a percentage interest in the restaurant, a smaller one, but I'll still want to keep an eye on my investment."

"Why do you need to watch over her?" She pouted.

"Jane, we have nothing going on. But she tends to drive away good employees and spends too much money on things she doesn't need, in short, the stuff she did when we were married."

Jane knotted her eyebrows together. "So, that's it then."

He vaulted off the stool and drew her into his arms, his mouth against her ear. "I won't go often, but when I do, I'd like you to go with me. I like to show you off to Polly. What harm is that?"

She clutched him close, hip to hip, and they kissed

just as the oven timer went off. The timer went off for a while. Finally letting loose, Jane walked on air to the oven and drew the steaming steak out.

"Wow. My mouth's watering." Dale breathed in the aroma. *And that's not the only reason it's watering,* thought Jane. Maybe the pushup bra was too much. Usually modest, she never allowed her cleavage to show before.

She shifted the meat to a platter and plunked the skillet onto the gas burner, then added dry red wine to the meat drippings, stirring all the pieces stuck to the bottom of the pan. Next, she poured the au jus over the steak and transferred the dish to the high-top table in the kitchen nook.

She started up her Jackson Browne CD, as Dale brought their wine glasses to the table.

"I wish you had explained about the restaurant that way before." Jane didn't have much appetite herself, but watched Dale dig in.

"Maybe I would've if you dressed that way more often." He gave her a slow wink and a warm buzz tingled up her back. He popped a piece of steak in his mouth, but stopped chewing to ask, "What have you been doing on your week off?"

Jane told him about the club's trip to the weather station at the campground and their visit to Ben Malkon. She ate a few bites as she elaborated, making the story seem more exciting than it was.

Dale poured more wine. "Are you going to tell me what else you're up to?"

"What do you mean?" She tried to keep the grin off her face.

"That's what I mean." He gestured at her with his

fork.

"Okay. I was going to tell you, anyway. Tomorrow, I'm driving up to Rifle Falls to talk to the campground hosts. Their names are Gene and Holly Toavne, and they knew Mike Quadtrini, were friends of his."

The smile slipped a little from Dale's face. "Is that safe?"

Her excitement faded as she tried not to scowl. "Nothing to worry about. They're campground hosts, there to help people. Because of Fourth of July weekend, the park'll be packed. Safety in numbers and all."

"You're probably right, but I'm going with you." His black mood threatened to return.

"All right, then." She gave him a hesitant smile. "It'll take over three hours to get there, so it's going to be a long trip."

"We'll have breakfast on the way out of town and lunch on the road." Dale was grinning now. "We can make a fun day of it."

But when he came by Jane's house early the next morning, she had fried eggs and bacon on the griddle. "We eat out a lot. I thought I'd make you breakfast since you enjoyed my cooking so much last night."

"That wasn't all I enjoyed." His voice sounded husky. Perhaps she shouldn't have dressed this morning in tight shorts and a thin tank top.

She flipped the eggs off the hot skillet onto plates. They sat at the kitchen counter and ate the meal while the food was piping hot. After Jane filled the dishwasher and Dale let the dogs outside and back in, they loaded Dale's company pickup truck with bottles of water and snacks, then headed to I-70 westbound.

"You don't mind missing work?" Jane gave a blissful sigh. No chance of running into Polly today, and maybe she didn't care if they did.

"You couldn't keep me away. Look at this sight." They came up Floyd Hill to the panoramic point with the glory of the Rocky Mountains displayed before them. Behind buffalos grazing in the field alongside the road, pine trees, mixed with aspens, marched up to the tree line. Snow topped only the tallest and farthest peaks and reflected white in the azure sky.

"I've never seen bluer skies than in Colorado." Jane rolled down her window to breathe in the piney scent as they barreled past the trees along the highway. "Look at the waterfall." Her hair whipping around her face, she jerked her fingers toward the side of the road at a small run-off from a melting glacier.

"I think I'm falling in love with you, Jane." Dale was looking straight forward, both hands gripping the steering wheel.

"You are?" Jane touched the nape of his neck, then twirled her finger around his ear. Her hair whisked upward, this time toward the open sunroof in the cab.

"How do you feel about that?"

She leaned toward him and gave him a kiss on the ear, then whispered, "I feel the same way." They held hands over the gearshift in the console for the rest of the drive. Take that, Polly Capricorn!

Once at Rifle Falls, they had difficulty finding a parking space and left his truck on the side of the road next to a camper. Dale's hands encircled her waist to lift her petite frame from the pickup cab to the ground. They wandered arm-in-arm down the path to where three separate waterfalls cascaded over the top of the mountain to a pool below, swirling and bubbling, before the water made its way to the Colorado River. The spray from the falls soon soaked them to the skin. They explored the limestone grotto and hiked to the top of the falls as their damp clothes dried in the warmth of the sun. Dale kissed her inside one of the caves and again at the top of the cliff.

In a high overlook, Dale held her close. Jane extracted herself from his embrace. "Don't you think we should go see the campground hosts?"

"Is that why we came up here?" He had on a sheepish grin.

"Yes." She walked in front, holding his hand behind her back, as they descended the steep steps from the top of the falls to the pool of water below. They laughed as they ran once again through the mist into the dry air away from the falls. Tiny rainbows shone where the water vapor met the sun's rays.

A teenage couple came out of a cave, then darted back inside. "Watch out. An old man and old lady coming."

Jane and Dale stared at each other. Jane pointed to herself and mouthed, "They can't mean us."

Dale laughed as they kept walking. "Every generation thinks they invented sex. But the truth is, they're just discovering for the first time what others have discovered before them."

They strolled along the road to the site closest to the ranger station. The hosts' camper was obvious. A "firewood for sale" sign leaned against a stack of cut logs, and the camper appeared to be a permanent structure with a satellite for television and a generator.

A bumper sticker read, "Welcome to our RV—the Toavne family."

Jane took a deep breath. "I'm not sure what to say."

"Just come out and ask if they know anything about Quadtrini. Honesty is the best policy."

"You're right, but I just thought of a way to bring it up."

As they walked into the campsite, a man came out of the trailer. "Do you want to buy some firewood?" He was wearing weathered jeans and a flannel shirt, even though the summer day was warm.

"No, thanks. But there's something we'd like to ask. We're planning a group camping trip for next summer, and we're checking out the sites here."

"This is a great park for reunions and groups. We have separate areas for RVs and tents. But make your reservations six months in advance or there won't be enough sites left for a group."

"I know we'll have to plan ahead. We just had a group campout at Yellow Mountain. We had to reserve those sites, too."

"Yellow Mountain Campground? When did you camp there?"

"Weekend before last."

"That's when the campground host was killed." High spots of color appeared on the man's cheeks.

"You knew him?" Jane pressed her fingers to her the small of her neck and gave what she hoped was a surprised look.

"Yes. We did." The man's shoulders drooped and his lips turned down. "Did you know him, too?"

Jane's eyes flicked over to Dale, who gave her an

189

encouraging nod. "Not really. By the way, I'm Jane and this is Dale." The two men shook hands.

The host pointed his thumb in the direction of a screened room. "You want to sit down?" When they nodded, he ushered them inside, where a picnic table was cluttered with camping implements—lanterns, water jugs, and fishing gear. Jane perched at one end of the picnic table bench, and Dale reclined next to her.

"So, you were a friend of his, then?" Jane brushed a strand of hair from her face.

"Sure. One summer he lived in a trailer park in the town near here and came over to the falls every day to fish in the upper ponds."

"What did you think of him?" Jane steepled her fingers and pressed them to her lips.

"He was lonely. Didn't know a lot of people. Some girl broke his heart a long time ago. Never married because of it."

Jane gave a strained laugh. "Do you know who that was?"

"No. It was years ago. Her name might have been Lisa or Laurie. No, that wasn't it. Something more unusual."

"Could her name have been Lucy?"

"No, no." He rubbed his chin.

"Lois?"

"No, that's not it either."

Her mouth went dry. "Lauren. Lila. Leah. Lily."

"No."

"Libby?"

"Yes, that's it." He slapped the picnic table. "They were engaged, and she called the wedding off at the last minute."

Jane swallowed a couple of times. "Did you tell the police about that?"

"No, didn't think to."

"You're right, probably no need. No need at all," she croaked.

"You want a drink of water?"

"Yes, please." Jane cleared her throat.

The host poured a paper cup from a water jug and handed it to her. "Anyway, Mike, he was over here on the western slope because he was a ranger at another park that closed for the season. So, he was sorta laid off, temporarily, until the park re-opened. He was only here the one summer. Then later, when he quit the Forest Service, he became the campground host there, like we are here at the falls. So, we kept in touch."

A woman came out of the camper with a dishtowel in her hands. "Oh, I didn't know we had company, Gene."

"Holly, I was just telling these people about Mike Quadtrini."

"You friends of his?" She passed into the screened room.

Jane put her hand to her throat again. "I was at the park when he was killed, but I didn't know him. I'm sorry he died."

"It was a shock." Holly glanced to her husband.

"Mike had a lot of regrets. Wasn't a happy camper." Gene chuckled.

Holly slapped his arm with the dishtowel. "Gene. Honestly. What will these people think?"

"Sorry, you're right." His expression went black. "He killed a kid in a car accident a couple years back and never got over it. Then, there was the business with the camp closure. Someone blamed him for the whole hullaballoo. I really don't know what it was all about, because Mike didn't want to talk about it."

Holly added, "I know they found asbestos, and there was some big investigation into it."

"Really?" Jane's eyebrows elevated in a question. "I don't suppose you know whether he had any enemies from that time?"

Holly said in a low voice, "I don't know of any," but Gene cut in, "He was worried someone was stalking him, even followed him over here."

"Why would someone stalk him?" Dale tilted his head in a question.

"Don't know." Gene picked up one of the lanterns and turned the light upside down. He opened the bottom and extracted the batteries. Holly dug around in a bin on the table and produced a new package. Maybe they felt it was time Jane and Dale took off.

"Is there anything else you can tell us?" Jane nudged Dale with her elbow to get going.

"No, not really." Gene shook his head. "We did go to his memorial service at the mortuary. Not many others were there."

"Did you recognize anyone?" Jane stopped in midrise from the picnic bench and plopped back down.

"There were some people from the Forestry Service and some locals." Holly gathered up the towel.

Gene added, "The weather observer was there. Don't know his name. I heard Mike was cremated after the service. Wasn't even buried."

"Yes, he was cremated." Jane didn't mention she was the one who spread his ashes. Dale didn't know, and perhaps the Toavnes would feel slighted for not being asked to join her. Instead, she handed him the phone displaying the picture of her campsite with Ben Malkon and Connie O'Hennessey standing near the Ladners' tent. "Were either of these people at the funeral?"

Holly inched over to stand beside her husband and study the photo. "Yes. I think they were both there. Don't you think so, Gene?"

He nodded and handed the phone to Jane. "I don't know who they are, though."

"Those two were also camping at Yellow Mountain when Quadtrini was shot." Jane gave them a long, level look, but neither had anything further to say.

Dale stood up and took Jane's hand, drawing her up with him. "Thanks for your help."

"You're welcome. I hope your group camps here next summer. Do you have a tent or a camper?" Gene walked them to the road.

"Our group has tents." Jane continued to hold Dale's hand.

"You should check out the tent sites, then. They're nothing like the camper side over here. The tent-only area is remote, and there's a hike from there looping around to the falls."

"Okay, we'll do that." Dale tugged Jane away as they both waved goodbye. When they were out of sight of the Toavnes, Dale turned in the opposite direction from his truck. "Let's walk over to the tent sites and see what they're like."

They strolled past the ranger station, crossed a parking lot full of vehicles, and set off down a wide path. Seven tent-only spots were spread out the distance of a football field. Each camping area was secluded.

The last site was nestled in the bend of the creek next to a path leading farther into the woods.

Dale gripped Jane's hand. "You up for hiking the trail? If the path loops back to the falls, it can't be too long."

"You think we have time?" Her cheeks burned under Dale's intense gaze.

"Sure, let's do it," Dale murmured into her hair. They set out on the path over a footbridge. In no time the trail made a turn to follow the creek to the falls. They ambled alongside an irrigation ditch. The path was deserted, in spite of the holiday crowd, until a deer stepped out of the woods, stared at them, and then darted into the trees.

"Dale," Jane began, "Libby did not tell me she was engaged to Quadtrini. In fact, she implied it was not a big deal."

"Maybe it wasn't a big deal. Maybe Quadtrini just assumed they were engaged and thought differently about their relationship than she did. Give her a break. Friends give friends the benefit of the doubt. They trust each other."

Jane nodded. "You're right." Her feet slowed to a stop.

"What is it, babe?"

"You'd tell me if you had PTSD, wouldn't you?"

"I don't have it." He jerked her to his side with some force. "I'd know if I did."

"You seem to have difficulties with relationships."

"I thought we cleared everything up between us." His lips crushed hers as he held her tight. She slid her arms around his neck. They certainly had physical attraction, but was everything else as good?

They took their time returning to Dale's pickup, then stopped for a late lunch in the town of Rifle at a restaurant where the wait staff wore revolvers strapped to their hips. The food was excellent, the premises clean and cozy, and the staff friendly, so there was no need for gimmicks to get customers in the door. But there it was—a gun toting restaurant like in the Wild West.

On the drive home along I-70, Jane's phone pinged five or six times. "We must have been out of range. I've got a bunch of text messages coming through at once." Her eyes scanned the screen and her mouth dropped open. "Olivia's been taken back to the police station."

"What?" Dale glanced away from the road to give Jane a wide-eyed stare.

"She said she's back in police custody, and I'd better solve this murder quick, or she won't make it to Estes Park for Fourth of July." Jane's fingers rapped frantically on her phone. "Cheryl and Libby sent me texts about Olivia, too. I'm replying now." But a message popped up that her texts failed to go through. "Darn it. I'll need to wait until we get closer to Denver, or at least on the other side of the Divide, to find out what's happening." Jane raised her feet up onto the seat, her heels jammed against her bottom, and hugged her arms around her knees.

Dale puckered his lips. "It'll be all right. They can't possibly arrest her for murder."

But Jane had her doubts, having been involved with police investigations in the past. After they went through the Eisenhower Tunnel, Jane's phone ping-ping-pinged again. She dialed Olivia's number, but there was no answer. Next, she called Cheryl.

Her friend's voice came over the speaker phone.

"Olivia hasn't been released yet, and Doug's at the police station, waiting. Bruce and I are still planning to go up to the cabin tomorrow. You should come too, because there's nothing you can do about this. Olivia will be let go when they're done questioning her, you'll see."

"I'm surprised Doug's allowing her to be questioned this long. She needs an attorney."

"He got one. An attorney's with her."

Instead of being encouraged, Jane's heart sank. The police were treating Olivia as a serious suspect, not just a witness.

After she hung up, Dale said, "Cheryl's right. We should still plan to go to the cabin. Besides, you want to see Cheryl again before they leave."

"Okay." Jane drummed her fingers on her lips as she stared out the window.

One last ping sounded and Jane read a new text. "Caleb and Erin want to meet us for dinner. It's been a long day. I'm not sure we should."

"We still have to eat. Let's meet them."

They drove the rest of the trip without much conversation, content in each other's company, listening to jazz on low volume. Once in the city, Dale had difficulty finding a parking spot, but after he did, they exited the truck and hurried across half a dozen blocks to the brewpub where Erin and Caleb had a table. First things first. They ordered drinks from the Happy Hour menu.

Caleb stowed the drinks list behind the salt and pepper shakers. "The food truck parked outside is for Asian Fusion. Decide what you want and I'll get our dinners."

"They don't mind you bringing in food from outside?" Dale tugged Jane in tighter so she was sitting with her arm crammed under his shoulder.

"Not at all. It's part of the arrangement. The brewery doesn't serve anything but drinks. A different food truck parks outside each night, and everyone grabs some eats—the trucks specialize in natural and locally grown ingredients." Of course the young couple would favor this type of food fare, since they belonged to a grocery co-op and bought from local produce growers.

Dale gave Jane a questioning look. "I don't know what I want."

She turned to her son. "Can you order for us, Caleb?"

"Is Thai curry okay?"

"Uh. Well," she started to backpedal.

"I'll just get you a noodle bowl."

"Okay," Jane acquiesced. Dale said he would have one of those too.

Erin twined her fingers through her auburn hair cut in an asymmetrical style. "On first Fridays, there's a food truck gathering in the park across the street. The organizers construct a stage, and local bands play. A portable outdoor bar is set up, too. There's even a truck where you can buy clothing. It's all free trade and natural fibers or vintage."

"Does that mean the first Friday in the month?"

"Yes. Next time we'll go on a first Friday."

"Sounds wonderful." Jane must not be too un-cool to be included in their plans.

After the waiter returned with their drinks, Caleb and Dale wended their way outside to place their orders at the food truck. The pub was getting crowded and loud—not a scene she preferred, but it was all about the company. The men soon returned with their hands full of takeout containers and scooted into their seats at the table.

"Any news in the murder investigation?" Erin peeled the paper wrapper from her chopsticks.

Jane opened her to-go box containing a noodle bowl in a plastic container with steam escaping from a hole in the lid. Since Erin asked and Caleb didn't appear concerned, Jane brought them up to speed on the investigation, including their talk with the Toavnes.

"So, who do you think did it? Who killed that man?" Erin lifted her curry with the chopsticks, balancing the food perfectly.

Jane's eyes darted to Caleb, but he remained relaxed. "Either Ben Malkon or the woman who ran into me, uh, I mean, the woman I overheard talking about how Quadtrini caused her a lot of grief. Connie O'Hennessey's her name. There's also a couple of others." She explained her suspects, but did not tell her son and his wife about being forced off the road or her confrontation with O'Hennessey at the campground last Saturday.

Caleb assured her, "The police will figure it out."

But Jane only slurped her noodles. She had her doubts. "So, what's up with you two?"

Erin replied, "Caleb told you about the job offer in Durango?" Caleb sat with a frown on his face and his chin in his hand.

"Yes, he did." Jane said a silent prayer they would decide not to go.

"He should take the job. Tell him, Jane." Erin scowled with a pinched expression.

"No. That means you'd have to give up your job, and we'd have to move. I'm not going to make you do that. Tell her, Mom." Caleb glared at his wife, and her eyes flashed back at him.

Jane swallowed hard. Dale was concentrating on poking his chopsticks around in his noodle bowl. Their shoulders bumped. Jane shoved her bowl away. "You need to decide together. You'll reach an agreement, you'll see. Somehow these things work out." That advice sounded lame to her own ears. "Don't you agree, Dale?"

But he stared at his noodles and jabbed them even harder with his chopsticks.

Jane faced the couple. "Okay. What are the pros and cons? Pros first." Caleb and Erin interrupted each other as they both tried to put the other's needs first. Then they hashed over the cons, but could not come to an agreement.

"Pray about it." Jane gave them a small smile and patted Caleb's back. "We'll talk again soon."

Once outside, the young couple stomped down the street without speaking to each other. There was a distant space between them. Jane's mouth went dry, but she was confident they would work it out.

She and Dale climbed into a Mile High Pedicab for a ride to Dale's truck parked some blocks away. They whirled along busy Blake Street past Coors Field where a baseball game was being played, dodging cars and buses, and proceeded east on Seventeenth Street. She was glad to hop out of the pedicab when the ride came to an end. Dale tipped the driver, a young woman they had learned was working her way through college, and he helped Jane into his truck.

After that long day, Dale dropped her off at her house and kissed her goodbye. "I'll miss you. Can't wait to see you Saturday in Estes."

Jane missed him, too, after he left and thought about him all evening as she packed a bag for the weekend.

Her phone rang around ten, just as she was getting ready for bed.

"Jane, it's Doug. Olivia's been arrested."

Chapter 17

With hardly any sleep the night before, Jane yawned and yawned again, as she assembled the Peachy French Toast Casserole early Friday morning. She forgot to include the peaches, so just sliced them over the top of the dish instead of layering them on the bottom according to the recipe. Then she remembered the bacon was still in the refrigerator, uncooked. After frying the bacon and letting it cool, she crumbled the crispy strips on top of the peaches. Hoping it'd taste all right, she carefully set the heavy, covered casserole dish in a large cooler full of ice.

She took the dogs for a quick walk around the block, stopping at the dog sitter's house to make sure she still had a house key. Jane gave her the address of where she'd be staying Friday through Sunday.

Yellow Mountain Campground, with the nearby Forest Service office, was not on the way, since it was many miles south of Estes Park, and farther west, but she had all day. So, she pointed her car in the direction of the mountains. It wasn't long before she stopped at the forest agency. Only one other car occupied the parking lot.

She hustled inside where a uniformed young man looked up from his desk. "What can I do for you?"

"I'd like to talk to Marshal Marsh...'em, Agent Marshall please."

"He's not here."

Jane tried to keep the disappointment off her face. What a waste of time. She should've called for an appointment, but had imagined surprising him by showing up unexpected.

"He'll be back in about an hour, though."

Jane sighed with relief. "Oh, good. I'll just leave and come back then."

"If you give me your name, I'll let him know you want to talk to him."

"That's okay. You don't need to bother," she murmured. She left the building and sat in her car. The campground was not far away, so she drove over to wait there. Since it was July third and the start of the holiday weekend, the campsites were all taken and the day-use area was almost full.

The club's camping trip of two weekends ago was a bittersweet memory. Enjoying the gourmet camp meals, sitting around the fire pit with cigars and good stories, hiking up to the outcropping in the beautiful mountain setting—it was all good—until they found the body. Then, the last time she was here was with the dinner club to question the weather watcher. That's when Olivia was enjoying her freedom, sunning herself at the picnic table just across the grounds, not knowing an arrest was around the corner.

She noticed a text she missed during her drive up the mountains and scanned it quickly. Doug had arranged to post bail the night before. They were on the way to meet with the attorney again and would motor up to the cabin afterward. Doug had written that Olivia did not want to miss this dinner club outing, plus she needed to take her mind off everything, since her arraignment was scheduled for Monday, when the charges would be read and she would enter her plea.

Jane put her head in her hands. Olivia was to be arraigned on Monday. She had to catch the killer and now.

So, who did it?

She didn't want to believe Ted was the murderer, because Gloria would be all alone if she lost Ted.

She didn't want to believe Ben was the murderer, because he had a family—a wife and young children—and he professed to have forgiven the man who caused the accident that killed his son.

That left Connie O'Hennessey. But she had no known motive. And what about Ed Koopmer? Had she considered him thoroughly?

The sun went behind a cloud, casting a gloom over the day, and Jane was suddenly lonely and aware of being on her own. Wanting to call Dale, she picked up the phone, then put it down. She hadn't told him, or anyone, about her side trip to see Marshall. Would that cause a problem with Dale? They were getting along so well now—why worry him?

Maybe she'd been in the car too long. She got out to stretch her legs by hiking the length of the gravel road through the campsites.

After peering through the trees to campsite one, with a large tent assembled near the picnic table, she trekked past the smelly latrines, down to campsite eight where Ted and Gloria had stayed in their tear-drop trailer. A family was camping there this weekend, gathered around an early campfire with hotdogs on sticks. The site O'Hennessey had occupied now held a large camper and a couple of pickup trucks.

Feeling as if she were being spied upon, she peered into the woods, but shook off the sensation and glanced at her watch. Maybe Marshall had returned to his office by now. Her feet beat a path to her car, and she climbed in and cranked on the engine. Distracted by her musings, she barely noticed a car exiting the park behind her. Speeding along the highway, she took a curve a little too fast and tapped her brakes. The red car behind slowed, too. In a few minutes, she steered into the parking lot and traipsed inside the U.S. Forest Service office to ask for Agent Marshall, saying his name correctly this time.

He came out to fetch her. "Come with me." He propelled her along the hallway to his office.

"Olivia Ladner's innocent." Jane's voice came out tight.

"Do you have any evidence, something to tell me?" He looked at her with interest.

Jane fumbled around, tugging on her shirt sleeves, then stretching her neck and adjusting her collar. Remembering the body language signs of guilt, she forced her hands into her lap to appear relaxed. "Yes. Olivia scraped her knuckles on a cheese grater. I was there. I saw her do it. Her fingers were bloody, and I put Band-Aids on them. She simply twisted her ankle hiking, like she said. She was with me or Doug the whole time. I'll give you a statement under oath."

"We already have your statement."

She puffed out her cheeks, then let out a long breath. "About the woman in the red car who ran me off the road, I know her name now."

"What's her name?"

"Connie O'Hennessey." Jane tossed her head back.

Agent Marshall flipped open a top-bound spiral notepad and held a pencil poised over it. "Okay. How did you find out?"

"I saw her name on the reservation tag on the post at her campsite." Jane scooted her chair closer. "Did you ever find a link between her and Quadtrini?"

He didn't answer as the moments ticked past.

"How about her and Malkon?" Jane leaned forward on his desk when he didn't respond. "At least let me know if casements were found at the scene."

"You mean casings." His lips twitched as he threw his pencil down and closed the spiral. "Revolvers don't eject brass. If the shooter used a revolver, no casings would be left at the scene, unless he or she stopped to reload." He rose from his chair and sauntered over to a coffee maker sitting on a rickety table and poured a cup. "Would you like some coffee, Mrs. Marsh?"

"Yes, thanks. It's Jane."

"You don't go by Marjorie?"

"No. My mom called me Marjorie Jane, but no one's ever called me just Marjorie. How did you remember my full name?"

He handed her a steaming cup of coffee. "From the sworn statement you already gave us. You can call me Marshall."

"You go by your last name?"

He smiled. "Why not? That's what people usually call me, anyway. I've even been called Marshal Marshall, so I thought I'd just make it easy." She blushed at her own mistake. "And Jane, there were no casings or bullets found at the scene. Most likely a revolver was used, that's why there were no casings. Then, the bullet causing his death passed through the body and disappeared into the woods."

"I was hoping new evidence had been found."

"No, we're confident we have our perpetrator."

Jane sloshed her coffee, spilling the brown liquid on his desk. She wiped the spot in a circle with her shirt sleeve. "Are you sure no one could've hiked to the campground from outside? Maybe someone drove to the firing range and hiked over?"

"Remember the road was closed. No one could get in or out by car or on foot either because the road crew would've seen them. Plus, everyone who signed in at the range was staying at the campground." He peered at her over the rim of his coffee mug as he took a sip. Then he made a face. "This coffee's awful. There's a coffee shop down the street. I could use some espresso."

Jane placed her mug on his desk. "Me too."

"Okay. Let's go." He rose from his chair and pocketed a set of keys. She trailed behind him to the front desk where he told the clerk, "I'll be at the Beanery down the street. Back in a few."

They strolled past the red car in the parking lot to the coffee shop where Jane ordered a mocha latte with a double shot and Agent Marshall ordered a plain espresso. They sat at a table in the patio area with their drinks.

"Why was I never a suspect?" Jane tilted her head and lifted her chin.

"You don't own a gun or shoot. There was no residue on your hands." His eyes were crinkling at the corners. "Are you telling me you shot Quadtrini?"

"Me?" Jane's voice rose an octave, but when she saw the smile in his eyes, she snorted. "I can be scary.

I'm the widow of the waves, after all." Remembering to watch the body language, she tried to keep her knee from bobbing up and down.

He cleared his throat. "Whoever shot Mr. Quadtrini was either a lucky shot or knew a thing or two about guns. He was killed with one bullet through the heart. Would you be able to do that?"

"No, not likely. And neither would Olivia."

"She's knows about revolvers and left her glasses with the body."

Jane scowled. "The killer planted her glasses."

"That's what she claims. What're you doing in the mountains today anyway?"

"My friends and I rented one of those big cabins in Estes Park for Fourth of July weekend." She ran her hands through her hair. "I took a little detour and drove here first."

His eyebrows shot up. "You're a bit out of the way coming here."

"I thought I'd take the Peak-to-Peak Highway. It's not too far if I cut across." Jane hugged her arms over her chest. "I don't know how we'll enjoy ourselves with all that's happened, but we'd rather be together than apart right now."

"You're a pretty tight knit group, sounds like."

"I'm a widow. My children are grown. The dinner club has become like family, and we've drawn even closer since we're under suspicion of this murder. It's been awful." She was about to lose them all. Cheryl and Bruce were flying home to Portland on Monday. Olivia was going to her arraignment hearing on Monday. And Libby—she'd lied to Jane about her engagement to Quadtrini…what kind of friend does that? She'd confront her by Monday.

Agent Marshall drained his cup and carried their mugs inside the shop. When he returned, they sauntered to the Forest Service office, and Jane thanked him before climbing into her car to leave.

She made good time on the road to Rocky Mountain Park, ahead of the other drivers waiting until the end of the workday to leave for the mountains on this holiday weekend. After turning into the parking lot at the cabin, she texted Olivia to ask how she was doing.

Olivia replied they were five minutes away, so Jane waited in the cool mountain air listening to the birds in the pines. Soon, the Ladners' car rounded the corner and rolled up next to Jane, leaning against the hood of her vehicle outside the large A-frame cabin overlooking the park.

Olivia lowered the window on the passenger side. Her eyes were red rimmed. "Doug and I are going into the rental office for the key, and we'll meet you back here."

"Okay. See you in a few." Jane gathered all her belongings from her trunk to take into the cabin. Before long, the Ladners returned with the key. Jane gave Olivia a tight hug, saying, "Everything's going to be all right."

"Doug keeps telling me they don't have a case. My attorney says the same thing."

Doug looked down at the ground, shaking his head with his hands clasped in fists. "I don't want Olivia to think about it anymore this weekend. I just want her to relax."

"I agree. Let's put his death out of our minds."

Jane gave Doug a curt nod.

Once in the door, Olivia dropped her turquoise handbag on the floor. The color was the same shade of blue as her earrings. "Since we're the first ones here, we get our choice of rooms." Olivia and Doug picked a bedroom off the front hall, and Jane contented herself with one of two smaller rooms on the upper level. She planned for Dale to take the other bedroom across from hers when he arrived the next day.

After setting her open suitcase on the luggage rack and hanging a dress in the closet, she tiptoed down the stairway of the quiet cabin to return to the family room. Rustic sofas made out of heavy logs held squishy cushions. A gigantic, stuffed brown bear rose eight feet up from the floor next to a large fireplace. A picture of dancing bears hung over the wooden mantelpiece, and a chandelier made out of antlers lit the room. Potpourri of cinnamon, orange, nutmeg, cloves, and vanilla scented the air.

Jane slid the Peachy French Toast into the refrigerator, along with the two bottles of white wine she'd packed in the cooler.

Olivia drifted in from the hallway. "I just talked to Cheryl, and she and Bruce are only now sitting down to have lunch with Megan, then they're heading up. I got a text from Libby that she and Wes haven't left yet either. Doug laid down on the bed and fell asleep. So, we're on our own this afternoon."

"What would you like to do?" Jane sank onto an old wooden rocking chair.

"Something fun. Let's go shopping." Olivia snatched up her turquoise handbag.

"Okay. I can drive." Jane unfolded herself out of

the rocker and plucked her black purse off the kitchen counter, then they headed out. "Do you know a good place in town to park? It's pretty crowded today." Jane steered her car onto a back road behind Elkhorn Avenue, the main street through town.

"Turn here and go over that bridge." Olivia waved her manicured hand out the window.

Jane braked the car. "The bridge looks too narrow."

"There's a parking lot over there on the other side of the trees. Go ahead." Olivia clutched the dashboard, craning her neck to see past the end of the bridge.

Jane turned the car onto the wooden structure, barely fitting between the railings. As the wheels passed over the wooden slats, they heard a clickety clackety, as if each board were popping up like piano keys during a glissando. Once across, they found themselves on narrow pavement.

"This must be a one-way road. There's not enough room for two cars," pointed out Olivia.

"But there's no sign that says 'one-way.' I don't have a good feeling about this." Jane rested her hands on the steering wheel wondering where she could turn around.

"Keep going. We can park over there." Olivia motioned to the left through the sparse woods. A parking lot abutted the back sides of several buildings. But how to get over there?

A man ran out of the trees, yelling and flapping his arms over his head. "Stop! Stop! You can't go this way." He was wearing a white, double breasted shirt and white toque.

Jane stomped on the brakes and rolled down her

window. "Everett."

"Jane?" Her former boyfriend skidded up to her car, almost bouncing off the door. "What in the world are you doing here?" His mouth fell open as his question hung in the air.

"We're in Estes for the weekend. What are you doing here?"

"I mean, what are you doing driving on this bike path?"

"We're just heading to the parking lot over there." Jane twitched her thumb in the direction of the trees. "What're you doing? I thought you worked in Vail."

"I'm catering the wedding you are about to drive into."

"What did you say?" Jane widened her eyes. "What bike path?"

"This bike path you're on."

She peered down the paved path to where the cement curved and a woman wearing a long, white gown and veil stood with her groom in front of rows of ribbon-bedecked chairs. A photographer was capturing the happy couple on film.

Jane's eyes darted over to Olivia who shrugged her shoulders.

Her voice came out shaky and halting. "What should I do? I can't turn around here."

"Return the way you came in."

"I'm afraid to go back over the bridge." Jane gripped the sides of her head and pinched her eyes shut.

Olivia pointed through the windshield. "If you drive up to the curve in the path, there's space to turn around."

"You can't do that. They're taking the wedding

pictures. You have to back up." Everett's small blue eyes flashed.

Jane jerked the car into gear, but only pressed her foot lightly on the gas pedal to move the car forward. Everett walked with big strides alongside the car, as Jane carefully maneuvered to the curve. He positioned himself at the tail end of the car as she attempted a three-point turn around. He held up his hands to give directions, and she inched the car first forward then backward, to swing in the other direction.

As soon as she had the vehicle pointed the opposite way, she said, "It was nice seeing you again, Everett," then screeched out of there.

Instead of returning over the bridge built to carry people only, she continued down the pedestrian path until they came to a metal chain barrier blocking the way. On the other side of the barrier was their destination, the store parking lot.

Olivia, who had been silent this whole time, asked, "What now?"

Jane risked a backward glance over her shoulder to see Everett and the bride watching them. The woman's fist was raised in the air, and her mouth was formed into a snarl.

"Come with me." Jane leapt out, leaving the car door yawning open, and Olivia did the same. They sprinted over to the barrier. Jane, taking one end with Olivia at the other, dragged the heavy metal structure to the side of the path out of the way. They both hurtled to the car to speed over to the parking lot. Jane drove to a close spot right next to the store entrance, and they beat a quick path inside.

She breathed a shaky sigh of relief. "I wonder if

we'll get in trouble for driving over the bridge."

"What are they going to do, arrest me?" Olivia put her hand on Jane's arm and sagged against her. Out of her mouth came, "Hee hee ha ha HA HA!"

Jane laughed out loud, too. "Adrenaline must have given us superhuman strength to move that barrier, but I was not about to go back over the bridge." She imagined the bridge collapsing, and her car floating down the Big Thompson River with her and Olivia inside.

Olivia brought herself up short. "There should've been a sign saying 'pedestrians only' or 'no motorized vehicles' or something…"

Another customer entered through the door, so the pair of them had to step out of the way. Olivia tugged Jane over to a display of earrings, and soon they both had bags with jewelry purchases under their arms. Once they snaked their way through the store and out onto Elkhorn Avenue, Olivia said, "I want to go to that dress shop across the street."

"I wouldn't mind going into the pet store on the corner." Jane remained at the curb to peer down the length of the town's main thoroughfare.

"Let's separate and meet back here. What, say, half an hour?"

"Okay."

A swarm of tourists jammed the pavement. The sweet smell of caramel corn assaulted her nose. Dodging the crowd, Jane glanced into storefront windows displaying Rocky Mountain Park T-shirts and souvenirs.

She hesitated at a window filled with fishing rods and gear. On display was a pink sweatshirt with the words, "Never Trust a Man Who Can't Fish or Shoot a Gun," and a drawing of a fishing pole. Instead of fishing line, smoke curled off the end of the pole. Movement in the store drew her eyes to the counter, where the clerk was unlocking a gun cabinet. A customer, wearing a red jacket, had his back to Jane, but he turned to examine the pistol in the clerk's hands. The man was Ben Malkon.

Chapter 18

She gasped and wrenched away from the front of the window, then wriggled sideways to peer in, just as Malkon plowed his way through the door. She spun around and stuffed her face into the bag containing her jewelry, as if looking for something. He strode right past her, so she fell into step a little distance behind him. He halted at the corner to toss an empty water bottle into the trash can, as she slunk down onto a bus stop bench, twisted her face away, and rummaged through her purse. He turned, taking another direction. She hopped up and followed.

The narrow side street was empty. The sidewalk led to the wooded part of town, near the river and away from the shops. The wind blew between the unbroken line of brick-walled buildings, and with it, whisking along the pavement, were paper cups, napkins, and a crumbled bag from McDonalds. Ben Malkon's boots made sharp, clopping sounds. Jane's footfalls were soft and made no noise as she tiptoed along behind. If he turned around, though, he would see her, since there was nowhere to duck and hide this time. Ben stopped in his tracks, and Jane took a few steps backward. She clutched at the cold bricks in the wall next to her, but there was no escape.

He looked at his watch, then continued down the road. When he reached the end of the block, he crossed a parking lot and unlocked a pickup truck. She waited behind the edge of the building. Her eyes followed the truck out of the parking lot and down the street. A gun rack with a rifle hung in the rear window.

She stepped out from behind the corner and ran smack into the weather watcher, Ed Koopmer. "Oh my gosh. What are you doing here?"

"What? Do I know you?" His expression was puzzled.

"You're Ed Koopmer."

"Yes. And you are?" His confusion appeared genuine.

Jane swallowed hard. "I was with the group at the campground asking about Quadtrini the other day."

"Oh, right." He gave a curt nod, his mouth pinched, but he still didn't appear to remember her. "Look out where you're going next time."

Jane sidestepped as he jerked past. Then she turned on her heels down the narrow street back to the crowds of tourists and hurried into the dress shop. Olivia was speaking with the cashier at the counter. After finishing, she asked Jane, "Did you like the pet store?"

"I didn't go in. Before I got there, I saw Ben Malkon. He was coming out of that fishing shop, and he'd been looking at guns. And then, get this, I ran into Ed Koopmer."

"What? How'd you know Malkon was looking at guns?" One of Olivia's eyebrows raised in a question.

"I saw him through the window. He was talking to the clerk at the gun display. When he left, I followed him, but he got in his pickup and drove away." Jane was panting a little.

"Did he buy a gun? If his revolver was confiscated

by the police, like ours, maybe he bought another one."

"Good point, but more importantly, what's he doing in Estes at the same time as us? And what is Koopmer doing here, too? Do they know each other?"

"Who's he again?"

"Koopmer's the weather watcher at Yellow Mountain Campground." She gripped her friend's arm. "It's very strange, don't you think? Let's go back to the cabin and talk about this."

"Okay."

Jane hightailed it to the parking lot with Olivia on her heels, then they zoomed to the cabin, avoiding the bike path and sticking to the roads this time.

After letting themselves in, Olivia plugged in the tea kettle. "Tea first. Something calming."

Jane opened one cabinet after another to find tea bags. Locating the bags on the shelf above the mugs, she asked, "What kind do you want?"

"Is there peppermint?"

"Yes. And I'll have that kind, too."

After Olivia poured the steaming water into mugs, they trailed out to the deck while dunking their tea bags. Olivia collapsed into a deck chair. "Could it be a coincidence that you saw both Malkon and that weather guy here in town? It is the holiday weekend, and everyone's come to the mountains."

"And Estes *is* a popular destination. Do you think that's all there is to it?"

"It's possible."

"But how likely?" Jane sank into the deep cushions on the deck chair. "Although I do believe in coincidences."

"Police say there aren't any." Olivia shot her a

level look.

Jane sputtered, "You were the one who said it's possible. Which is it?"

"How am I supposed to know? I have no idea what they're doing here." Olivia waggled a finger in Jane's face.

Jane slapped her hand away, but stopped herself from barking back. "Okay, okay. I wasn't accusing you of anything."

"Sorry. I'm just stressed out about Monday. I was hoping to forget about it this weekend." Olivia pressed a finger to the corner of her eye.

"Certainly." Jane struggled to keep the smile on her face. "Let's talk about something else." The pair put on their new earrings and looked at fashion magazines while the afternoon waned and their tea cooled. She refrained from bringing up the subject, although her thoughts kept returning to Malkon and Koopmer.

With perfect timing—at the cocktail hour—the Breewoods arrived with the Powells right behind. After hugs and greetings, Olivia and Jane helped their friends unload. Doug ambled out from his nap to lend a hand by carrying in their bundles, and in no time at all everyone had chosen their rooms and settled in.

They soon gathered in the family room with glasses of wine. Cheryl turned to Olivia. "So, you've been arrested. It's too unreal."

"It's all circumstantial." Doug exchanged a look with his wife. "I don't want Olivia to worry about it this weekend."

Bruce asked, "What's the evidence?"

"They figure the bullet that killed Quadtrini came from the same type of gun as Olivia's, and her

Derringer had been fired recently. That's all."

Wes pointed at Olivia. "Did they find out she's a good shot?"

Jane paused with her glass halfway to her lips and sucked in her breath.

Doug clenched his jaw. "Yes. But please, Olivia needs to put it out of her mind for now."

"And her glasses were under the body…and those cut knuckles and sprained ankle," Libby said, as Jane watched, spellbound. "But what's your motive, Olivia?"

"I haven't got one, although the police don't seem bothered by that." She had a dangerous glint in her eyes and snapped, "It's all circumstantial, like Doug said. And why aren't you worried? You were engaged to Quadtrini."

Sloshing her wine, Libby's face went white.

Wes growled, "What's this?"

Jane might as well dive in. "You won't believe who I saw in Estes today. Ben Malkon. He was buying a gun. And I saw Ed Koopmer, too." She looked around at their stunned faces.

Libby squeaked, "Oh no! What'll we do?"

Olivia butted in. "I didn't see them, only Jane did."

"Did you talk to them, Jane?" Doug's eyebrows hovered near his red hairline.

"No. Only to say, 'excuse me,' when I bumped into Koopmer."

"No other words exchanged?"

"I don't think Ben Malkon even saw me, and Ed Koopmer didn't recognize me." But goose bumps rose on Jane's arms just thinking about it.

"Nothing to be alarmed about." Bruce gave Doug a

serious look. Did they have a secret police defensive plan in mind?

Olivia smacked her glass down hard on the table. "I'm going to lay down. I need a break."

Doug stood up fast. "Let's go." She and Doug disappeared down the hall.

Bruce rose from his place on the couch, tight lipped. "Whew. That was tense. I'm going to make a cocktail. I found this drink in one of my cigar magazines that I want to try."

"Make a glass for me." Cheryl spoke up for the first time.

"I'll make everybody one." Bruce strode into the kitchen and lifted out several bottles from the brown, cardboard box he'd brought to the cabin. After mixing vermouth with orange bitters and poking a twist of orange peel in each glass, he handed the tiny aperitifs around. The drink was nasty and tasted strong to Jane, so she took only one teensy sip before setting the glass on the table.

Libby took a deep breath. "Wes, let's start making dinner."

"Good idea." He clambered out of his seat, and the rest of the group followed him into the kitchen. "I know we're assigned dinner tonight, but I can't remember who's responsible for the rest of the meals."

Cheryl answered, "Jane has Saturday morning breakfast. The Ladners have lunch. Saturday night we're eating in town. Bruce and I have Sunday breakfast."

Jane reclined at the kitchen counter with an open bottle of wine in front of her, so she dumped her aperitif in the sink and reached for the wine.

"That's for the chicken." Libby whipped Jane's hand away.

"It is?" Jane poured from the bottle anyway to taste it. "It's good. Not like cooking wine."

"No, but it's a pretty cheap table variety. We're making chicken thighs in garlic and white wine. That's the wine we're using in the recipe."

"Well, I like it." Jane drank some more, as Bruce popped open his iPod and dance music poured out.

Libby performed hip-hop steps around her husband. Wes waved his knife in the air. "Watch out! Those are some dangerous moves…"

She threw Wes a wine bottle opener. "Open up the wine we brought to drink. The Sauvignon Blanc. It's one from the western slope."

He did. They sipped that good wine and munched on chips with guacamole dip for their Happy Hour appetizer.

Jane wanted to ask Libby more about her engagement to Quadtrini, but now was probably not the time. Everyone appeared relaxed, the tension forgotten. No one said a word about Olivia and Doug's outburst or about Malkon. Or about Koopmer.

As Jane stuffed a loaded chip in her mouth, a face loomed up in the kitchen window. Connie O'Hennessey stared at her with teeth bared and nostrils flared.

"Aaaah!" Jane screamed, spitting out her chip. Libby jolted upright, Wes dropped his knife, point down, missing his shoe by millimeters, and Cheryl dumped Sauvignon Blanc on her blouse. Jane's chip landed salsa side down on the floor. Everyone gaped at her as Cheryl grabbed a towel. "What the hell…"

They hadn't seen the face vanishing from the

window.

The initial shock retreating, Jane shot out of her chair and lunged at the door, throwing it open. A stepstool was on the deck beneath the kitchen window, but she raced past it, flying down the stairs two at a time. She halted near the hot tub, but O'Hennessey was nowhere in sight.

Heart thumping, she vaulted up the steps to the deck, where the dinner club members were waiting, mouths agape. Bruce said, "What's the matter? Did you see a bear or something?"

"I thought I saw…" gasped Jane, "…I thought I saw that woman. The one who ran me off the road." Leaning over with her hands on her knees, she took a deep breath, then straightened up. "Connie O'Hennessey. She must've followed me here. Spied on us through the window." Jane yanked open the door and crossed into the kitchen, as the group trooped in behind her.

"Why would she do that?" asked Wes.

"How did she follow you here?" asked Cheryl at the same time.

Olivia rushed in from the hall with Doug at her back. "What the heck's going on?"

"I saw Connie O'Hennessey." Jane's voice was still breathless as she flicked her hand toward the window. "Out there."

"I'm going to take a look around." Doug bounded out the door, and Bruce ran after him.

Wes retrieved his knife from the floor and placed the sharp instrument on the cutting board before snatching a towel to wipe his hands. Libby stopped him as he aimed for the door. "Please don't leave me to finish. Stay to help get everything on the table. They'll be back in a minute."

"Okay, sure." Wes looked disappointed, but stepped to the stove top and stirred the steaming pot.

Olivia jabbed both fists onto her hips. "Why are you the only one to see these people, Jane? Malkon and Cooper, or whatever his name is. And now that woman. This can't be another coincidence."

Jane's jaw dropped open. "His name is Koopmer, not Cooper."

Cheryl's voice came out quiet. "Jane's observant. She pays attention and notices things the rest of us don't." Olivia had a skeptical look, but Cheryl ignored her. "Jane, how could she have followed you?"

Jane chewed on a fingernail. "I stopped at the forestry office before heading here. And at Yellow Mountain Campground, too. Maybe she happened to see me and followed me."

"Whaddaya stop there for?" Olivia drew her head back with her chin down, looking over the top of her glasses.

Before Jane could answer, Wes pointed out, "Connie had to have known Jane overheard her outside the latrines. Maybe she said something about the actual murder...like, maybe, she killed him. That's why she followed Jane home after the camping trip and now here."

"She probably saw me coming out the latrine." Jane's eyes narrowed. "And figured I must've heard everything she said, but I didn't. I wish I had."

Olivia's firm stance crumpled. "I wish none of this happened. And it's all we can talk about now."

Libby steered her to a chair at the table. "Olivia,

we can learn something here to help with your defense." Olivia looked tired and drawn as she lowered herself, tucking her feet under the chair.

Jane wrung her hands. "This is what I think happened. Connie's the killer. Ben suspected her, too, and confronted her at the latrines. She thinks I overheard her confessing. And now she's trying to bump me off. Rub me out. Silence me! They both are…Malkon bought a gun in town, remember? And I admitted to him I overheard them talking. Why did I do that?"

Libby handed her a head of lettuce. "Here, put that nervous energy to use and tear this up." She plunked a bowl on the counter, and Jane ripped the lettuce apart with great force, just as Doug and Bruce returned.

"Did you see anyone?" Jane knitted her brows together.

"No. Didn't see a thing." Bruce patted her arm. "Try to relax. You're with us. Nothing's going to happen."

"I really did see her at the window. And Ben Malkon in town." Jane's chest was tight and her voice shaky.

"We believe you, honey." Libby ran her hands through her spiky hair.

Doug gave Jane a pointed look. "Did I hear you say Malkon bought a gun in town?"

"I don't know if he bought one, to tell the truth, but he was looking at one in the store."

Cheryl pointed a finger at her husband. "Bruce, call the police."

"I'd rather not see the police again so soon." Olivia's lips were white and drawn in a thin line.

Everyone was staring at Jane. The decision was hers. She took a deep breath. "Let's eat dinner while we think about it. Maybe we won't see any of them again and nothing else will happen."

"Are you sure, Jane?" Bruce's fists jiggled some loose coins in his pockets. "Looking in someone's window is a criminal offense. The police have reason to question her."

"That's right, we should call the police." Doug gripped Olivia's shoulder. "It's the best thing to do, hon."

"I don't want to see them," Olivia wailed.

Jane blew out her cheeks. "You aren't going to. Wes and Libby worked so hard to make us a nice dinner. Let's not spoil it. Remember, that's what we're here for. We're a dinner club. We should enjoy the food and each other's company."

A long moment passed, then sizzling from the frying pan got Wes's attention, so he rushed to the stove. Libby opened a plastic dish with a loud pop and rattled the chopped tomatoes, peach wedges, and red onion slices around inside the container.

"All right, then. But if one more thing happens, we're calling the cops." Bruce snagged a peach wedge and tossed the piece into his mouth. "What's all this for?"

Libby gave him a stern look. "The salad. Stay out of it." She dumped the peach mixture on top of the lettuce in the large wooden bowl.

"Jane's right that we need to eat." Sliding onto the chair next to Jane, Cheryl asked, "What kind of dressing do you use with this, Libby? I've never put peaches in a lettuce salad before."

"Vinegar and oil." Libby shook a pint-sized jar of dressing, then emptied the contents over the greens. She handed Jane a pair of tongs. "Here, stir the dressing around."

Jane made a feeble attempt, as Libby toted a bowl of steamed vegetables and the platter of chicken to the table.

Wes waved a spoon in the air. "Dinner's ready. Sit down everyone." Like obedient children called from mischief to the dinner table, they shuffled to their places. Wes reached for Libby's fingers, and then they all held hands as he gave a blessing over the food.

Doug poured more Sauvignon Blanc. "Let's toast to our good friends, the Breewoods, for coming all the way to Colorado to be with us on the Fourth of July."

They bumped glasses, and Jane started to relax and enjoy the meal. After dinner, the friends pitched in to clean up the kitchen. Then Cheryl asked, "Did everyone bring swimming suits like I told you to?"

"Yes, we did." Libby's head bobbed up and down.

"Go change and meet at the hot tub." Cheryl jerked her head toward her husband to follow her. The others dispersed, as well.

Jane was left alone in the kitchen, so she wandered up to her room to change and rustle up a towel. After stepping into her modest suit, she wrapped the towel around her hips and stuffed her feet into flip-flops, before heading outside to the hot tub beneath the deck.

"I fired this up before we ate." Doug stuck a finger into the water. "It's nice and hot, the perfect temperature."

They each slithered into the bubbling, soothing water as the sun set over the Continental Divide.

"Ahhhh."

"Ooooh. This feels great on the ole' back."

"Nice!"

"Okay. So, you might be a redneck if you think a hot tub is a stolen bathtub." Bruce chuckled.

They all groaned. Before long, Jane and several others climbed out of the tub. Jane slipped to her room to change into yoga pants and a sweatshirt. She returned to the family room to read her Kindle. Glancing out the door, she noticed Bruce was still in the hot tub. She tugged open the window above the sofa and spoke through the crack. "You'd better not stay in there too long. I don't think it's good for you."

"But it's so relaxing."

"Have you been in there this whole time?"

"Yeah. But I'm getting out now."

Jane shut the window and sank into the overstuffed cushions. She poked a throw blanket around her legs and got ready to start a new mystery she'd been wanting to read. But when Bruce walked through the door, his face was bright red and he stumbled into the table, then held his hands out to catch himself as he fell onto the sofa.

"Bruce! You all right?" Jane shot up.

"Lightheaded. Don't feel good."

Jane ran into the powder room across the hall, jerked the hand towel off the rack, and twisted the cold water faucet wide open. She soaked the towel and raced back to Bruce. She placed the cold cloth on his back just as Libby walked in. "Libby! Get some more cold towels. We need to get Bruce's body temperature down."

"What happened?" Libby's eyes were large, and

her hand flew up to cover her mouth.

"He was in the hot tub too long. I think he's got heat stroke."

Bruce moaned, as Libby dashed out to the kitchen and returned with a tray of ice cubes and some kitchen towels. "Will it shock his system to put ice cubes against his skin?"

"I don't know, but I think it could. Let's wrap the cubes inside the towels." Jane pressed a cold towel full of cubes against his forehead, while Libby ran cold water from the sink in the powder room.

Wes flitted into the room next, and Jane soon explained the problem. He galloped up the stairs to find Cheryl. Soon the whole dinner club was replacing cooled-down towels with cold ones on Bruce's back and arms. Cheryl shoved a cold sports drink into his hand, and he took some sips.

His wife admonished him with a few words. "You were steaming yourself in a slow stew in that hot tub!"

Jane knew he was feeling better when he said, "I'm okay. Quit fussing." He stood to test his legs. "I think I can make it to the bedroom now. I'll go lie down."

Cheryl held his arm and walked him down the hall, with Olivia and Doug trailing behind, as the three remaining friends sank onto the sofas and chairs.

"Well, that was a little scary," Jane said, just as a blood curdling scream rent the air.

Chapter 19

Wes raced down the hall with Jane and Libby running behind. Another small scream sounded from the Ladners' bedroom. Wes banged open the door to find Doug, lying in his robe on top of the bedcovers, and Olivia, white-faced, swaying in the bathroom door.

"There's a huge spider in the sink!" Olivia screeched, pointing with a shaky finger.

Libby ran her hand through her spiky hair. "I'm sorry. I put it there. It's fake. Not too funny now after everything that's happened tonight."

Olivia laughed as she sank against the door frame. The rest joined in, and Libby said with relief in her voice, "Gotcha!"

Doug ran a hand over the top of his head. "Weren't you the one who bought that fake spider, Olivia? You were the first to prank someone with it. How come you didn't know it was fake?"

"I don't have my glasses on." Olivia giggled.

Jane put her hand on her friend's shoulder. "We all needed a good laugh. But I'm tired. I'm hitting the sack."

Reaching around, Olivia gave Jane a quick hug then let her go. Jane left to retrieve her e-book reader from the sofa. Once in her room, she closed the door and climbed under the blankets.

She slept soundly after that busy day, then awoke

at the first light of dawn, threw on her robe, and sauntered into the kitchen to put her breakfast casserole in the oven and start a pot of coffee. Libby padded into the room in her pajamas. Jane said, "Good Morning. It's a peach themed weekend because I'm making Peachy French Toast."

"Whaa?"

"Remember, there were peaches in the salad last night."

"Oh, yeah. I'm not awake yet. Need coffee."

Jane poured them both steaming, fragrant mugs. "Here ya go."

"Gosh, that breakfast casserole smells good." Libby took a sip, then blew her breath out over the top of the scalding drink. Wes walked in, fully dressed in golf clothes and prepared for the day.

"When's the tee time?" Jane felt a little guilty because she was the only one not planning to golf.

"It's at nine-thirty."

"The casserole will be out of the oven by eight."

"Plenty of time, then." Wes smiled at his wife, and she reached up to tousle his hair.

Both women headed to their rooms to get dressed. Jane returned first and set the table. She placed a jar of genuine maple syrup and a dish of real butter in the center. She started to ask, "Anyone know how Bruce is doing?" when the man himself walked in, followed by Cheryl. Olivia and Doug were on their heels.

Jane emptied the first pot of coffee into mugs as Bruce assured everyone he was fine. "I'm planning to golf." He and Cheryl were both dressed in bright green golf shirts and black pants.

"Indeed. You can't miss golf." Olivia put one hand

on a hip.

"As long as you're not planning to get back in the hot tub," added Wes.

"I'm staying out of hot tubs from now on." Bruce adjusted his glasses. "They don't agree with me."

"The problem was you were in there too long." Jane rolled her eyes. "But I'm glad you're better this morning." She wrestled open the oven door to check on the bubbling dish. Bruce and Cheryl helped finish setting the table, and Libby, having joined them, started another pot of coffee.

Once it brewed, Jane slid the casserole out of the oven and set the dish on a trivet in the middle of the table. "We're eating family style. Dig in." They each took the same chairs as the night before.

"Oh, this is surprisingly good. I want the recipe." Olivia licked her lips.

Jane paused to think about Olivia's compliment. "Thanks, I guess." She was relieved the casserole was edible, hoping she hadn't forgotten any more of the ingredients.

After they had their fill, Jane cleared the table, and the golfers loaded their clubs to make their way over to the Estes Park golf course. There were several false starts—Olivia forgot the sun visor that matched her golf shoes, and Bruce came back for his cellphone, then Olivia returned for the sack lunches she'd brought for everyone to take with them on the course, reminding Jane there was one for her in the fridge. Finally, her friends departed, and Jane was alone at the quiet cabin.

She wiped the table clean, began yet another pot of coffee, since seven people emptied the last one, and turned on the dishwasher. She carried her Kindle out to the deck and arranged a wicker lounge chair to face the glory of Rocky Mountain National Park. The scent of pine needles was heavy in the air. A common mule deer skirted the yard where someone had placed a salt lick. A mountain blue jay provided a bright spot of color in one of the pines. She would need to tell Cheryl she'd spotted a jay.

What an idyllic spot.

But after finishing one cup of coffee and two chapters, she was restless. Her gaze darted around the woods on the other side of the deck. What if Connie O'Hennessey came back to find her alone? Or Ben Malkon? Ed Koopmer? Heck, maybe Gloria and Ted would show up.

The setting didn't seem so idyllic after all.

She returned her book to her room, tugged on her walking shoes, and donned a pair of sunglasses. Grabbing the key off the kitchen counter, she locked the cabin, and deciding to leave the car this time, joined the crowd of tourists hastening on foot toward the downtown section of Estes Park.

The Big Thompson River, flowing east out of Moraine Park through the town, cascaded with loud crashes around rocks and over fallen logs, as she trekked along the walking path beside the fast moving river. An animal swam under the overhanging branches, its wet, brown head and whiskered nose sticking out of the water. Jane hoped the animal was a muskrat, not a common rat.

Shuddering, she turned away from the river to follow the path to the main street, then went straight to the pet store. After some time, she exited with a bag containing two doggie T-shirts. One was stamped, "if you are close enough to read this, why aren't you scratching my back?" and the other, "a big dog in a little package."

A throng of visitors strolled past shops selling ice cream and caramel corn, past the T-shirt shops and jewelry shops and craft shops. Families with small children in strollers, teenagers on skate boards, elderly couples, and other folks, who appeared to move along with purposeful strides, flowed around Jane when she stopped in the middle of the sidewalk.

Stepping out of the stream of pedestrians, she peered into the reflection of a shop window.

Connie O'Hennessey stood behind her.

Jane's heart leapt to her throat, where her breath also seemed to have stuck fast.

Was she imagining things?

She pivoted around and clutched her plastic sack in front of her with both hands, shielding her chest. It was Connie, even bigger than her image in the glass window. "What do you want?" Jane screeched.

"You need to quit being nosy." O'Hennessey was poised with hands on hips, feet apart. "You spied on Ben and me talking outside the latrines at Yellow Mountain. You followed me to the campground last weekend. I heard you even showed up at Ben's house. Really, who do you think you are?"

Jane's eyes darted up and down the street, before she was compelled to look O'Hennessey in the eye. "You rammed into my car! I could have you arrested for leaving the scene of an accident."

"I didn't ram into you. You braked suddenly. I could sue you."

"Uh, no. No, you can't. You were following too

close. I know what I'm talking about." Jane glared into O'Hennessey's face.

The two women continued to glower at each other for a moment, then Jane said, "I don't know why you feel threatened by me, Connie. I know nothing about you."

O'Hennessey smirked, as if in disbelief.

"What is it you think I know?" Jane drew back a step.

The woman's forehead wrinkled. "You heard Ben and me talking. Quit pretending you didn't."

"But I didn't hear much." Jane lowered her bag of T-shirts a tad. "Does it have something to do with the asbestos found at the campground?"

O'Hennessey's eyes bulged out and her mouth pinched into a small line.

"You're the whistleblower?" Jane's heart hammered in her chest.

"What's that?"

"The one who blew the whistle to the EPA, you know, got the Forestry Service in trouble for the cover up?" Jane's voice ended in a question because O'Hennessey's features had relaxed.

Barking out a laugh, O'Hennessey took a step toward Jane, reaching for her arm. Jane raised her flimsy bag to shield her body and took a couple more steps backward. Her heel hit against the bricks at the shop front—she was up against a wall. What was she doing, backing down? She'd had Krav Maga lessons, well, one lesson.

O'Hennessey seized Jane's arm in a tight grasp. Jane tore herself away and launched into the defensive position, raising her right arm and coming down with the heel of her palm onto O'Hennessey's solid, formidable shoulder.

"Ow. That hurt." O'Hennessey rubbed the top of her arm and gave Jane an offended look.

Jane rubbed her own arm, which was tingling in pain from the jolt. "Sorry. I meant to hit your neck."

"What?"

"The neck's supposed to be a vulnerable spot." Jane exchanged a look with her foe, then startled when she heard a car horn and her name.

"Jane! I'm on my way to the cabin." Dale had nosed his car over to the curb. "What are you doing in town?"

She ran over, jerked open the passenger door, and hopped in. "Let's go! Gun it!"

"What's the matter?" He steered away from the curb to join the heavy traffic on Elkhorn Avenue. "Who were you talking to?"

"You remember what I told you about Connie O'Hennessey?"

"The woman who ran you off the road?"

"Yes. That was her." Jane's heart pounded in her chest.

Dale peered into the rearview mirror. "I don't see her now." He turned the corner and drove up the side street to the cabin. "You'd better call the police and tell them you saw her."

Jane managed to squeak out, "I'm going to." Yes, the time had come. Olivia may not want the police to show up, but they needed to know what was going on. She dug her cellphone out of her purse and punched in the number. Trying to keep her voice steady, she asked for Agent Marshall, then told him in a few words about

O'Hennessey looking through her kitchen window and also confronting her downtown.

"I'll alert the Estes police, and in the meantime, someone will drive by her house." Agent Marshall's voice sounded calm and reassuring.

"Does she live up here in the mountains?"

"Yes."

"By the campground?" Jane guessed.

"Not too far from there. But don't go near her."

"I won't." Jane glanced over at Dale, listening to her side of the conversation as they sat in the car outside the cabin. "She lunged at me, so I gave her a Krav Magna chop on the arm, but it was in self-defense."

"I'm glad you told me. She'll be sure to tell the officer you hit her when he catches up with her. By the way, it's Krav Maga, not Magna."

Jane flushed. "Anyway, she started it. She came up behind me, and she's got quite a few pounds on me."

"Duly noted. I'll be back in touch with you. Call me if you see her again."

"Okay." Jane disconnected and sat still and small in her seat.

Dale squeezed her hand. "She peeked in your cabin window?" He gave her a slanted look.

"Ye-yes."

"I'm glad you talked to the police."

"Me, too." Jane mustered a smile.

"I'm worried about you." He stroked her hair with an intense expression on his face.

"I'm all right now."

"Krav Maga?" His eyes crinkled at the corners.

"Yes. I'll tell you about it another time."

She carried in the sports coat from Dale's backseat where the jacket had been hung on a hook, as he brought inside a small, overnight bag. She showed him the spot where Connie stood on the stool to spy in the window, then escorted him to his bedroom across the hall from hers.

Just as they finished settling Dale in his room, they heard Bruce's Expedition drive up, car doors banging, and happy voices entering the cabin.

"Hello, Dale." Bruce shook his hand as everybody else said their hellos.

Dale said right off, "Tell them what happened to you, Jane."

She waved her hands around in the air, palms wide. "I saw Connie O'Hennessey again, this time in town. She came up to me and grabbed my arm, but Dale showed up, so I got away from her. I called Agent Marshall to let him know."

Olivia's eyebrows shot upward and her mouth dropped open.

"Did you tell Marshall you also saw Ben Malkon yesterday, too?" Cheryl touched Jane's arm.

"You didn't mention that, Jane." Dale's calm look was slipping.

Bruce had a grim twist to his mouth. "I'm glad you called the agent. In the meantime, let's be sure to keep the cabin doors and windows locked." They all murmured their agreement.

Cheryl gave Jane a quick hug. "We should stay together as a group from now on."

Dale pulled her close to his side. "I won't leave her alone."

Wes strode over to the front door to lock it. "I'm

going to check the windows to make sure they're all shut and locked."

Libby made to follow him. "I'll go with you."

Doug turned toward the hall leading to his room. "I'll check our room, then I'm going to take a shower."

"Everyone meet in the family room in an hour, and we'll head over to the restaurant for dinner." Olivia accompanied her husband down the hall.

"How was the golf game? Did you play well?" Jane contrived a smile as she faced the Breewoods.

Cheryl answered, "We played scramble, so it was easy. But I only had one best shot."

"What does that mean? Only the best shots count toward the score?" Jane maneuvered out from under Dale's arm onto a seat at the counter next to Cheryl.

Bruce got out his scorecard. "No. That's best ball you're thinking of. In scramble, all the players tee off, choose which shot is best, and everyone hits their next shot from that one."

"Another game with a lot of rules, it sounds like." Jane scratched her head. "What was your best shot, Cheryl?"

"I happened to hit an amazing putt from one side of the green to the other."

A knock sounded at the door, so Dale answered it. Agent Marshall stood hat in hand on the porch, and Dale invited him inside. Declining a seat or cup of coffee, Marshall explained, "Officers showed up at O'Hennessey's home, but she wasn't there, and they didn't spot her around town, either."

"Tell him about Malkon, too." Cheryl rose from her stool.

Jane turned to Marshall. "I spotted Ben Malkon

looking at guns in a sporting goods store here in town yesterday. I saw him through the store window, and I don't think he noticed me, but it's a weird fluke that he's here in Estes, at the same time as all of us. And Ed Koopmer, too."

Agent Marshall's eyes narrowed, and he nodded. "And where did you see Koopmer?"

"I ran into him on the street. He didn't appear to recognize me." Jane clasped her hands together. She was glad that the Ladners remained out of sight, so Oliva didn't have to deal with any questions.

"Call my number if you see any of them again."

"I will," Jane agreed.

After the agent left, Cheryl said, "Well, that means they're all still out there somewhere."

No one moved for a moment. Jane put on her brave face. "When's that reservation at the restaurant?"

Bruce glanced at his watch. "Six. We have half an hour before we need to leave."

****

After dressing in a new sundress for dinner, Jane joined Dale in the hall between their rooms, and then they met the others downstairs. Olivia was coordinated in a pink tank dress and sandals. Libby wore a sundress, too, but Cheryl had on a summer top with a short, jean skirt. The guys wore their typical uniforms of golf shirts and Dockers. After locking the door behind them, they set out to walk to the restaurant.

A cool breeze ruffled their hair and the women's dresses as they crossed busy Elkhorn Avenue, engorged with cars making their way in and out of Rocky Mountain National Park.

"It's a good thing we made reservations because

this city is packed with people," said Wes to Bruce, as they broke into groups of twos on the crowded sidewalk. Dale gripped Jane's hand and drew her close to keep them from getting separated. They veered away from the traffic-jammed road to stroll on the walkway along the Big Thompson River and up to the restaurant with outdoor seating. A round table for eight was set up for them near the water.

They each ordered a glass of wine and examined the tall cardboard menus. Jane and Dale decided to split a thirteen-ounce Angus beef ribeye steak. The others ordered pork chops, lamb, and steak entrées, and to share, an appetizer of bacon-wrapped dates stuffed with blue cheese.

Bruce gave a sarcastic wink. "This menu isn't as fancy as your breakfast casserole, Jane."

"What was in that dish, anyway?" Olivia flipped her napkin open and laid the cloth in her lap. "There was some kind of meat along with the eggs and peaches, but it wasn't bacon."

"Not tellin.' Secret recipe." Jane grinned back at them.

"I think it *was* bacon." Libby wrinkled her nose. The waiters arrived with their dinner salads, and once the bowls were on the table, they twisted enormous pepper mills over the greens with a flourish.

Jane answered, "Yes, there was bacon. There was a second meat chopped into small pieces, Olivia, and it was chicken, I'll tell you that much."

"Poultry and pork." Bruce wiggled his eyebrows up and down. "That explains why some of us pigged out and others chickened out."

"It was piggy-licious!" Cheryl ran the tip of her

tongue around the outside of her mouth.

"Did you buy the casserole ready-made?" Olivia had a suspicious look in her eye.

"No, I swear." Jane caved. "All right. I got the recipe from the Food Network website under 'easy breakfast recipes for a crowd.' You can download it."

"Sounds delicious. You'll have to make a smaller version of that casserole for the two of us some time," Dale chirped in.

"I sure worked up an appetite on the golf course." Wes forked a tomato from his salad bowl into his mouth.

Doug raised his wine glass into the air. "A toast. May we never live without good friends or good food."

Each of them hoisted their glasses with a "Hear, hear."

A man loomed up behind Dale. He was wearing checkered pants, a white, double-breasted jacket, and a toque on his head. "Hello Everett." Cheryl's eyes swept up his tall frame.

"Hey, good to see everyone. Welcome to Veneta Jo's Grille." He threw his arms out wide.

Jane stuttered, "Wha-what are you doing here? I-I thought you were only catering that wedding."

"I did that yesterday. Today I'm the head chef at this restaurant."

"But you took a job in Vail." A warmth crept across her cheeks.

"I did for a while, then I moved to Estes because I was offered a head chef job here." Everett flapped his hand in dismissal.

Bruce gave him a thumbs-up. "Congratulations on the new job. This is a wonderful place."

Everett beamed as he glanced around their table. Dale's voice rang out, "I found your car keys in my salad. I put them back on your desk in your office. You'll have to be more careful."

Jane's heart caught in her throat. Everett's smile faded and his strong jaw clenched as he stared at Dale out of his small, narrowed eyes, but Bruce laughed and slapped him on the back. "Good one, Dale!" The people at the next table chuckled, too, and Jane let out her breath.

"Yes. Congratulations on your new job, Everett. We'll certainly be back," said Doug. Everett thanked him, wished them all a good evening and an enjoyable meal, and then strode off.

"What a thing to say to Everett. What did the other diners think?" Libby made a face at Dale.

"Actually, I came up with that joke. I said the same thing to, um, to somebody else at another restaurant once." Jane gave an exaggerated shrug of her shoulders. She didn't met Dale's eyes. He'd sure gotten even.

Olivia's eyes looked amused. "I remember. You told me about that." Her gaze flicked past Jane to stare over her shoulder.

Jane spun around, thinking Everett had returned, but she stopped and ducked. Connie O'Hennessey and Ben Malkon were eating at a table on the other side of the outdoor patio. She turned her whole body around and scrunched lower in her chair.

"Nothing can happen. You're here with all of us, Jane." Dale's chest puffed out, and his fists clenched.

Bruce said, "Let 'em try and come over here. We'll show them," and Doug agreed.

"Are they having an affair?" Olivia frowned as she

continued to peer their way. "Maybe that's all there is between them, and you imagined a connection to the murder. They don't want to be caught in their affair, that's all. But if that's the case, I'm disappointed one of them isn't the killer."

Libby added, "Connie might think you overheard something about their affair, not about the murder."

Jane stared at Libby, wanting to ask about her engagement to Quadtrini. Was there more to their relationship, just as there might be more between Connie and Ben? Jane's gaze darted to the couple across the crowded, noisy patio. "There was no hint of an affair in their conversation at the latrines. And they aren't acting like lovers now."

Ben and Connie appeared to be scowling at each other.

After that, everyone claimed to be too full to order dessert, so they shoved off without sticking around for coffee.

Once at the cabin, they snagged jackets and sweaters and met on the wooden deck, overlooking the park on one side and the city on the other, to watch the Fourth of July fireworks. Jane brewed a quick pot of coffee and carried out cups on a tray right before the show started and the sun set behind the Great Divide. The lights exploded in blazing colors at the top of the celestial dome and cascaded in receding brightness onto the tree line below as booms ricocheted off the mountains. The smell of gunpowder and puffs of black smoke hovered in the air after the show ended.

The club members carried their empty coffee cups into the cabin to head to their beds. Everybody stretched and yawned with gaping mouths, but Wes was silent and stiff, with a white face and glassy eyes.

Jane pulled Libby aside. "I need to talk to you in private."

Her friend raised her eyebrows, but gave a slow nod. "All right. Be right back." Libby took Wes's arm as they crossed the hallway. In a matter of moments, she strutted from the other room to join Dale and Jane on the couch.

"Wes is getting ready for bed. I have a few minutes. What's this about?" Libby elevated one foot, then the other, onto the ottoman.

"About you and Quadtrini being engaged..." Jane trailed off.

"But we weren't really engaged." Libby ducked her head low and stared at the floor. "Why are you asking?"

"Some friends of Quadtrini's said you broke his heart and that's why he never married."

Libby swallowed. "It's not like he knelt down on one knee and put a ring on my finger. Well, we did talk about it, and we sorta said, yeah, we'd like to get married, but it's not like we sent out invitations in the mail or anything. It's not like it was the week before the wedding—"

"Oh my God, Libby! Did you leave him at the altar?"

"No. It wasn't like that. Not exactly. I still had time to return the dress."

"You did break his heart!"

Libby hesitated, as if considering it. "No. I'm sure that's not why he never married." Her head jerked from side-to-side in a quick, curt negative.

Jane sighed. "So you say."

Libby yanked her feet down to the floor. "I want to check on Wes. Goodnight you two." She fled down the hall to her room.

"There was more to the relationship than Libby will admit." Jane yawned. "It's my bedtime. I'm heading upstairs."

Outside her door, Jane gave Dale a lingering goodnight kiss, and they parted for their own rooms. The day had been tiring, so she had to force herself to brush her teeth and cream on her moisturizing lotion before falling into bed.

It felt like her head had just hit the pillow when she was awakened by a boom in the night. She rose onto her elbows, but laid down again, rotating to her side and jerking the comforter tighter around her shoulders. Another loud sound rent the air. *Crrracckk! Kaboom!* Then, "Aaiiee!"

Jane shot out from under the blankets and flew through her door.

Chapter 20

She smacked into Dale in the hall. He eyeballed her thin silk chemise pajamas, so she ran into her bedroom for her robe. By the time she joined the others on the first floor, Libby was in the middle of apologizing for Wes's outburst.

"His PTSD flared from the noise. This is never a good night for him." Libby wrung her hands as another *whiiizzz, boom* burst into the air close by the cabin.

"Somebody started up more firecrackers," Cheryl stated the obvious.

"Wouldn't he feel better in here with us? I don't mind sitting with him until everyone quits with the fireworks." Jane put her hand on Libby's arm. "I could make some hot tea."

"Hot whiskey might be better. I could use some of that myself." Bruce fished inside a kitchen cabinet for cocktail glasses, then retrieved a flask from the box he'd left on the counter. Jane plugged in the tea kettle as they all took places on the squishy couch and chairs.

"I'll go get Wes." Libby was gone a few minutes before returning with her husband in tow.

He had a sheepish look. "I'm sorry I woke everyone up."

They responded with, "No problem," and "Don't worry about it."

Jane told a white lie. "I couldn't sleep anyway."

She passed around mugs of hot water and set the boxes of tea bags with a stack of spoons on the ottoman. "Everyone help themselves, unless you want some of what Bruce has." Doug poured a couple of teaspoons of Bruce's whiskey into his tea, while the others opted for plain tea without embellishment.

"Wes, do you want to talk about it? Might help." Dale held a steaming mug in both hands.

Wes drew in a long quivering breath. "No. I'd rather talk about something else. Get my mind off it." Another *whiiizzz, bang, rat-a-tat-tat* sounded outside the cabin's window, so Wes said after all, "Sudden noises bring it on. I feel like I'm back in the combat zone." His hands shook, and his eyes blinked rapidly.

Each of them sat as still as stones.

"Gunfire all around, bright lights and sounds, kinda like these fireworks. The hard part is, why did I survive? Why me? I feel guilty I was the one who came home. And then, once I got home, nobody asked me about the war, no one wanted to talk about it, including me. War veterans were not treated as heroes, but as war mongers and killers. That's not what we were. We believed in our country, we were patriotic, we wanted to do something worthwhile, we were fighting for a cause." Wes broke down.

The men leapt over to him. Bruce patted him on the back, and Dale, with a pale face of his own, snaked his arm around Wes's shoulder. "It's okay, buddy."

"We love you. We're here for you." A tear fell off Jane's cheek into her mug of tea.

Libby rose to her feet. "I'll be right back." She left and returned with a photo album in her hands. "Wes brought this to show everyone. Let's look at it now."

An hour went by as they poured over photographs from his overseas tour. Wes talked and talked. Dale shared some stories of his own as Jane listened with rapt attention, since he had not given away any of those feelings before. The fireworks sputtered out, then ceased. Afterward, they all trooped back to bed, except for Jane.

She rinsed out the tea kettle and stacked the mugs in the dishwasher. She double checked to make sure the front door was locked, then went into the kitchen one last time to test the knob on the patio door. She peered out the window, and a light caught her eye; someone with a flashlight was near the hot tub.

She cracked open the door, stuck out her head, and said barely loud enough to be heard, "Please don't let off any more firecrackers. It's too late, and we're trying to sleep here."

Someone seized Jane's arm, and she stumbled out onto the deck, the door closing softly behind her. Connie O'Hennessey's and Ben Malkon's faces soared out of the darkness, and Ben held a revolver in his hand.

"What do you think you're doing, waving that gun around? Get out of here." Jane's voice failed her and came out as a whimper.

Ben lowered the revolver a fraction. "Keep quiet. If you wake up your friends, there'll be trouble." He brandished the gun once more, then stepped back under the cover of darkness.

Jane widened her eyes in sudden understanding. "You both did it. You killed Mike Quadtrini together, didn't you?"

"I told you she'd heard us talking. I was right,

wasn't I?" Connie's face was red and puffy in the light cast by the kitchen window.

"Connie, be quiet." Ben couldn't be seen in the black shadows.

"But I didn't hear everything you said. I don't know anything." Jane's heart thudded in her chest as she imagined the gun aimed at her from beyond the circle of light.

Out of the corner of her eye, she saw a curtain twitch in a window at the far end of the patio. Wes's face appeared in the crack of light. His lips jerked and his eyes had a wild glare, unseen by the threatening pair, who had their backs to the window. As her heart thumped harder, she forced herself to look away, hoping Ben and Connie would not turn around. "How did you know we were staying here?"

Connie took a step closer and wagged her finger. "I overheard you talking to Agent Marshall yesterday morning. I followed you from the campground to the Forest Service office, then to the coffee shop."

Ben added, "That didn't matter, because I saw a Facebook posting by one of your friends. Libby Powell posted that your group was coming up for the weekend, even gave the name of the cabins. Then she 'checked in' on Facebook. I knew right where you were."

"How did you know Libby's name to find her on Facebook?" Jane couldn't keep her eyes from darting to the window, but she could no longer see Wes in the sliver of light. He was sure to come outside any moment now. What if he didn't know Ben had a weapon? What if Wes came outside and Ben shot him? Jane's heart pounded hard, and her palms sweat.

"You introduced yourselves when you came to my

house, don't you remember?"

"Oh yeah, we did." She raised her voice, hoping Wes would hear. "You'd better put that gun away. I'm sure the police are on to you, and they'll show up any minute. I called them and told them you were here in Estes, threatening me."

"Keep it down!" Ben's deep, gravelly voice spoke from the dark shadows. "I want you to walk slowly down the deck steps. Stop at the bottom. We'll be right behind you, and I'll have the gun pointed at you the whole time." The nose of Ben's pistol poked out into the light. "We're going to walk into the woods. You're going to shoot yourself out of remorse for killing Quadtrini. Nobody will notice one more loud bang on the Fourth of July."

"No one would ever believe I'd kill myself." Jane's voice trembled as her hands stretched backward for the doorknob. But then she stopped. If she went into the woods with them, she could lead these two crazies away from the cabin, away from her innocent, sleeping friends, away from shell-shocked Wes, away into the dark, scary woods where her friends couldn't get hurt. "All right. Don't shoot and I'll go with you."

The patio light flashed on as the cabin door burst open, and Dale dashed out onto the deck. He pushed past Jane, forcing her behind him, and she stumbled around like a drunkard, at the same time Doug and Bruce bounded up the steps at the other end of the patio.

"Watch out! He has a gun!" Jane waved her arms around in circles, regaining her balance.

Shielding Jane, Dale barked, "Hand over your gun. The police are on the way here and you can't escape."

He had a wild, savage expression.

Bruce and Doug stationed themselves at the top of the deck steps, but they stood on the balls of their feet, fists clenched.

Ben stepped into the light, the pistol first aimed toward the men at the stairs, then at Dale, then back. "I'm not handing over my gun. And you're going to do as I tell you."

Her rescuers exchanged looks, while Jane's heart thumped even more.

"Stand over there." Ben motioned for them to group together, but no one stirred. "Jane, you first, get a move on." She started to shift past Dale, who grabbed her arm and thrust her behind him. Dale took measured steps to join the other two men, pulling Jane along and placing her between them. He grasped her hand as she gave Bruce and Doug a questioning look, but no one said anything.

"Okay. Now, everybody go down the stairs," ordered Ben.

They were forced to descend to the hot tub area below. Ben and Connie crept down the steps after them. Ben jerked the gun. "Get into the hot tub."

Bruce turned white. "Why?"

"Just get in."

Doug lowered himself in first, then Dale with Jane following, her bathrobe soaking up the water like a sponge. "It's hot. Did we forget to turn the hot tub off this whole time?" Jane sank up to her waist.

Bruce put a toe in the steaming bubbles, but halted. Beads of sweat popped out on his forehead, and he hadn't even stepped in yet.

Out from behind a pillar rushed Wes, eyes firing

sparks.

He sprinted at Ben Malkon, head down like a charging bull. But before Wes could reach his target, a shot rang out, and the gun flew out of Ben's hand, landing on the ground. Bruce leapt from his perch on the side of the hot tub and snatched up the gun, just as Wes ran full blast into Ben, striking him to the ground.

Olivia stepped forward, out from behind the pillar, holding a pink Derringer in her right hand. "Those shooting lessons paid off, wouldn't you say?"

Chapter 21

They stood as a tableau vivant for a moment, then Libby and Cheryl sidled out from the shadows. "We called the cops already."

"Okay, that's good." Wes towered over Ben, who appeared to have the wind knocked out of him.

Jane's tense muscles finally eased as she hauled her dripping body out of the hot tub and strode over to Ben, with Dale right behind at her back.

"You were pretty convincing when you said you'd forgiven Quadtrini for the car accident. But you didn't, did you?" Jane glared into Ben's gasping face, but he only moaned.

"How could anyone forgive something like that?" Connie's voice was hard and low, barely audible. "Quadtrini never asked for Ben's forgiveness. Ben told the police that story to get them off his trail. Quadtrini was not a nice person, not a nice person at all."

Jane eyes swiveled to Connie. "Tell us, what did Quadtrini do to you?"

Olivia pulled the hammer back and continued to aim the pink Derringer at her, so Connie said in a hushed voice, "My dad was the one who worked on the campground renovation. He was demolishing some old buildings and got real sick. My dad's going to die, but Quadtrini had gotten off with a slap on the hand." Her eyes glistened with tears. "He wasn't punished for what he did."

"But what exactly did he do? It wasn't his fault the asbestos was there."

"He was worried the campground would be closed for good, so he hid the asbestos, covered over the old roofing materials with a bulldozer. Then he hired my dad for demolition. My dad went in and started working. He worked a couple of days with that asbestos in the air before he realized it. He alerted the EPA, and the camp was closed."

"I'm sorry that happened." Jane's throat caught a little as she glanced around at her friends. "Is your dad still alive?"

"He's in hospice." Connie's eyes went from teary to steely. A siren reverberated from a few short blocks away, with an *oooweeeoooh...*

Olivia twitched her pink revolver and jutted out her chin. "So, which of you pulled the trigger? You or Ben?" Jane half expected Olivia to twirl the gun on her finger, like a gunslinger.

Ben stirred at the ground at their feet. "Don't tell. Don't say anything, Connie."

But Connie said, "I did."

Doug piped up, with Bruce standing behind looking over his shoulder. "So you met Quadtrini at the amphitheater, shot him, and planted Olivia's glasses."

"Yes. I started a fire in the pit in the middle of the night, and Quadtrini showed up to check it out."

"You planned it."

"Ben thought it through. Afterward, we changed our clothes, and he carried the gun and the clothes up to the mountain lake and threw them all in. I took a shower, and I think Ben did, too, before daybreak. We had no gun residue, no gun, nothing. We would only be suspected along with everyone else. Ben was the only one with a known motive, and I was to be his alibi."

"That you were both at the latrines?" Jane asked Ben, now sitting up. He groaned again, but didn't answer. The *ooweeeoooh* of the siren grew closer. "What about your families? Did they know?"

"No. They didn't." Connie was pale in the light from the basement window. Eight pairs of eyes narrowed at the shaking woman.

"They had to have noticed you were gone. Especially when they heard the gunshot." Bruce's eyebrows formed a question.

"George? My husband can sleep through anything." Connie gave out a crazy bark of laughter as her eyes swept over Jane. "Speaking of husbands, I overheard you talking to Agent Marshall about being called 'widow of the waves,' and I looked you up on the internet. We figured the police probably suspected you, not Ben, and especially not me."

"So, you thought if I shot myself in the woods out of remorse, they'd close the investigation." Jane's face grew hot with anger. "How did you two ever get together in the first place?"

"We met when we were both camping at Yellow Mountain. I complained about Quadtrini, and Ben told me his whole story. We found we had a common enemy."

"Are you a sharpshooter?"

Everyone took a couple of steps closer, and Olivia flashed her pink pistol once more. "Answer the question."

Connie gave a little shudder. "No. I fired all the

bullets into the woods, emptied the gun, but one lucky shot actually hit Quadtrini."

Lights flashing, an Estes Park Police cruiser careened into the parking lot, and the siren flipped off. Connie and Ben were caught in the headlights, like actors on a stage. Two officers strode over. The friends all talked at once, and after their jumbled explanations, one of the officers handcuffed the two guilty parties and escorted them to the backseat of the patrol car.

****

They slept late on Sunday morning, having been up half the night before. Jane awakened first and went outside to sit on the deck and read her devotional as the mid-morning sun warmed her. She prayed a prayer of thanks for the heroic rescue by her friends and that the murder was solved.

Then a prayer that Caleb and Erin would not move away. It was selfish, but heartfelt all the same. Immediately after, a text message pinged on her cellphone. The text was from Caleb. *I turned down the job offer in Durango. The cons won.*

She pressed her palm to her heart as she let out a huge breath and put down the phone. Sometimes prayers were answered right away, like this one, and sometimes not. She snatched the phone up one more time and texted Caleb, then her secretary, Evelyn, that the murderers were caught and to be prepared to hear the whole story when Jane got back in town. She'd need to call Luke, too.

Tires sounded on the gravel in the parking lot. Agent Marshall's car nosed into a space, and he climbed out and ascended the steps to the deck. "I heard all about what happened last night from the Estes

Police." He glanced around. "Where is everyone else?"

"They're still in bed," Jane said, as he took a seat.

"I can come back." He started to rise again.

"Not at all. Those sleepyheads need to get up soon anyway. Do you want a cup of coffee?"

"Sure."

Jane slipped into the kitchen and back with a steaming mug for Marshall. He told her, "O'Hennessey and Malkon were moved to a federal facility after they both signed confessions. O'Hennessey stepped on Olivia's reading glasses on the way to the amphitheater, so she picked them up thinking they were her own. Then, after she noticed they weren't hers, she dropped them at the scene hoping to deflect suspicion."

"She picked the wrong person to frame. We weren't going to sit back and do nothing about that. But why wasn't she a suspect? She threatened me, after all, and I expected you to look closely at her, find the connection." Jane tried to keep the irritation out of her voice.

"Her name was different from the asbestos victim's. We just now found out she was adopted as a little kid by her stepdad, so even her maiden name wasn't the same as her dad's. There was nothing to connect her specifically to Quadtrini or the campground."

"Humph." Jane beetled her brows. "Tell me, was Ted a suspect? Gloria said his fingerprints were on Quadtrini's gun."

"No. That gun hadn't been fired. Not even loaded."

"I wish I'd known. I was worried about him and Gloria." Jane sagged back in her chair. "And what about Koopmer?"

"We did look at him pretty close."

"I wonder what he was doing in Estes."

"In the mountains on the Fourth of July weekend, like everyone else."

"So, a coincidence, then. I'll have to tell Olivia." She smiled, then went on to provide him the details of the previous night. "Wes is the hero. He spotted me with Ben and Connie right here on this deck and alerted the others. Then he formulated a rescue plan."

"I'm not a hero." Wes, holding two coffee mugs, stepped out the cabin door.

Libby shuffled out behind him with the carafe. "Yes, you are."

"I just went into a zone. I hardly remember what happened," he argued, but neither Jane nor Libby would hear of it.

"Your quick thinking saved my life." Jane squeezed his arm.

The rest of the group, except for one, meandered outside and joined them at the patio table. Dale dropped into the chair next to Jane's. Olivia asked the agent, "Will the charges against me be dropped now?"

"Yes." He nodded. "Your attorney probably already got a call that the arraignment hearing's cancelled."

Doug had a satisfied smile, and the anxious look on Olivia's face was gone.

Wes said, "I guess now the investigation is over, the police will return our guns to us."

"Yes. Bring your receipts to the Forest Service office in Denver," Marshall said in his slow and matter-of-fact way.

"What gun did you use last night, Olivia?" Jane

cradled her steaming mug in both hands as she examined her friend's face.

"I got a spare Derringer from my mother."

Doug added, "Lucky thing because none of the rest of us brought any weapons."

"Where's Bruce? Is he still in bed?" Libby strained her neck to look past everyone through the window into the cabin.

Cheryl answered, "He's inside frying bacon and eggs for breakfast. There's plenty if you want to stay and eat." She glanced at Agent Marshall, but he shook his head and said he needed to get going.

After he left and breakfast was laid on the table, they talked about the excitement of the night before. Libby explained, "I wish I had been outside to see Olivia shoot the gun out of Ben's hand. Cheryl and I stayed in the cabin with 9-1-1 on the phone. I wanted to come out, but Wes said I would be in the way."

"I didn't even want Olivia to come with us, but she insisted." Doug gave his wife a sharp look.

Dale added, "Good thing, too. That was some shooting." They all peered at Olivia, who beamed, pointed with her right hand, first digit out straight and thumb up like she was taking aim. She clicked her tongue as her thumb went down and her hand came up, then she blew over the top of her smoking gun finger.

"Good job. Thanks, Olivia." Jane gave her a broad smile.

"I'm so relieved it's solved and done with before that hearing tomorrow." Olivia tucked a strand of her black hair behind her ear.

"I'm glad it was solved before we need to leave for Portland." Cheryl's eyes were wide as was her smile.

"I can't believe you're heading back tomorrow." Jane frowned. "Your visit went by too fast."

"You know what they say. Time flies." Olivia handed a folded newspaper to Jane. "The Sunday paper was delivered to the cabin this morning."

"Is the news of the arrests in the paper already?" Dale asked.

"No, but go to page three."

Jane spread the paper out flat on the table and turned the pages with Dale looking over her shoulder. There, in a color photo covering the top half of page three, was Jane in the front seat of her car, eyes wide open and hands gripping the steering wheel, together with Olivia in the passenger seat and the bride and groom in the foreground. The caption read, "Car Photo Bombs Wedding."

Jane gulped, then swallowed hard several times.

"And that's not all." Olivia screwed up her face.

"What else could there be?" Jane stared at her friend. Olivia held up a cellphone for all to see. On the screen was an internet news site with the headline, "Wedding Photo Bomb Goes Viral."

"Oh no, not again," wailed Jane. "That photographer! I'll bet he gave the photo to the newspaper and posted the picture on the web for publicity." She threw the paper down with force and crossed her arms. "I could shoot him!"

Everyone laughed, but Wes said in a stern voice, "Don't say that. Neither Ben Malkon nor Connie O'Hennessey could forgive Quadtrini for what he'd done to them. And look what that led to."

Their laughter was brought up short. Dale clamped a hand on her shoulder. "Jane didn't mean it that way. It was just a manner of speech."

Jane patted Dale's hand. "But I hear you, Wes. Ben and Connie's hatred of Quadtrini is what they had in common. And I should've seen it earlier."

Cheryl disagreed. "But no one could have linked O'Hennessey to her father, and then to Quadtrini."

"The police should've made that connection anyhow." Bruce scowled. "By not making an arrest, they allowed those two to follow us to Estes and attack Jane."

"Let it go." Wes swatted the air with one hand. They turned to look at him. "I'm learning about forgiveness in counseling. It's important. Otherwise things just eat at you." They sat in silence for a moment.

Dale's lips were in a thin line. "I know what you mean, buddy."

Jane gave her boyfriend a long thoughtful look, then asked Wes in a small voice, "Are you doing better?"

"I am. I'm learning to forgive." Instead of the stressed look of last night, Wes appeared relaxed with a smile.

Jane knew she, too, was holding on to unforgiveness. She glanced at Dale again. Yes, Dale, for his continuing relationship with his ex-wife. Her eyes went to Cheryl. Yes, Cheryl, for moving away and Bruce for taking a job in Portland. Libby, for not telling the whole truth. Olivia, for her cutting remarks. Doug, for taking command of her investigation. Herself, even, for surviving her husbands. And that wedding photographer!

But all those feelings evaporated in the crisp, cool

mountain air. A peace fell over her, while a blue jay called from the pines and the sun reflected purple off the slopes of the awe-inspiring mountains.

Doug took a swallow from his mug, draining it, and set the cup on the table. He tapped the cellphone with Jane's face in the viral photo and looked at the time. "We have to check out of the cabin by eleven, don't we?"

Olivia nodded.

Wes added, "Remember, we're meeting the fishing guide at eleven-thirty behind the dam." As a finale to their holiday weekend, he had arranged a two-hour fly fishing excursion with someone he knew at an outfitters.

Doug and Olivia rose from their seats and the rest followed suit.

The men hoisted suitcases into the trunks of their vehicles, while the women looked in cabinets, under sinks, and in drawers to make sure nothing was left behind.

Slam, slam...slam...slam, slam went the car doors with the final loading of bags and bundles. Doug and Olivia left first. "We're going to drop off the keys at the rental office. See you at the dam."

Dale hugged his arm around Jane's shoulder. "Do you want to leave your car here and ride to the lake with me?"

"No. I'll follow you to the meeting place. After fishing, we're all going home, and I won't want to come back here for my car." She glanced around, but the cabin in the woods looked safe and peaceful in spite of the events of last night.

They piled into their vehicles and caravanned to

the dam, Jane's car close on Dale's bumper.

The outfitter was waiting with supplies of fishing poles and nets. He was already dressed in waders and a fishing vest with flies pinned to his chest. Sitting on a hard, flat rock while the others climbed into gear, Jane listened to the guide explain how to make a roll cast and use wet flies. Was there such a thing as a dry fly and how could anyone keep the fly from getting wet?

Dale asked her, "Don't you want to fish?" His fierce protectiveness was still in evidence.

"I've never fished in my life. I'll enjoy watching all of you. I'll keep you honest. No one can boast about the fish that got away because I'll be a witness."

The outfitter wound a fishing line around a bobbin. "About this time last year I took out a kid, musta been 'bout ten years old or so. He caught a twelve pound brown trout on his first cast."

The others chimed in with, "See, it doesn't matter if you've never fished before...Jane, come on...don't be a spoil sport."

Cheryl urged, "What's the matter with you? You're usually game for anything. It's just catch-and-release for fun."

Jane hopped off the rock. "Okay. You asked for it. Now, you'll really have competition, like that ten-year-old." She found a short set of women's waders and yanked them on, then grabbed the pole the outfitter offered to her.

Standing at the edge of the water, Dale held out his hand to help her in. She seized his fingers and stepped into the cold, strong stream.

**Recipe Suggestions
For A Gourmet Camping Experience**

Breakfast Burritos by Barbara Buchanan

2 medium potatoes, cut into small cubes and cooked
1/2 cup of onion, minced
4 scrambled eggs
1lb. breakfast sausage, browned and crumbled
4.5 oz. can green chili (medium or to taste)
1 cup shredded cheese
Warm 4 taco shells
Mix all ingredients and divide onto the four taco shells.
    Roll, and bag. Use freezer bags for camping. Thaw
    overnight and warm in fry pan over the campfire.

Potatoes in Foil Packets by Karen Whalen

4 medium or 2 extra-large potatoes
3—4 tablespoons butter (or more, to taste)
1 medium onion, chopped
1—2 garlic cloves, chopped
1 can whole kernel corn
Salt and pepper

Thinly slice potatoes and nestle in squares of heavy duty aluminum foil, dab with butter, add chopped onion, chopped garlic, several spoonsful of canned corn, and salt and pepper to taste. Close aluminum foil tightly by folding edges over and pinching shut, creating more of a flat packet than a round one, one potato per aluminum packet. Cook on grill or over fire for approximately 20 minutes (campfires have inconsistent heat so check the packets, when they are soft and sizzling, they're done. Don't poke with a fork, because this will release the butter. Just squeeze with your hand in an oven mitt.). You can serve individually out of the foil packets, or scrap the potatoes into a bowl for serving. Some of the potatoes may have blackened and stuck to the foil, but I like them that way. If you want to make these potatoes as a side for breakfast, substitute bacon, fried and crumbled, for the corn. Serves 4.

Kevin Wagner's Famous Chili

Start with a large (12 quart) cooking pot. Add the following:

5 lb. can of Bush's Baked Beans

46 oz. can of tomato juice

1/2 cup of brown sugar, stir after adding

1 large sweet onion, chopped

Float a layer of Mrs. Dash Original Blend seasoning

Stir everything together, then add:

Another 46 oz. can of tomato juice

2 packets of Shelby Chili mix

Stir everything together and add:

3 lbs. hamburger, browned with Mrs. Dash

Simmer for at least 1 to 2 hours, stirring frequently

Yield: 40 bowls of chili—cut in half for a normal-sized dinner club

Cinnamon Hot Chocolate by Barbara Buchanan:

Thought this would sound good in a chilly evening around a campfire. Doesn't need refrigeration and is easy to pack in a zip lock bag.

1 3/4 cup nonfat milk powder

1 cup confectioners' sugar

1/2 cup baking cocoa

1/2 tsp. ground cinnamon

1 cup miniature marshmallows

To make a cup of hot chocolate, use 3 tablespoons of mix to one cup of hot water or hot milk, if desired.

You won't want to miss the next book in the series.
Here's a sample:

A Stewed Observation

by

Karen C. Whalen

Dinner Club Murder Mysteries,
Volume 4

Chapter 1

"We survived the drive." Dale yanked the parking brake of the tiny, white rental car in front of Lomán Castle, the medieval, ivy-covered, romantic's dream destination.

"Good job." Jane gave him a shaky grin, not wanting to admit she was nervous traveling on the left side of the narrow motorways. Excitement tingled in her already churning stomach as he opened the hatchback and piled their luggage onto the gravel next to a white-blooming, sweet-smelling rowan tree. She stepped alongside him as he wheeled their bags through the double, iron-clad doors.

She studied the possible spots for Dale to pop the question.

Although they were in their early fifties and both had been married before, she still held out hope for a romantic proposal. Would it be in the wide, stone-flagged entry hall with the arched, diamond-paned windows, or near the miniature, book-crammed library next to the lobby, or on top of the curved, blue-carpeted stairway?

They paused at the marble registration desk.

"Fáilte. I'm Griffin O'Doherty. Welcome to Ireland." Only it sounded like "Oireland." Crow's feet slightly edged Griffin O'Doherty's aquamarine eyes, and his thatch of strawberry blond hair was in a longish, shaggy style, unlike the precision cuts of the Americans. His melodic, Irish tongue was as captivating as his long hair and blue eyes, but Jane tried not to notice since she only had eyes for Dale.

"Reservation for Dale Capricorn." He took hold of one of her hands, his calluses scratchy and hard. He did not look his age, since his thick, brown hair and dimples gave him a youthful appearance.

Griffin O'Doherty's fingers typed on the keyboard. "Let me find your booking."

Dale said, "We're with a group. There are two other couples joining us."

"The dinner club, right? The others beat you here, and they've already checked in. May I have your passports?" After making copies, Griffin slid a plastic card out of a drawer. "Here's your room key card."

A hardy, geriatric version of Griffin O'Doherty came out from a room behind the reception desk. "I just don't understand why you had to change all the keys to these silly plastic cards, Griff." Although fairly fit, he appeared to be north of eighty years by a few notches. His voice held a tremor, shaky and crackly. His sullen face was well-lined, his hair so thin it only required two fingers to comb over.

"Uncle, it's so much easier to replace a card when a guest loses the key."

"Who lost a key?" He turned an angry scowl toward Dale. "Did you? Do I know you?"

"No, I just got here!" Dale's eyebrows shot up along with his voice.

Jane gasped. Was this old man going to ruin the big event? Keep Dale from asking for her hand on bended knee?

A cacophony of American voices sounded from the hallway. Everyone swiveled in that direction, as the dinner club members trooped in. Cheryl and Bruce Breewood, original members of the club, had planned the trip to Ireland to visit Bruce's relatives. Olivia and Doug Ladner decided to come along, and so, of course, Jane and Dale had to come, too. The Breewoods were the ones who picked the hotel.

Cheryl's words rose above the other three, "Jane, Dale. We thought you were right behind us on the road, but we lost you." Her eyes widened as she took in the old man with the angry, red face. "What's going on?"

Griffin came out from behind the desk, his tall frame soaring above everyone else. "Uncle, go on back to the tower. I'll join you in a minute." With his right arm around the old man's shoulder and his left hand holding him in a vise grip, Griffin propelled his uncle through the door and slammed it closed after him.

The friends stood in silence, as if caught eavesdropping on an embarrassing family moment. Griffin said, like he had been dealing with a difficult child, "He doesn't like change." Dale edged to the desk and snagged the key card, jamming it into his pocket. Griffin asked, "Can I help with your luggage?"

"No, thanks, I can manage." Dale turned to the others. "We'll meet up after we stow our bags." He grabbed his black suitcase with one hand and the handle of Jane's with the other, and wended his way through the group. The two other couples stepped aside to let him pass.

"Wait. I have my own separate room." Jane held firm at the desk. "Do you have my reservation, Mr. O'Doherty? Under Jane Marsh?" Dale spun around to wait.

"Oh, sorry." Griffin's eyes darted from her to her boyfriend, then a mischievous smile broke out on his face, a smile that hinted he was up to something. "The room next to Dale Capricorn's."

Jane seized the slippery plastic card from his hand. "Thanks." She supposed it natural he would assume, since they were adults of a certain age, they were all married, and in fact, everyone was married except the two of them.

Cheryl brushed her long chestnut bangs out of her eyes. "If you need us, we're in room four and the Ladners have six."

"Okay, see you in a few," Jane said over her shoulder as Griffin led the way along the massive hallway and up the curved staircase, with a whiff of furniture polish on the banisters. Dale followed at their heels. Stopping at Jane's suite, the Irishman unlocked, then held the door open for her. He gave her a grin behind Dale's back.

****

The friends occupied the far table in the massive dining hall. Even though the hall was majestic, with huge crystal chandeliers hanging from tall ceilings, stone walls and floors, two long, dark wooden tables under white tablecloths, and oversized, heavy chairs—everything you'd expect in a castle—dinner consisted of simple bowls of Irish stew.

Olivia flicked her napkin open and draped the flimsy paper across her lap. "Douglas had a power nap while you and Dale were unpacking. Cheryl and I ran across the street and bought postcards. Aren't the rooms fantastic?"

"I love my view of the Shannon River from the second floor." Jane slid a chair out from under the table and plopped down.

"It's called the River Shannon." Griffin lowered a wide tray of steaming bowls and stacks of soda bread onto the table. He placed full bowls in front of them, and the aroma of peppery, browned meat assaulted their noses. "So, you six are in some kind of a club?"

Doug, a bold, red-headed, take-charge kind of person, being an ex-cop, answered for them all. "A dinner club. We host gourmet meals in our homes. The idea is to try new recipes on like-minded foodies."

"There's one other couple in the club, but they couldn't come on this trip." Jane breathed in the steam from her bowl. "What's in the stew?"

"It's an old Irish recipe, made with lamb, potatoes, carrots, and good ol' Irish stout, and the bread is to sop it up." Griffin tipped the empty tray on the table edge and leaned against it. "Can I get you anything more?"

Bruce answered, "I'm good," before glancing at the others, who all nodded in agreement, like people in a group do, and then he added, "When you have a moment, though, I have a question."

"I always have time for questions." He gave Bruce an encouraging smile, a look that said he was in business-ready and customer-pleasing mode.

"Can you tell us more about the history of the castle? Is there a brochure in the lobby?" Bruce adjusted his wire-rimmed glasses.

"Ah, no, I don't have anything like that, but my uncle would love nothing better than to answer your questions." Griffin gestured to his uncle across the room and called out, "Uncle, these guests would like to talk to you."

The old man shuffled over and stuck out his weathered, but meaty fingers. "Fáilte. I'm Alsander O'Doherty."

Bruce stood up to grip his hand. Doug shook his hand, too, but Dale remained in his chair, his arms crossed over his chest. Jane took in a sharp breath, wondering if the old man was in a better mood and if he would behave himself.

Bruce returned to his seat. "Would you please join us? We'd love to talk to you about this place."

"Certainly." Alsander scraped a chair out from the table.

"Griffin, can you join us, too?" Cheryl scooched over so Griffin could sit down next to his uncle.

"Are you sure?" Griffin appeared to hesitate, but when everyone else urged him, too, he took a seat.

Alsander began, "Most people think all the castles are owned by the government, but they aren't. Not all are national monuments." Everyone gave the old man their attention. He went on. "That's right. People own them, they buy them up and own them. I bought Lomán Castle about, let's see, twenty-five years ago now. It's medieval, built in the fourteen hundreds. A clan chieftain named Lomán built it on this hill next to the River Shannon as a defense against invaders." He rubbed his hands together. "I was after turning this place into a bed and breakfast. My daughter wasn't interested, so I got my young nephew to run it." His right hand came down heavily on his nephew's shoulder.

"I'm not young anymore, Uncle. I'm almost the same age as you when you bought the place."

"Not quite, not quite, lad."

Jane didn't think Griffin was much older than herself, and possibly he was the same age. Relieved that the conversation was relaxed and easy, she asked the old man between bites of the crunchy soda bread, "Does your daughter live close by?"

"She lives in Dublin mostly, has a job there, but she's often here to visit."

Bruce leaned forward with his elbows on the table. "I have family in Limerick. My cousin is a pharmacist, Ryan Breewood. Do you know him?"

"Breewood, you say?" Alsander's eyes widened for a second, then narrowed. "Oh, the chemist." Beads of sweat appeared on his forehead.

"Yes. He married a Falon."

"Oh, them. Humph." Alsander wiped a handkerchief across his sweaty face.

Cheryl and Bruce frowned at each other. Jane stiffened and glanced at Dale.

Olivia put down her spoon. "What's wrong? Don't you like the Falons? Or is it the Breewoods you don't like?"

"I don't have to like everybody." Alsander's eyes bulged out as the water poured off him.

"Not again," Griffin groaned, his hand over his eyes.

"I'm done here." Alsander stood up. His face was bright red, and a vein pulsed at his temple.

Griffin followed him through the doorway into the kitchen. "Did you take your medication, like I told you to?"

When they were out of sight, Jane let out the breath she'd been holding.

Bruce glanced around the group. "Jeez. Do they still have clan feuds here?"

"Well, Bruce, you were the one who picked this place." Olivia snorted. "Should we look for another hotel?" Her husband, Doug, shot her a silent *be-quiet* message.

"I reserved this B&B months ago, and you want to change plans now?" A dangerous light glinted in Cheryl's eyes.

"Of course not. This place is fantastic, Cheryl, good job." Jane stuck her thumb up. She wanted to stay, still envisioning a marriage proposal at this romantic castle. They eased into a conversation about the flight and the drive from the airport. Then they talked over plans for the next day. Finally, explaining she was tired from traveling, Jane excused herself and slipped from the room, but instead of heading upstairs, she sidled over to the reception desk.

A young lady, with dreadlocks in her blonde hair and piercings in her nose and eyebrows, was reading a magazine. "Ha-ware-ya?" Pinned to her clingy top, a badge read, "Fiona."

"Ah, what?" Jane scratched her head.

"Need, anytink?"

"Yes. Could I have the key to room four?"

"Here ya go." Fiona gave her the key card.

That was too easy. Jane raced down the hall and used the card to enter room four. She retrieved a black plastic spider with hairy legs from her pocket and tucked it under one of the pillows. Then she slid a fake, furry mouse under the sink in the bathroom. She stuck her head out the door, and not seeing anyone, returned to the receptionist. "I'm sorry. I meant to ask for the key to room seven." Once she had the new key card, back down the hall she went to leave similar pranks in the Ladners' room.

But after opening the door, she stood as still as a mouse, a real one. Someone was sleeping in the bed, snoring with a loud wheeze out and a deep breath in. Moonlight slanting from the uncovered window struck an open book, a bottle, and a glass of water on a table, and the bed with Alsander's head on the pillow. She backed from the room on tiptoe, closed the door with a soft click, and took in the room number. Room seven. Hmmm. She must've heard the number wrong.

She jumped when she felt a tap on her shoulder.

A word about the author...

Karen C. Whalen is the author of a culinary cozy series, the Dinner Club Murder Mysteries. First and second in the series are *Everything Bundt the Truth* (2016) and *Not According to Flan* (2017).

She previously worked as a paralegal at a law firm in Denver, Colorado and has been a columnist and regular contributor to *The National Paralegal Reporter* magazine.

She has hosted dinner club events for a number of years.